DEADLY CONVICTION

A detective seeks the truth against all odds

ROBERT McCRACKEN

THE
BOOK
FOLKS

Published by The Book Folks

London, 2023

ISBN 978-1-80462-104-2

www.thebookfolks.com

Deadly Conviction is the seventh book in the DI Tara Grogan mystery series.

What's past is prologue.

William Shakespeare, *The Tempest*

PROLOGUE

Christmas Eve, 19 years ago

The driver hit the brakes. Hard. He drew a sharp breath. The car slid on icy tarmac then slewed sideways thudding against a grassy bank.

'What the hell?'

He peered at the figure of a woman standing in the road, captured in the glare of the headlights. Trembling, she clutched a silk dressing gown around her slender body. The driver's companion was already climbing out of the patrol car. The woman's cries overcame the silence of the country lane, and her hands gripped her face as the shock of what so nearly happened suddenly registered.

'Are you all right, love?' Constable Anne Farnham asked. 'We nearly had you then. What are you doing out here on your own?'

The woman, with dishevelled brown hair and quivering lips, stared vacantly at the fresh-faced constable. The young rookie officer who had been driving the car emerged from the vehicle and stood beside Farnham. He looked as shaken as the woman.

'It's my daughter,' the woman struggled to say. 'I'm looking for my daughter. She should have come home by now.'

'Where do you live, madam?' Farnham asked.

'Right here.' With a shaky arm she pointed to the driveway of her home. A brass nameplate embedded in a stone gatepost read Briarwood Manor. In the frosty gloom the outline of a large imposing house, fifty yards beyond the open gates, drew the attention of the police officers.

Christmas tree decorations filled the window of a ground-floor room and two lanterns set either side of the front porch cast light over the frosted lawn.

'Let's get you indoors before you freeze to death,' said Farnham, taking the woman by the arm.

'But I must find my daughter. I'm worried about her. It's very late, and there's been talk of a prowler in the lane.'

The woman didn't protest further as the officers led her along the drive.

'Is anyone else at home?' Farnham asked her.

'My husband and son. They've just arrived. They're phoning around Rebecca's friends.'

'We'll go inside and take some details about your daughter.'

Within a few seconds, security floodlights illuminated the drive and garden, and the voices trailed off as they entered the house. Less than a minute later, however, the police officers rushed back outside, ran to their car and sped off.

Two hours of searching country lanes around Briarwood Manor elapsed before they made a stop next to the ruins of a two-storey building sitting close to the roadside. They had already driven by several times in their search for Rebecca Winters. Not for a second did either constable imagine that they were looking for a body. Rebecca was twenty, a student home for the holidays. She was most likely partying with friends in the city. Her father had said as much to the officers when they'd met briefly in the lavish entrance hall of the house. Rebecca's mother, it seemed, had been overreacting.

With torches in hand, the officers picked careful steps through rutted and frozen mud strewn with bricks and broken planks. The derelict farm labourer's cottage still had its roof intact but there were no doors or windows. Farnham, a twenty-six-year-old constable, was sturdily built and did not scare easily. She had no fears about venturing inside. A cursory look around revealed three empty rooms with stone floors. Two of the rooms were bare of furniture except for a tiled fireplace in each. The remnants of flower-patterned wallpaper coated with black mould were peeling from the walls. The kitchen contained no fittings at all. Water pipes ran to the spot where there had once been a sink. A narrow wooden staircase led from the kitchen to the upper floor. Farnham's junior colleague checked there was a floor above on which to stand before ascending.

Blue lights flashed in the distance as if to awaken the night. The search for the missing woman was scaling up. It was a faster response than usual for a person who had been missing for less than six hours, particularly if you believed Rebecca Winters was probably enjoying a Christmas party or a romantic tryst before struggling to get a taxi for home on one of the busiest nights of the year.

'Up here!'

Farnham, responding to his call, raced up the stairs and came to his side. At first, she saw nothing. Her colleague pointed downwards. He couldn't summon words.

She shone her torch from the opening to illuminate the ground below. There, amongst bricks and weeds lay the body of a beautiful young woman. She lay face up. There was blood on her forehead, her arms were trapped beneath her body, and her right leg sat askew.

'Hell of a Christmas present,' said Farnham with a deep sigh.

Her inexperienced companion still had no words.

CHAPTER 1

Present day

Stephen Lloyd called to his parents as he stepped outside.

'See you later.'

He hadn't done that for such a long time. Hadn't been able to, not for years.

'Bye, son. Mind how you go,' Gladys, his mother, replied.

He closed the door and paused to look around. This street was the place of his childhood. He breathed a lungful of Hornsey Road fresh air and recalled his days of kicking a ball up and down the street until his feet ached or darkness descended and his mother ordered him in. He and his mates, Burnsy, Phil Weed, Fat Billy and Marsha. Oh, to relive just a minute of those times, he thought, as he sauntered to the junction with Anfield Road. He'd forgotten just how close he lived to the stadium, nowadays host to a bunch of highly paid internationals with exotic-sounding names. His heroes had been Robbie Fowler, Stevie McManaman and Jamie Carragher. All local boys from Bootle or Toxteth. God, he'd grown up closer to Anfield than any of them. His dream had been to score a goal there. He would have loved it to have been for the reds, but Everton was the first club to take an interest. He'd signed for them at fourteen. Alone in his bedroom, beneath his Liverpool scarf hanging on the wall, he told himself if he were to score for Everton at the home of Liverpool then so be it. But at thirty-eight that ship had sailed. It had disappeared over the horizon in a flash on the day his life changed forever.

He looked at each house as he walked by. Hornsey Road was so like that street on the Channel 4 continuity scene that appeared most nights, the big four ident kicking a football with a bunch of kids. He knew that it was Cardigan Street in Wavertree but so what? It could just so easily be Hornsey Road; he and his pals getting chased after smashing a window with their football.

He passed the former home of Fat Billy, long dead in a car accident at the age of twenty. Opposite to Billy's house was Marsha's. Stephen wondered where she was now. The last he'd heard, she was married with three kids. His first kiss had been with Marsha, although at the time he'd felt little excitement. Next door to Marsha was the house where Burnsy had lived with his brother Phil, nicknamed Weed because of his skinny frame. Stephen knew little of what had happened to them. Burnsy had managed a few first-team appearances for Tranmere Rovers then sank into the reserves and was never heard of again in football. Stephen would have loved to remain friends with at least one of his mates, but life had swept by. Even without the tragedy, Stephen doubted that he would have ever remained in contact with his childhood buddies.

The action of boarding a city-bound bus shook him from his wistfulness. Taking a seat and staring vacantly at the streets flashing by, Stephen switched his thoughts to the evening ahead. He'd done the homecoming with his loving parents Gladys and Winston. He'd even reconnected with extended family and endured a welcome-home party, but it was time to get down to business. He had someone to meet and maybe afterwards, if he was lucky, he could attend to a more basic need.

He hesitated at the door of the bar. Friday evening and punters were coming and going. He watched them all, wondering if any were quite like him, if any had the same history. Was his friend already inside enjoying a cool pint? The teenage Stephen hardly had the chance to enjoy a social life before it had been snatched away. Eighteen years on, tonight was his fresh start.

Two women, quite merry, stepped from the pub. He had to move out of their way. Both were much younger than him and not his type, if he was even inclined to engage them. They smiled and laughed. Whether it was at him, for him, or he was irrelevant to their joy, he didn't know. His heart thumped in his chest as finally he summoned the courage to venture inside. His glasses immediately misted over from the stuffiness. He pulled them off and gazed around the dingy palace. No one took him under their notice but for one guy, alone in a corner. The man raised his glass, Stephen smiled, relaxed, and went to join his friend.

It was the first and would be the last night of Stephen's resumed social life.

CHAPTER 2

A recently slimmer DS Alan Murray posed for photographs with his new bride Trudy Mitchell. It was an unseasonably warm Saturday but fortunately lacking in the bright sunshine that would interfere with the photography. The couple stood by a decorative fountain at an exclusive wedding venue in the Oxfordshire countryside. The forty guests looked on as a fussy man with his camera composed each shot with an air of over-importance. But no amount of scurrying around was going to upset the newlyweds. They appeared as happy as any couple might be, surrounded by close friends and family.

For Murray they amounted to his parents, his younger brother as best man, two elderly aunts, and his colleagues from Merseyside Police. His immediate boss and closest friend DI Tara Grogan smiled with deep affection for the man who had been at her side for her entire career in the Serious Crime Squad managed by Harold Tweedy. Harold and his wife Eleanor observed the couple with pride as if Murray had been their own son. DC Paula Bleasdale and newly promoted, now DS, John Wilson watched alongside Tara.

For Trudy Mitchell, former television presenter and now producer, the guest list included several notable celebrities. Tara observed them all, intrigued to see how the mildly famous behaved at social gatherings. This was Tara's first outing since her violent experience at the hands of serial killer James Guy and the tragic death of her friend Aisling. She pictured Aisling standing beside her now, wonderfully dressed and on the hunt for the rich man of her dreams.

Despite the cheerful occasion, for Tara, everything was tainted with sadness. If it hadn't been Alan Murray's big day, she would not have bothered coming. There was no joy in her recent past and she couldn't imagine a happy future. She would have consigned her police career to the dustbin but for one single and frightening thought. What else could she do? She'd done nothing with her life since graduating from Oxford except to hunt down the vilest killers in the country. Recently, she'd struggled with a depressing feeling that beyond police work there was little meaning to her life.

As she watched Alan and Trudy embrace each of their guests, she could hardly wait for the day to end. It was too joyous an occasion for someone like her. How low must she be sinking when she longed for work on a Monday?

'Smile, Tara, it might never happen,' Murray quipped then gave her the tightest hug she could ever remember, lifting her slight frame off the ground. Tears sprang to her eyes, and she struggled to get the words out. She summoned a smile then a kiss on the cheek for her cherished colleague.

'You clean up well, DS Murray. I hope you're happy, you deserve to be.'

Murray hugged her again. He knew how difficult life had been for his beautiful boss.

'And don't think I didn't notice, you calling me Tara.'

'Not working today though, are we?'

Trudy approached and Tara kissed her on the cheek and complimented her dress.

'Look after him for me,' Tara said. 'I want him ready to work in two weeks' time.'

'Thank you for coming,' Trudy replied. 'It means so much – to both of us.'

'So, you're definitely starting back on Monday?' Murray asked, when Trudy moved on to greet another guest.

'What else would I do, Alan? But I need you with me, understand? Be happy with Trudy but remember I can't do this without you.'

The pair embraced once more, and Tara sobbed discreetly against his shoulder until Superintendent Harold Tweedy stood before them.

* * *

'Welcome back, ma'am,' said Paula Bleasdale with a warm smile, standing at Tara's desk. Still in her twenties and quite athletic, her brown hair retained some of the styling she'd had done for Murray's wedding.

'Thanks, Paula. How's the head?'

'Paracetamol did the trick and early to bed last night.'

'Hair of the dog for me,' called a jovial DS Wilson from the far side of the office.

'Glad to hear it,' Tara replied. 'Newly promoted officers with hangovers are not what we need in this place.'

Tara had had no such problems. She'd managed only two glasses of champagne and a glass of white wine during the wedding meal. Then she had an early night as her colleagues enjoyed the celebrations into the early hours.

No sooner had Tara taken her seat and switched on her computer than her desk phone beeped. Lifting the receiver, she knew it would be Tweedy.

'Good morning, Tara. Come and see me when you're ready.'

'On my way, sir.'

She put the phone down, took several deep breaths and got to her feet. Turning around, she noticed that everyone in the room was watching her. Bleasdale smiled. The atmosphere unnerved her. As if her first day back wasn't already harrowing. Now she had the feeling that everyone was waiting for her to crack. Defiantly, she marched from the room, knocked on Tweedy's door and bounded in with as much confidence as she could muster.

CHAPTER 3

Superintendent Harold Tweedy smiled warmly at his cherished detective.

'Did you enjoy the wedding?'

An icebreaker, Tara sensed, but she had to play along.

'Great to see Alan settle down at last. He deserves to be happy.'

'How about you, Tara?'

She replied with a shrug largely of indifference.

'I'm fine, sir. Happy to be back at St Anne Street, ready to get started.'

The two officers momentarily studied each other. Tara's reply had been rehearsed, her way of avoiding a discussion of the recent past. Looking at his eyes, filled with genuine compassion, she realised that Tweedy knew that she was not about to open up. He was a man edging closer to retirement. His wrinkled and pinched face belied his caring style of management. It had been suggested that Tweedy's face had a wrinkle for every case he'd brought to a successful conclusion.

'My intention had been to let you get settled in,' he began, and to Tara's relief filling the uncomfortable silence. 'No direct involvement in cases for now, until you find your bearings again.'

She bristled at that. This was his way of pussyfooting around her just like the others in the office, all waiting for her to fall to pieces. But Tweedy hadn't finished.

'Unfortunately, and while we were enjoying ourselves in Oxfordshire, a fresh murder inquiry has been handed to us. The weekenders passed it on to me yesterday evening. With Alan on leave I need your eyes on this one.'

She felt a sudden yet familiar rush of adrenalin as she was about to be confronted with a new case.

'Yes, sir,' she replied, unable to prevent a tear rolling down her cheek. Embarrassed, she wiped it away with the back of her hand. Tweedy rose swiftly, reaching for his coat.

'If you're ready, we can head down to the crime scene.'

'Yes, sir.'

* * *

They could have walked. It was less than a mile from St Anne Street police station to the junction of Victoria Road with the entrance to the Queensway Tunnel. Instead, with flashing blue lights and siren blaring, the distance was covered in less than two minutes. It should have been quicker, but the morning traffic was snarled in a logjam with the Birkenhead-bound lanes of the tunnel remaining closed since the discovery of a body in the early hours of Saturday morning.

Tara and Tweedy sat in the back of the Vauxhall Insignia driven expertly by Wilson. Paula Bleasdale sat in front beside him. They pulled into a parking area outside a building used as the Mersey Tunnel Police Information

Point. Climbing from the car, Tara's gaze was drawn to the white incident tent erected on the pavement beneath a coppice of trees close to the road junction. Immediately, she noted just how much of a public space it was as the venue for a murder. She waited for Tweedy to emerge from the car then fell in behind him as he strode purposefully to the tent. She felt as though it was her first ever murder scene. Her head became light and her stomach queasy; her eyes darting nervously around looking for refuge from what was about to unfold. Traffic crawled by on those lanes that were open. Indicators flashed as drivers attempted to find a functioning lane that would lead them out of the mêlée and onwards to their destination.

A uniformed constable held the flap of the incident tent open for the four detectives to enter. Tara sighed with relief. Tweedy smiled his understanding. The body of the victim had already been removed. At least she had been spared that horror. Tweedy had visited the scene the previous evening. He related the pertinent information to his team.

'The victim is male, thirty-five to forty years old. There was no ID on the body. He was found by a police officer at 2.45 on Saturday morning.' Tweedy paused to consult his notes.

Tara examined the chalked outline of where the victim had lain. There had been a huge loss of blood, judging by the stain on the tiled pavement and how it had seeped into the soil beneath the bushes.

'The post-mortem results should be with us by lunchtime,' Tweedy resumed. 'It was apparent to the first responders that the victim suffered a severe beating, and the likely cause of death was loss of blood from several blows to the back of the head.'

'Any witnesses?' Tara asked.

'No one has come forward yet,' Tweedy replied. 'Tara, I'll leave you to get on with things. We can meet in my office sometime this afternoon. Perhaps you could have a plan of action drawn up by then.'

Tweedy was suddenly gone, and Tara felt as though someone had whipped the duvet from her bed while she slept. She looked at Wilson who sensed that it was time for them to step outside.

Tara drew a deep breath, realising that if the body had been in situ she would not have coped well. But it was time to get on with it. Sympathy was reserved for the family of the victim and not for a fragile police detective chasing down a killer.

CHAPTER 4

Wilson and Bleasdale were doing the work: gathering information, speaking with officers who had been first on the scene, and re-entering the incident tent to examine the spot where a man had lost his life. Tara felt a chill seeping through her bones. She knew what to do next, but she merely gazed around her, feeling lost and lonely.

'If you're finished, ma'am, we can head back,' said Wilson, slipping a notebook into his jacket pocket.

For a second, she looked vacantly at the large frame and round face of her DS. They'd shared many horrific experiences at crime scenes, and she could usually tell when he was being the consummate professional or the considerate friend. This morning, however, he was nothing but a voice penetrating her turbulent mind.

'Ma'am? You OK?'

'Yes, John. I'm fine, just thinking,' she lied.

He smiled at the petite and beautiful woman, who happened to be his boss. He had still to get used to the change in her appearance. The shoulder-length blonde hair had gone, replaced with a style resembling an old-fashioned short back and sides. Her blue eyes had lost their cheerful gaze. For the first time, DI Tara Grogan looked much older than her age.

* * *

Back at her desk, Tara browsed the information gathered on the murder victim. Precious little so far. No ID, no post-mortem report, no witness statements, no CCTV footage, nothing except for what had been collected from the road junction in the city centre. She knew it wouldn't be long before they were swamped with detail, but she was impatient. How was she supposed to get on with things, put the past behind her, when she had so much time to dwell on her ordeal and the murder of her precious friend Aisling? The thought that Aisling's death had been her fault never faded. For the second time within an hour, DS Wilson nudged her from depressing visions of rape and death.

'Dr Witney's secretary just called, ma'am. We can see the victim now if you're ready.'

'OK, lead on,' Tara replied, getting to her feet. She drained the coffee from her mug, grabbed her bag and fell in line with Wilson and Bleasdale as they walked out of the office.

At the city's mortuary they found Dr Brian Witney in the post-mortem suite speaking with an assistant. Tara was always astounded by how routine and businesslike the autopsy process seemed when she observed those who had to perform it. Witney was a highly experienced pathologist, a man, like Tweedy, fast approaching the days when he might consider putting his feet up, travelling the world or working an allotment. He had always had a soft spot for DI Grogan as if he knew she needed more love than others to get her through harrowing days. He had a warm smile for his favourite police detective, but he couldn't hide his shock on seeing her worn-down appearance.

'Tara! Good to see you back. How are you?'

'I'm fine, thanks, Brian. Can't say it's good to see you in this place but I hope you're well.'

Her eyes went to the centre of the room where a green sheet covered what she assumed to be her latest murder victim. Witney did not waste any more time and got down to business. The three detectives gathered around the stainless-steel bench ready for the lecture. Without ceremony, Witney pulled back the sheet to reveal the head and torso of the victim.

Tara winced. Every horrific vision she had endured in this room surged through her mind. Bleasdale noticed her wavering and gently grasped her arm to steady her.

'As you can see, the victim is male,' Witney began. 'Approximately late thirties, five feet nine inches tall, thirteen stone six pounds – give or take for the massive loss of blood. He is of mixed race: European Caucasian and Afro-Caribbean, I would say.'

'Cause of death?' Tara asked, sounding impatient.

Witney cleared his throat. He was not used to being rushed while giving his report. Of the police officers he dealt with regularly, Tara was not known to display such irritation.

'The back of his head has been beaten to a pulp,' Witney continued in stark language rather than technical explanation. 'The perpetrator struck him multiple times with a heavy weapon. An iron bar, a hammer, metal pipe or something similar. The victim sustained several fractures to the skull. He would probably have been unconscious after the first or second blow and then bled out. As for other wounds, there are multiple bruises to his upper body. I would guess that he'd been kicked before being struck on the head or perhaps as he lay dying.'

'More than one attacker?' Wilson asked.

'Could be. One striking the head, another kicking the victim as he lay on the ground.'

'Anything found that might help identification?' Bleasdale asked.

Witney shook his head.

'We're processing DNA samples. They might help. I'll have the results this afternoon. There was no wallet or mobile phone recovered from the scene, just a pair of spectacles in his coat pocket. One more thing, the fly of his trousers was open.'

'A vicious mugging or a sexually motivated attack,' Tara remarked, sounding dismissive as she stepped away from the corpse. She'd seen and heard enough for now.

Wilson drove them back to St Anne Street. Tara remained quiet where usually she would be posing questions and scenarios for her officers to mull over. The silence was awkward. Finally, Wilson succumbed, and his voice filled the car.

'So, ma'am, you think this is just a case of robbery?'

'That will start us off, don't you think? Let's see what we get from CCTV, witnesses, and a positive ID.'

Tara's response had quickly sealed off the discussion. Nothing more was said until they were getting out of the car at the station. Before Tara could release her seatbelt, Wilson placed his hand on hers. It was over-familiar with his superior officer, but he didn't seem to care.

'Ma'am, I am so pleased that you have come back to us. We care about you.'

They stared at one another, and Tara summoned a smile of understanding or gratitude. She didn't know which.

'Thanks, John. I know you do. I'll be OK, honest. Murder is never easy to deal with at the best of times.'

'Yes, ma'am.'

Tara's first day back after a four-month lay-off had not turned out to be as light as she'd been told to expect. Despite the initial findings, a murder investigation was never going to be simple. A brutal mugging or something more sinister, Tara would soon discover what it was to be.

CHAPTER 5

The examination of CCTV footage covering the immediate area of the murder scene was already in progress when Tara returned to her desk. Harold Tweedy stood behind a detective constable who was seated and paying close attention to her screen. Tara was invited to join the discussion.

'What have we got so far?' she asked, her eyes peering at indistinct images on the monitor.

'This is from a camera at the entrance to the Queensway Tunnel,' Tweedy explained. 'We're running through footage around the time we think the attack took place.'

'The tunnel was open,' said DC Irene Flowers, a woman in her forties with a heavy scouse accent. She fast-forwarded the recording. 'No road or tunnel maintenance in operation, little traffic at that time of the morning. But if we switch to the camera at the Whitechapel-Victoria Street intersection, we see this.'

Tara looked in amazement at the recording. A figure, in some distress, staggering and seemingly disoriented, emerged from St John's Garden, ventured onto Victoria Street and, after falling twice in the middle of the road, eventually reached the far side of the frame where his image was obscured beneath the trees.

'You think this is our victim?' Tara asked, her gaze fixed to the monitor. She watched again as the figure fell on the road and a car swerved to avoid him. A moment later, another vehicle slowed but did not stop.

'This next bit explains a little more of what occurred,' said Tweedy.

DC Flowers switched to another camera view. Suddenly a second figure, carrying what seemed to be a hammer, emerged from St John's Garden, ran across the road and disappeared beneath the trees.

'The time was recorded as 12.26 a.m. and the victim was discovered at 2.45 a.m. – over two hours later,' Flowers said.

'Anything more to see?' Tara asked.

'Not yet, ma'am. We're still gathering all available recordings in the area,' Flowers said.

'I want to see in which direction this second individual went after pursuing the victim. I want to see footage of both individuals at the time they entered St John's Garden and where they came from. While you're at it, get a trace on the two vehicles that drove past the victim but failed to stop.'

'Yes, ma'am,' Flowers replied.

Tara marched off leaving Tweedy, Flowers, Wilson and Bleasdale staring at each other, somewhat surprised by her abrupt manner. They had little time for further comment. Tara had lifted her jacket and bag and was making for the door.

'John! Paula! Let's get down to St John's Garden. It's now our principal crime scene. Sir,' Tara added, addressing Tweedy, 'I would appreciate it if you could alert uniform and SOCO. We need to have the place sealed off from the public.'

Tweedy had no time to respond. Tara had left the room.

* * *

Wilson and Bleasdale stood next to Tara watching a team of forensic personnel scouring the lawns and pathways of the square below St George's Hall, an oasis among the busy roads and surrounding civic buildings. So far, nothing of significance had been found, such as the victim's wallet or mobile phone. The spot where it was believed the initial attack had occurred was sealed off by tape. An array of yellow plastic indicators, so common at the scene of a serious crime, marked the areas where blood had been spilled. Samples were diligently collected from the pavement and lawn by officers in white coveralls. Several onlookers stood behind police incident tape strewn across the entrances to St John's Garden.

Tara caught Wilson checking his watch. It irked her. She didn't care to be standing here either, but it was her damn job. What else was there for her to do other than gather information?

Bleasdale answered her mobile, strolling off while she listened to her caller. It wasn't long before she said a thanks and bye, then came directly to Tara.

'Ma'am, we have a possible ID for the victim. The super wants us back at the station.'

Wilson couldn't help looking relieved. Tara frowned but did not protest.

'We'd better get back then,' she said.

* * *

'Nothing other than some blood stains,' Tara said in answer to Tweedy's inquiry on how they had fared at St John's Garden. 'With a bit of luck, though, we might get DNA from more than just the victim.'

Tweedy was seated behind his desk. Instinctively, and from years of habit, Tara glanced to the top-left corner where a leather-bound Bible occupied its usual place. She used to think it very touching and somehow comforting. Today she didn't even think it quaint.

'We have a probable ID for the victim,' he said as Tara, Wilson and Bleasdale took their seats.

'DNA results already. That was quick,' said Wilson.

'No, John, not DNA. A missing person alert was filed yesterday morning. A Mr Winston Lloyd reported that his son Stephen had not come home since going out on Friday evening. He had not heard anything from him in that time. It was out of character that he would not have contacted his family.'

'Does our victim match the description for Stephen Lloyd?' Tara asked.

'Entirely.'

'Has the father been informed?'

'Not yet.'

Tara rose abruptly.

'Best do it now,' she said, making for the door. 'Paula, if you can fetch the address we can head over there.'

It seemed that Tara was determined to get the case finished by the end of the day, as if tomorrow would be too late.

CHAPTER 6

There was a single bay window on the ground floor and a paved strip around it bordered by a low wall – a tiny piece of land to hold a few plant pots but hardly classifiable as a garden. Tara stared at the terraced house as Bleasdale stopped the car. The main mark of individuality in this street was to paint the exterior wall in a colour different from adjacent properties. The front doors varied also, but aside from that the houses on this road were identical. Yet it was what lay within that displayed true individuality. Families, happy or sad, functional or dysfunctional, childless couples, single parents, widows, divorcees, bachelors, spinsters and loners. Every street had them.

Tara hated this task more than any other. She was about to break the hearts of people she didn't know or had never met, and she had little to offer by way of comfort. Sickening nerves coursing through her slight body made her hesitate before ringing the doorbell. Winston Lloyd, seventy, dressed in a brown cardigan and well-worn slippers, opened his front door before she had another chance.

'Mr Lloyd? I'm Detective Inspector Tara Grogan.'

The man's pain seemed to overpower all further engagement. He stared to an infinite point while Tara fought to hold back tears and speak with a compassionate yet confident tone.

'May we come in?'

Suddenly, Gladys Lloyd, already hysterical, bounded to the door.

'Please, God, not my boy, not my Stephen!'

Tara stepped inside with Bleasdale following. The pair managed to usher the couple into their lounge. Bleasdale sat close to Gladys, a heavy-set woman with grey hair and a rosy face, while Tara related the news of what they believed had befallen Stephen Lloyd. Winston clasped his hands tight before him as if to repel the pain entering his body.

When Tara had explained what they knew, enough to sadly suggest but not yet confirm that Stephen Lloyd had been the victim of a brutal murder, she had to ask some difficult questions of the couple.

'Can you tell me everything you know of your son's movements until you last heard from him?'

'He went out on Friday evening,' said Winston Lloyd in a croaky voice. 'That was the last time we saw him.'

'Where was he going?'

'He said he was meeting a friend in town.'

'Do you know the name of this person or where they were intending to meet?'

Bleasdale brought mugs of tea from the kitchen.

Winston shook his head despairingly.

'I don't know any of these things. Stephen said that he was meeting a friend for a drink and not to wait up.'

'Was that normal for him?' Tara asked.

'No.'

'Can you give me some idea of what Stephen was like, his job and his interests?'

Winston Lloyd stared blankly at Tara. It was Gladys who managed to answer the question.

'Stephen didn't have a job. I don't know what his interests were.' She fell into heavy sobs. Her husband took over.

'He was a quiet lad. Read books, listened to music and watched football.'

'Do you know of anyone who might have wanted to harm him? Did he mention anything that was bothering him?'

'There is nothing like that, Inspector. I'm sorry I can't help you.'

'Would you have a recent photograph of your son? It would help our enquiry.'

Gladys rose from the sofa and lifted a framed picture from a sideboard. She handed it to Bleasdale. 'It was taken nearly twenty years ago,' she said.

Bleasdale examined the photo then passed it to Tara. She gazed at a handsome young man, late teens and wearing a blue track suit with an Everton badge on the chest.

'He was an apprentice for Everton until...' Gladys broke down again, her words lost in anguished sobs.

Winston Lloyd held his mobile and was searching for something.

'Here's a recent picture of Stephen.' He passed his phone to Tara.

She studied the image. It had been taken in the room in which they were seated. A thin-faced man with short dark hair and gold-framed spectacles, an arm around his smiling mother.

'When was this taken?' Tara asked.

'Last Tuesday,' Winston replied. 'We had a family party for Stephen.'

Tara looked quizzically at the man.

'It was to celebrate Stephen's release from prison.'

CHAPTER 7

Tara glanced at her watch. She scarcely believed she was still living in the same day. It was ten to four and on her desk was a preliminary report on the post-mortem examination for Stephen Lloyd. On her screen was the police file of the man's criminal record. She had a cursory read through Dr Witney's report in case there was something arising that she had not already learned while at the mortuary. Results of toxicology tests and DNA analysis were pending. After meeting with the Lloyd family, a formal identification had been arranged for the following morning.

Tara read from the criminal record file. Stephen Lloyd had been raised in Liverpool. His father Winston was born in Jamaica, and Gladys in Liverpool to an English father and Irish mother. At the age of nineteen, Stephen had been charged with the murder of a twenty-year-old Cambridge University student from Liverpool. He was found guilty and sentenced to life imprisonment with the recommendation to serve at least eighteen years.

At the time of his arrest, he was an apprentice professional with Everton Football Club. It seemed that the young man had had an exciting career ahead of him that was completely derailed by his murder conviction. There was little more to be gleaned from the record. Lloyd had no other convictions. Instinctively, Tara was moved to consider the victim of the crime for which Lloyd had been jailed. She entered a search for Rebecca Winters into the police national database.

The office door squeaked as it closed behind the last person to leave for the night. Tara hardly noticed that she was alone. Her thoughts were set on the information on her screen. This had been her first day back at work after a four-month absence. It should have been light duties then home early. Now it was after seven and Tara's mind raced with conflicting possibilities of what lay ahead in her investigation of the murder of Stephen Lloyd. It had begun with the idea that it was a mugging, a violent one, but still just a late-night robbery. It was her natural default to keep an open mind, to consider every possibility and not to rush to conclusions, but already Tara wondered if this was more than a straightforward crime.

* * *

Tara detested the place. It had been her only home since her days at Oxford, but now the apartment in the Wapping Dock complex next to the Mersey felt claustrophobic. When she had first moved here, she enjoyed a panoramic view across the river. Since then, new apartment blocks had risen, and her outlook was lost.

It was like the walls had eyes rather than the proverbial ears. They saw her in her most intimate, most vulnerable and lonely dispositions, and she didn't like the exposure. It was supposed to have been her happy place, her refuge from the horrors of her job, a cosy den where she enjoyed the company of her best friends, Kate and Aisling. But Aisling was dead, and it was her fault. And Kate blamed her too. She'd never said anything, but Tara knew, could feel that her one remaining friend now resented her because of the job she did, a job which ultimately had led to the murder of Aisling. Nonsense, of course, that the walls of her apartment knew all this, that they also blamed Tara for Aisling's death, but that is how she felt about her home. It wasn't made easier remembering that Aisling had lived in the same block, further along the hall and one floor down.

Tara couldn't stay here. In the four preceding months, while she recovered from her ordeal at the hands of serial killer James Guy, the beast who had taken her beautiful friend, she'd gone to stay with her parents in Caldy. It was never ideal, no matter how supportive and well-meaning her mother and father had been. The result was a different claustrophobia that she was relieved to finally escape with the excuse that she was returning to work. She was saddened that Kate had not invited her to stay. Was it proof that her friend blamed her for Aisling's death? Tara's fear was that the chasm between them might never be bridged.

It was well after nine and the TV was on with the sound muted, thankfully avoiding another dating show where singletons shared a house on a Greek island with a view to sharing each other's beds. Alcohol, though very welcome, had not been a sufficient crutch for Tara to lean on. After a week of drunken nights, it'd been her stomach that needed relief. That was just two weeks after her rescue from a cliff face in Anglesey. She realised then that if she didn't stop the heavy drinking she may as well return to said cliff and throw herself off.

In place of alcohol, she had self-pity and retrospection but tonight she also had contemplation of a case of murder. When she had finally left the station, she had brought with her several folders of freshly printed information. As she lounged on her sofa, a half-eaten chicken tikka wrap on the coffee table and a mug of strong coffee beside it, she read through her notes of an intriguing case. This was not the killing of Stephen Lloyd, a man only recently freed after eighteen years in Liverpool Prison. This was the case of his victim, the murder of a young student and the story behind her death.

CHAPTER 8

Elizabeth liked orange jelly. Lately, it was the one thing that made her smile. Once in her mouth she had little to do but let it slide down her throat. Her jaw moved as if she were chewing fillet steak and then she opened it again ready for the next spoonful. When it didn't immediately come, she grunted, hardly forming a word, until Jack obliged.

'You like that, don't you?' he said as she smiled again. 'If you finish all this, I've brought you some chocolate.'

There was little acknowledgement. Elizabeth merely smacked her lips. Eating jelly was her sole focus. Nothing else mattered. Her world revolved around eating titbits and staring vacantly into the centre of the room. Some days were better than others. She seemed to enjoy listening to the singers who came each Tuesday from the local parish church. At other times she would traipse around the corridors of her wing in the nursing home, pausing to gaze at the pictures on the wall. Each one seemed to have something to beckon her interest. Perhaps she recognised the images of the Hollywood greats – Humphrey Bogart, Spencer Tracy, Lauren Bacall, Richard Burton and Rock Hudson. At times, they sparked a personal memory. She had once even claimed to Jack that Gregory Peck was her brother Peter.

Jack visited on Mondays, Wednesdays and Fridays. He would spend the morning with his wife, feed her lunch and read the *Daily Mail* aloud. Not that she took much in. News was no longer news to Elizabeth. Not even family news. There had been, however, several random occasions when she had inquired about her father.

'Elizabeth, sweetheart, your father died twenty years ago,' Jack would reply.

'Oh,' she said. 'And what about Mum, have you seen her lately?'

'She's dead too, my love.'

'Dead? Oh, I didn't know.' Then she would retreat to her own mysterious thoughts leaving Jack to the silence of her room.

He was advised by one of Elizabeth's nurses that he should not correct her each time she asked such questions.

'It merely adds to her confusion,' the nurse explained. 'Memories of a long time ago come to the surface. It might be her childhood or teenage years. When she asks about her parents, she's reliving those times. She can't relate them to the periods in between. Each time you correct her it's as if she's hearing the information for the first time. That can be very upsetting. Ten minutes later, she's gone somewhere else. Your information has already been forgotten.'

Consequently, Jack got used to not putting Elizabeth straight on the facts of her past life. He played along with her questions, not lying to her, but hardly stating the absolute truth.

There were days also when the tricks in her mind played out in a performance for others to witness. One morning Jack arrived with newspaper, orange jelly and coffee to find Elizabeth embroiled in a face-off with the residents of the home.

'You can't come in here,' she was shouting. 'It's my office. You are not allowed. It's locked and I have the key.'

The room under guard from Elizabeth was the residents' day lounge. One of the carers was handling the stand-off.

'I'll take charge now, Elizabeth. The others won't do any harm.'

Elizabeth glared at the four residents, three women and a man with a walking frame. None of them had a clue what was going on.

'But I have the key.' She brandished a teaspoon in front of the female carer.

'Well then, you unlock the door, and we can both go inside. Without them,' she added in a whisper.

'OK,' said Elizabeth with a smile. She turned to the door and attempted to insert the end of the teaspoon into the lock. Nothing happened. Elizabeth was lost for what to do next. The carer took over and pushed the door open. The other residents shuffled inside behind Elizabeth and the carer. By the time Elizabeth had slumped into her armchair, the matter was forgotten. The carer smiled at Jack when he entered the room.

'Just another morning, Jack, nothing to worry about,' she said.

How Jack wished for such vigour to re-emerge in his wife. Nowadays, lucid conversation had all but disappeared. His one remaining joy was that she still recognised him. Once or twice, she said other names. She mentioned their son and confused him with their GP. She once said the name of someone he had no desire to hear of ever in his life, but Jack realised that Elizabeth didn't mean it. She had no motive in saying the name. It simply arose in her thoughts without relevance to anything. Then, recently, she spoke another name, a person she hadn't mentioned in a very long time. Jack was reading aloud at the time about the latest government proposals for tax rises. It could not have sparked anything in his wife to say the name.

'He came to visit,' she said, sliding another chocolate button into her mouth.

CHAPTER 9

The detectives in Harold Tweedy's team spent the entire day at St Anne Street examining various CCTV recordings from the area surrounding the Stephen Lloyd murder scene. Even Tara, with thoughts of this killing merging with those of the case she'd been studying at home the night before, had to do her share of watching.

Recordings from all cameras surrounding St John's Garden had been retrieved, including those from commercial premises. Tara, Wilson and Bleasdale sat together reviewing the first fruits of their work. Wilson controlled the mouse and scrolled through the timelines of interest.

'Firstly,' he said, 'we have our victim exiting St John's Garden at 12.26 a.m. He is pursued across the road by an individual and both disappear under the trees at the junction of Victoria Street and the tunnel entrance. Earlier, at 12.15, a camera near the roundabout at Old Haymarket and William Brown Street shows this.'

Tara watched two figures, indistinct but holding hands, stroll across the road, pause close to the Hillsborough Memorial then enter St John's Garden.

'Did any other camera pick up those two?' she asked.

'I've been watching all other traffic camera footage in the vicinity, ma'am,' said Bleasdale. 'Nothing else apparent in that time window.'

'Anything from cameras covering the other gates to the garden?'

'Just this,' said Wilson. He brought up a recording of a single figure running past St George's Hall. 'He or she is heading towards Lime Street station. The time was 12.25.'

'So, that happened just before our victim is pursued across the road towards the tunnel,' said Tara.

She paused for a moment.

'OK, since the initial attack seems to have occurred in a corner of the garden close to the entrance used by the couple holding hands, let's try to get more on them. Where did they come from? Is there anything that confirms one of them as our victim? Or one or both as our perpetrators?'

'One more thing, ma'am,' said Bleasdale. 'We've been trying to trace the vehicles driving by as Lloyd staggered across the road. No details of the registrations but hopefully another traffic camera further on can pick them out. Also, this might be worth checking.' Bleasdale selected another recording and pointed to the image of interest.

'This shows the fork in the road at Dale Street-Byrom Street. That's roughly forty yards beyond the final assault beneath the trees,' Bleasdale explained. 'Do you see the brake lights of that car? At first, I thought it was just slowing down but it had stopped. Twenty seconds later, it's gone.'

'The time was 12.28,' said Wilson.

'See what you can find out,' said Tara. 'It might be an accomplice to the attack, a possible witness or nothing at all.'

Tara left the detectives to their laborious task of peering at camera recordings and went to speak with Tweedy. She sat down in his office and ran through the latest developments in the case. Strangely, this morning, she felt as though she had never been away from her job. She was immersed in a fresh investigation and had no time for navel gazing. Today, she told herself, was going to be better than yesterday.

'So, you think you'll get what you need from CCTV?' Tweedy asked.

'Hopefully, we can establish a timeline and get an idea of the victim's whereabouts leading up to his murder. I have organised an appeal for witnesses that will go out on local TV and radio news this evening. Winston Lloyd will formally identify his son's remains this morning. I want to ask him a few more questions.'

'Good. I think you've covered everything. How are you feeling today? Yesterday was rather a plunge in the deep end.'

'I'm fine, sir. Getting on with it.'

'You know that my door is always open, Tara. You don't have to shoulder every burden on your own.'

'Thank you, sir. I appreciate that. There is one thing about this case that I'd like to run past you.'

'Fire away.'

'Lloyd had a conviction for murder. He'd only been released from prison last week, so there is a possible link to something there. Last night I read through the case file on Lloyd's conviction.'

'I recognised the name. It's an interesting background to our victim.'

'Indeed. I realise it was nineteen years ago, but I'm assuming you remember the events?'

Tweedy agreed with a slight nod of his head. 'It was a gruesome killing, and it was headline news at the time.'

'I suppose it's not every day that the daughter of the chief constable for Merseyside Police is murdered.'

CHAPTER 10

Winston Lloyd was tearful but composed, supported by his daughter Sylvia, as he confirmed to Tara and Bleasdale that the body they could see through the window was his son Stephen.

Tara thanked father and daughter for their cooperation and invited them for coffee. She had decided it might be less daunting to get it over with in a neutral setting rather than at the station or at the Lloyds' family home. They sat around a table in the restaurant of the hospital above the city mortuary.

Sylvia Waterson, one of Stephen's two sisters, was in her late forties with a close likeness to her mother Gladys. She wore a black overcoat and kept a hold of her father's arm as they sipped their coffee.

'I appreciate how painful this must be for your family,' said Tara. 'But there are some questions I have to ask.'

'Anything that helps you, Inspector,' said Winston.

Tara saw a thoroughly broken man sitting opposite her. She realised that no matter how carefully she might choose her words, they were bound to inflict more pain.

'We are doing all we can to track down your son's killer. We're trying to piece together Stephen's movements last Friday evening, where he went and who he may have met. There is a lot of CCTV evidence to go through and perhaps we can get all we need from that.' Tara hesitated over the intrusion that she knew would cause the man distress.

Winston looked her in the face.

'But we need to get some background on Stephen.' Tara realised she was going round the bushes, but how else could she handle this? She felt her tears rising. What the hell did that mean?

'I know you do, Inspector,' said Winston. 'Please, don't worry about me.'

Sylvia squeezed her father's arm.

'Can you tell me about Stephen's murder conviction?'

'Surely you don't believe that has anything to do with Stephen's death?' Sylvia's outburst caught Tara by surprise.

'It may not have, but I'm trying to build a picture of Stephen. It's worth trying to eliminate that aspect from our enquiries.'

Sylvia did not look impressed.

'Raking up the past won't get you anywhere. Stephen's life was ruined. He was going to be a footballer. Then he got mixed up with that damned family.'

'That's enough, Sylvia,' said her father. 'This is not helping the inspector.'

The woman continued to fume but turned her gaze away from the table.

'Do you think Stephen's conviction for that young woman's murder could be connected to his death?' Winston asked.

'It needs to be considered, Mr Lloyd.'

The man nodded his acknowledgement.

'Well, my son spent eighteen years in Liverpool Prison, Inspector. He was released last week. I know that the Winters family have grieved the loss of their daughter for all those years, but I can tell you this, Inspector, and it is the absolute truth. Stephen did not kill her.'

CHAPTER 11

Andy Greengates had good reason to be fearful when he heard the news about Stephen Lloyd. They had been mates. More than mates, he supposed, considering his circumstances and until last week Stephen's also. They had shared a cell for three years, and they had looked out for each other in this place. He knew things about Stephen, intimate secrets, including the story of how he had ended up serving a life sentence. And Stephen knew all about him, too. He'd told him everything he'd done in his past and not once had Stephen judged him. Besides, his victims had usually deserved what came to them. Twelve years he got for putting a sodding drug dealer out of business. The drugs had killed his girlfriend and in revenge he'd torn out the dealer's eyes. No real justice in that, Andy believed. He was looking at another three years before a possible early release. Inside, together with Stephen and a few others, he had tried to avoid trouble. But trouble had still come their way.

Andy reckoned he knew what had befallen Stephen but, stuck in here, he could never prove it or much less deal with the murdering bastard.

The Judas window on his door opened and he looked up from his book. He knew those eyes staring at him, laughing at him. On the outside, Graham Benson wouldn't stand a chance. In here, however, he was king, king-screw, and everyone knew it. One day, he thought. Only a matter of deciding which bit of him to cut off first.

'Sorry to hear about Lloyd,' said Benson through the slit. 'He would have been better off staying in here with you losers.'

'Fuck off and die, will ya.'

The hatch slammed shut but Andy could hear Benson laughing heartily as he moved along the landing.

* * *

When Tyrone Cunningham saw the news bulletin with the appeal for witnesses to the events that had occurred in the early hours of last Saturday, his first reaction was to call the police and tell them what he knew. His second was to cut the call mid-dial. It could so easily have been him. His mind raced to all manner of possibilities. Had someone Stephen knew been waiting to kill his friend? Or was it just a case of being in the wrong place at the wrong time? But if the killer was someone they both knew, was he likely to be next? It was for that reason that Tyrone decided not to go to the police. Let them work it out. Why should he put his life at risk? Stephen was dead. There was nothing he could do for his mate.

He refilled his mug with tea and wandered to his lounge window. Wet day, the bins were out, and the street was deserted. It was a normal day for him, and he hoped it would remain so. Angie had left for work, and he was free. In fact, he was free every day. He struggled to fill his time with anything but morning telly, a walk to the bookies after lunch then home in time to make dinner for Angie. Without her, he would have nothing. She understood him and tolerated him, asking for little, only that he tidy the house and prepare meals. If it wasn't for her, he would have been homeless after his release from prison.

He watched a car moving down the street, slowing when it neared his house. The front seat passenger peered out. Tyrone stepped back from the window. It was too late, he thought, they had already seen him. He didn't recognise the face, so why was the stranger looking in his direction? If it hadn't been for Stephen, he wouldn't have paid any heed. But now he felt an unease in the pit of his stomach. He hadn't felt that way since his first night spent in jail.

He knew that he'd made the right decision not to call the bizzies. Too dangerous. It had only been a few seconds, but it felt like hours before the car moved away. Its departure did nothing to soothe his nerves. He would have to be careful.

CHAPTER 12

Tara spent her lunch break online, browsing properties for sale on Merseyside and The Wirral. The notion of selling her apartment at Wapping Dock had surfaced immediately after Aisling's death. But she couldn't see it as a fresh start, not yet. It was simply a desire to get away. If she wasn't to pack in her job, then she needed to do something. Moving house was the only thing she could think of that might improve her state of mind.

She wrote a list of possibilities on a notepad. She didn't want to be plagued by estate agents hounding her day and night to make appointments to view properties in areas she had no desire to call home. Location was paramount. It sounded such a paradox, but she wanted freedom *and* security. The three addresses she highlighted were all on The Wirral. One afternoon she would leave work early and look for herself.

'How are things, Tara?'

It was Harold Tweedy standing over her. Tara knew that he wasn't enquiring about her house hunting. He was, however, asking about her well-being and not her current workload.

'Fine, sir,' she replied, closing her search on the computer. She was getting used to people tiptoeing around her. She would probably do the same if faced with the likes of her.

'We've had minimal response so far from the public appeal for information, but we are amassing a significant quantity of CCTV footage of the area surrounding St John's Garden.'

'Good. I'm sure it'll turn up something soon. Attacks in the city centre are usually well explained by CCTV evidence.'

'Yes, sir.'

Tweedy meandered off chatting to other officers, those pouring over the very evidence they had just been discussing. Tara browsed the file compiled so far on the killing of Stephen Lloyd. She felt impatient; she wanted to solve this case quickly. In some way she hoped it would spare the Lloyd family unnecessary pain. But the more information was gathered on the events of last Saturday morning, the more it appeared to be an opportunistic attack with robbery or mindless evil as the motive. Despite CCTV evidence, they might never find the killer.

She read through Stephen Lloyd's original case file again. At this point in her day, it was more interesting than the study of CCTV that occupied the others in Tweedy's squad.

Rebecca Winters had been described as attractive, and by some as promiscuous. She was a second-year politics and economics student at Cambridge and was ten weeks pregnant at the time of her death. Tara read the details of the murder, trying at first to regard it as she had any other killing. But within minutes, she was reduced to tears picturing her friend Aisling. Was this going to happen for every new case? Was each investigation going to be a mere excuse to relive her personal tragedy? She wiped her eyes with a tissue, furtively glancing around her. She imagined that everyone was staring at her. But her colleagues were busy: no one was paying her any heed. Feeling sheepish, she lowered her head again to read.

The body of Rebecca Winters had been found late on Christmas Eve on a country lane near Aughton and less than half a mile from her family home. Cause of death was stated as a broken neck resulting from a fall. Her body had been discovered below the first-floor window of a derelict building. Also recorded in the post-mortem report was a blunt force trauma to the forehead, either a consequence of the fall or inflicted by the perpetrator. The time of death was not definite but was estimated at between four and five hours prior to the discovery of the body.

Tara continued to read. She absorbed the details recorded of the crime scene, the subsequent investigation and the arrest, interrogation and charging of Stephen Lloyd with Rebecca's murder. A plethora of questions arose as she studied each report, an instinctive reaction from an experienced homicide detective. She was baffled as to why the file, a murder investigation file, was severely lacking in detail. Surely, there must be information missing. There was no consideration of the death having been an accident. Had Rebecca, for reason unknown, merely fallen from the window? Might she have been alone at the time of her death? Tara was surprised also to note just how quickly the case had been solved. Stephen Lloyd had been arrested on Boxing Day and questioned. The investigating officer was Detective Chief Inspector Ted Havers who at the time operated out of Admiral Street station. This puzzled Tara. Admiral was hardly the nearest main police station to where the crime had been committed. Even St Anne Street, itself a city station, was closer to Aughton.

After being released following his interview, Stephen Lloyd had been rearrested in late January and charged with the murder. At one point, Lloyd admitted to having been with Rebecca on that Christmas Eve but denied killing her. His DNA had been found in Rebecca's car and a single follicle of Rebecca's hair had been found on Lloyd's coat. No other suspects had been identified, questioned, or arrested in the intervening period. What Tara did not have was the transcript from Lloyd's trial. She made do with a brief online read of the publicity surrounding the murder, the subsequent media furore during the trial, and in the months afterwards the failed attempts to have Lloyd's conviction overturned.

CHAPTER 13

The late afternoon developed into a flurry of activity, snap decisions, numerous technical discussions, and officers despatched to several locations in the city. The study of CCTV recordings was bearing fruit. DS Wilson summarised the findings for Tara and Tweedy.

'We have traced the victim's movements all the way back to when he boarded a city-bound bus near his home.' Wilson peered at the screen. 'He boarded a number 27 bus on Anfield Road at 7.15 on Friday evening.'

The detectives watched the recording of Stephen Lloyd boarding the bus, taking a seat, alone, midway along the lower deck. Wilson then navigated to the point when Lloyd disembarked.

'He gets off fifteen minutes later at the Moorfields stop. A camera picks him up on Dale Street as he heads towards Crosshall Street. The next time we see him is three minutes later.' Wilson switched to another recording.

'Where are we now?' Tara asked.

'That's him entering The Docker's Rest in Cheapside. There's nothing more until 11.39 p.m. when the camera picks him up as he leaves the bar. But this time he's not alone.'

The detectives watched Lloyd emerge from the bar and turn right. The resolution was poor and both individuals wore dark clothing, but Lloyd was holding the left hand of his companion. The range of the camera only covered the entrance to the bar and ten feet to either side. It wasn't enough to get a clear picture of the person leaving with Lloyd. Tara clucked.

'Is that everything? Where did they go next? Did they go directly to St John's Garden?'

'We have nothing more so far, ma'am,' said Wilson. 'They may have merged with others or even split up before we see the victim again.'

'We need to know what happened next. Who was Lloyd's companion? How did they spend their time before Lloyd was attacked?'

'Yes, ma'am. I'll keep at it.'

'No. We're going to The Docker's Rest. It's our first opportunity to find some witnesses.'

* * *

Cheapside was little more than an alley between Dale Street and Tithebarn Street. It was the site of the Bridewell, a Victorian prison and now a hotel. Dotted along it were several small businesses – hairstylists, tattoo parlours, betting shops – but mostly it contained the rear entrances to large public and commercial buildings including blocks of student accommodation and private apartments. The Docker's Rest was situated forty yards off Dale Street. It wavered between its reputation as an Irish pub, a sport's bar and on occasions had gained popularity as a gay social spot.

Tara noted the position of the security camera directly above the doorway as she entered the premises. The interior was modern although the lighting was too dim for her liking, not personally, but from a professional point of view, in that poor light masked information that could be useful to an investigation. Contemporary pop music blared to a near empty bar. It could have been any of the so-called boy bands or, as Tara considered them, boy-blands. She preferred her music to be hard rock.

Wilson approached the bar where a youngish barmaid in white T-shirt and black jeans was restocking a cooling cabinet with bottled beers. She had long straight black hair and a thin face.

'Hiya, love. What can I get you?'

Wilson introduced himself and Tara, then explained the reason for their visit.

'Didn't you get our CCTV already?' she interrupted.

'We did, thank you,' said Tara. 'But there's been a development. Our murder victim was in this pub on Friday night. We'd like to ask you some questions.'

The woman's cheery demeanour had altered, although it seemed that her lively eyes would always present as friendly.

'Fire away, love,' she said, closing the door of the cooling cabinet. 'My name is Stella. I'm the manager, and I was here last Friday night.'

Wilson set a printed copy of the picture of Stephen Lloyd, taken from Winston Lloyd's phone, onto the bar.

'This is our murder victim,' said Wilson. 'He's recorded on your CCTV entering the bar at 7.33 on Friday evening. Do you remember him?'

Stella lifted the photo and studied it carefully.

'Er, yes. I remember him. Was he killed after leaving here?'

'I'm afraid so,' Tara replied. 'We're trying to track his movements earlier on Friday night. It appears that he spent several hours in here. Did you see him interact with anyone?'

'I can't say what happened later in the night because we got busy. It was Friday; the place was jam-packed. But when he first came in, he sat in the corner with another fella.' She pointed to a booth where there was a round table and upholstered bench seating.

'Not much I can tell you,' she said with a shrug. 'They seemed ordinary fellas if you know what I mean. Didn't bother anyone else, just sat with their pints and talked.'

'Did they leave together?' Tara asked. 'Mr Lloyd was recorded leaving at 11.39 p.m. He was holding someone's hand.'

The barmaid shook her head.

'Sorry, love. I've no idea. Like I said, the place was hiving until one o'clock.'

'If you looked at your CCTV recording,' Wilson began, 'would you be able to pick out the guy who sat with Mr Lloyd?'

'I could try.'

'That's great, thank you.'

Wilson gave Stella his contact details and asked her to call at St Anne Street as soon as possible to review the CCTV recording.

'Let's hope that the guy who sat with Stephen Lloyd is the same person he left with,' said Tara when they had stepped into the street. 'If not, then this investigation will get increasingly complicated.'

'At least, if it is the same individual, we might have a motive.'

'You mean a homophobic attack?'

'Yes, ma'am. If it was a male holding his hand. Maybe the pair were attacked.'

Tara's mind raised other possibilities.

'Then perhaps we should confirm whether or not Stephen Lloyd was gay.'

CHAPTER 14

When you were in prison there was no best time of the day. Early morning could be fine some days, with activity and chat about the match on TV the night before. Late afternoons were quiet once educational classes, sports and gym, and cleaning had finished for the day. You could be alone for a time unless something kicked off. That was a daily occurrence on his wing. It was one thing for two inmates to lose it with each other or with one of the screws, but it was bloody irritating when it was the screws who started the trouble. Andy tried his best not to get involved. When he'd first arrived here, he would have been at the centre of it, taking a beating, or a pumping from one of the pervs on the wing. He could dish it out too. But the tough nuts had either grown tired of harassing him or they were satisfied that he'd been put in his place. Now, only the screws messed with his head.

Benson was at the forefront of it, but he encouraged his lackeys to join in. Even the female screws couldn't be trusted. Having a vagina didn't stop them from sticking their boot in your groin or putting a knee in your neck while one of their pals did the kicking.

There was no best time of the day in a place like this, but night-time was definitely the worst.

This evening, for instance, he struggled to get comfortable. The pain in his ribs caught him when he drew breath. The taste of blood in his mouth after his face had been slammed on the tiled floor of the shower room had turned fetid and made him nauseous. When they'd left him cowering on the cold floor, walking away, laughing at their work, he'd decided on a little revenge. Instead of cleaning himself and then skulking back to his cell, he paraded down his landing stark naked displaying the scratches and bruises on his body, allowing blood to trickle from his mouth. He made sure he was picked up on the cameras. Maybe someone on the prison staff had a conscience. It was proof anyway that life was dangerous for the inmates, and someone would have to delete the recording to get rid of the evidence.

Of course, he should have realised that he was heaping more trouble on himself. Two screws grabbed him by the arms and frog-marched him to his cell. Lydia Jennings removed the clothes from his locker and took them away.

'If you want to go around bollock-naked, be our guest,' Benson jibed as he slammed the cell door.

He lay beneath a blanket staring at the ceiling. Lydia Jennings was another screw's name to be added to the list. And now there was more evidence of abuse to pass to the outside. Tyrone would know how to use it.

CHAPTER 15

'I have two new babies,' Elizabeth chirped.

'Have you, dear?' Jack had no enthusiasm for the ridiculous conversation. Lately, his wife seldom made sense and he was tired of the charade. He handed her a square of Dairy Milk and returned to his paper.

'The nurse brought them to see me. They're gorgeous. Twin girls, you know. I'm keeping them beside me.'

Jack gazed about the room. To his right sat Myrtle, a woman in her nineties and well beyond the stage of dementia that Elizabeth was currently experiencing. There was precious little of her, withered in an armchair staring to a point in the carpet and with a trail of drool on her chin. On Jack's left was Charles, an octogenarian with bottle-glass lenses and a bloated stomach. He was dressed each day in a three-piece suit as if ready for a tough day at the GPO where he had worked for forty-one years. He held the same newspaper in his hand as Jack, *The Echo*. Whilst Jack struggled to read between the wacko comments from his wife, Charles read nothing at all. His paper was upside down. At the far end of the lounge, morning television was in full swing with a wannabe celebrity confidently informing the British public it was unwise to over-indulge in highly calorific foods during Christmas.

'Father called in yesterday,' said Elizabeth.

'Did he now?' Jack passed her another piece of chocolate then resumed his reading.

Elizabeth had taken no notice of Jack's reply and licked melted chocolate from her fingers. After several moments, she surprised her husband by adding to her comment.

'He's in the room next to mine. Died in the bath. I told the nurse. Chocolate.' She held out her hand and Jack obliged. 'We carried him outside this morning.'

CHAPTER 16

Late autumn was hardly an ideal time of year to consider buying a house or flat, but Tara supposed that if she liked somewhere now it could only look better come summertime. Before venturing inside any of the properties she had chosen to view, she wanted to get a feeling for the location. If it didn't seem right, then there was little point in wandering through the place. Stepping from her car into a sharp wind with an icy sting to it, her eyes were immediately drawn to the end of the short road where it met the sea. A beach, no more than fifty yards from your doorstep, had a heart-warming appeal. She slipped her hands into her anorak pockets and held her face into the breeze. There wasn't a sound, not even from the shore. She smiled and cast her gaze upon the house she had come to view. First impressions were that it was much too grand for her needs. She had noted this and the lofty price tag from her online search but couldn't resist having a look. The first two properties she'd viewed were apartments, one too small and in need of renovation, the other in a less desirable location. She had now set her mind on a place close to the sea and preferably near Hoylake.

A car drew up behind Tara's. A young woman got out and greeted her with a warm smile and a cheery 'hiya'.

'Hi there. I'm Tara Grogan.'

'Ah yes, I'm Mandy Wetton from Clark's. You're here to view number 47?'

Tara guessed Mandy to be in her early twenties. She was dressed in a warm overcoat and flat shoes, the wind playing merry hell with her long fair hair that she had to sweep continually from her face. She led Tara along a winding tarmacked drive to the front door of the two-storey house. It was fifty years old in red brick with the lounge and bedroom windows positioned to capture a partial sea view.

From her first step inside the hall, it was clear to Tara that this house had been a family home, well lived in. Carpets throughout the ground floor, a cosy fireplace in the lounge, bookcases in a study, and then she fell in love instantly with a kitchen that oozed country appeal. She was not a great cook, but she often longed for time to spend in a space such as this, fumbling through celebrity recipes, having the girls over as her guinea pigs. Barbecues and cool wine in the summer, lounging in the garden gazing at the sea. Tara was going to have a battle in her mind to walk away from such visions.

Mandy Wetton didn't need to add much as she observed the woman taking everything in without comment.

'What do you think?' she asked, finally.

'It's much too big for me,' said Tara, wistfully.

'You live alone?'

'Yes.'

Mandy smiled sympathetically and Tara sensed that she was being pitied. Did she really appear that lost?

'We have several lovely apartments in the area if you're interested.'

Tara swept her hand over the granite counter and gazed through the window.

'No, thank you. I think I'll submit an offer for this place.'

She had a rare tingle of elation as she drove back to the city. Fresh start, a new outlook, or running away, she couldn't decide. She told herself it was simply moving on. She prayed that her offer would be accepted, and she could soon be free of Wapping Dock. Her mind bubbled with plans for her new home, fresh décor, new furniture, a huge bed overlooking the lawn to the sea, albeit a tiny strip of seascape viewed between other houses. But then she was only a few yards from the beach. There, she could walk, or maybe run again, come home to a hot shower, and round off her day with a mug of drinking chocolate in front of the telly. Perhaps Kate would bring Adele to stay and the three of them could have picnics and games in the garden. It was all going to be wonderful.

Back in the flat at Wapping Dock, the files on the coffee table captured her attention and thoughts of a new life were swept beneath those of her latest murder case.

Tara could not dismiss the notion that Stephen Lloyd's death might be connected to his conviction for the murder of Rebecca Winters. Or was it mere coincidence that he was killed only a few days after his release from prison? The question of Lloyd's sexuality puzzled her. She'd read that his conviction for murder had centred on a sexual motive, but surely Lloyd would not have felt that way about his victim if he was gay. There had been no evidence of sexual abuse having taken place and yet he'd been accused of stalking and finally killing Rebecca because she had rejected his advances.

CHAPTER 17

Stella Ramsey, the manager from The Docker's Rest, turned up promptly at ten thirty at St Anne Street station. Tara greeted her at reception on the ground floor.

'Thank you for coming, Stella. We really appreciate your help with this.' Tara led the way upstairs to their operations' room.

'Don't know if I can be of help. So many faces going in and out of the bar. I hope they don't roll into one.'

Tara sat the woman down in front of a computer monitor and went in search of Wilson.

Stella smiled meekly as he took a seat beside her. Tara left them to it and busied herself with a backlog of emails.

'We want to run through the recording from around the time when Stephen Lloyd came into the bar,' Wilson explained. 'If you see anything out of the ordinary, just stop me. I'll speed up the playback when there's nothing happening.'

Stella sat rigidly, gripping her bag as Wilson played through the CCTV footage taken from The Docker's Rest.

It began at the point when Lloyd had entered the premises. Stella made no comment. She watched for thirty minutes as several people either entered or left the bar.

'Anything?' Wilson asked. Stella shook her head slowly.

'Sorry. I don't recognise anyone.'

'OK. Maybe the person Lloyd met was already inside when he arrived. We'll go back to a period before then.'

Wilson left Stella browsing and went to fetch coffee for them both. When he returned Tara was sitting next to the woman. They were staring intently at the screen.

'How certain are you, Stella?' Tara asked.

'Definitely him. That's the guy who met with Stephen Lloyd. He's been coming in regularly of late.'

'Name?'

'Tyrone.'

'Surname?'

Stella shook her head and accepted a cup from Wilson.

'I only know him as Tyrone. Sometimes he comes in with a couple of other lads and a few times with a woman. We share a joke. One of his mates asked me out but I didn't accept.' She held out her left hand showing an engagement ring on her third finger.

'Congratulations, Stella,' said Tara. 'When's the big day?'

'Next September. Just booked the reception last week.'

'That's lovely. I wish you all the best. And thank you for your help this morning. Can you tell us anything about Tyrone? Even the most trivial detail might help us to trace him.'

'Can't think of anything,' Stella replied. 'He's just an ordinary bloke.'

Wilson scrolled through more of the recording from that Friday night. He stopped and replayed another short piece for Stella to watch.

'Is that Tyrone leaving?' he asked.

'Yes, that's him. I remember him wearing that white baseball cap,' said Stella. 'He's worn it every time I've seen him.'

Wilson then retrieved the footage showing Stephen Lloyd's departure from The Docker's Rest over two hours later.

'It's clear now that Tyrone is not the person who left the bar with our victim,' said Wilson.

'Yes,' Tara agreed with a sigh. 'So, we're searching for this guy Tyrone and another individual we have yet to identify.'

They looked again at the image of Stephen Lloyd leaving the bar holding the hand of another whose image was unclear.

'Do you recognise the person leaving with Stephen?'

Stella shook her head.

'Sorry,' she said. 'It's hard to make anything out from that footage.'

Tara even doubted now that the figure was male. Perhaps the victim's sexuality was not relevant at all here.

Tara thanked the young bar manager for her help. Stella agreed to alert them the next time she saw Tyrone in The Docker's Rest.

At least it was progress, Tara thought. Soon they would have someone to question over the death of Stephen Lloyd. But what rankled with Tara was that Lloyd had left the bar that night with another stranger and they had no clues so far on their identity. She would have to content herself with tracking down the man named Tyrone and hopefully it would give them a lead to follow up.

While her colleagues continued to work on tracing vehicles recorded on CCTV at the time of Lloyd's murder, Tara's thinking switched again to the case of Rebecca Winters. The files she'd read prompted as many questions as they had answered, but what she really wanted to do was to speak to the people involved at the time. She realised, of course, that once she began asking questions, she would have to explain her interest in an old case of murder, one which had been closed successfully eighteen years ago.

CHAPTER 18

Tara drove to the Lloyds' family home on Hornsey Road. The door was opened by Sylvia who did not look pleased to see her.

'Hi, Sylvia. I would like to ask a few more questions about Stephen.'

'Mum and Dad aren't here. They've gone to the funeral home.'

'Perhaps you can help me.'

Resignedly, Sylvia opened the door wider allowing Tara to enter, and led her to the kitchen at the rear of the house.

'Can I get you some coffee?'

Surprised, Tara accepted the offer, feeling that a more casual chat between two women was better than her playing the role of a brash police detective. On their first meeting, she hadn't found Sylvia terribly cooperative.

'What do you want to know?'

Tara sat down at a small dining table and looked on as Sylvia prepared the coffee. She brought her up to date on the investigation of Stephen's murder and explained her difficulty in identifying the people he'd met on the night he died.

'Can you tell me if your brother was gay?'

Sylvia paused and glared icily at Tara.

'How is that relevant? Is that why he was killed?'

'Can't say that just yet, but we have Stephen recorded on CCTV leaving a city centre pub holding someone's hand. The image is indistinct, but it looks more male than female.'

'My parents don't know,' Sylvia explained, placing a coffee mug in front of Tara. 'There's little point in upsetting them now that he's gone. He told me a long time ago that he was gay. Since he was locked up in prison, I didn't feel it was right to tell Mum and Dad.'

'At the time of his trial did you know that he was gay?'

'Why ask me that?'

Sylvia sat down opposite Tara, cupping her hands around her mug. She was answering the questions but remained indignant. Tara could understand Sylvia's coldness where law enforcement was concerned. She believed that her brother had been wrongfully convicted of murder. His life had been ruined and the police were responsible.

'I've been looking at Stephen's conviction, his trial and the news reports at the time. There is no mention of his sexuality despite the prosecution's argument that the murder was sexually motivated.'

'Back then I don't think anyone would have known that Stephen was gay. Don't think he would have been sure himself. But I had my suspicions. For one thing, he didn't have girlfriends, especially at a time when he should have had girls chasing after him because he was going to be a footballer.'

'Did he ever talk about such things?'

'I'm nearly ten years older than Stephen. We didn't share secrets like that. Not then. He didn't open up to me until after he'd gone to prison.'

Sylvia pulled a crumpled tissue from the pocket of her cardigan and blew her nose.

'Do you think Stephen's death has something to do with Rebecca Winters?' Sylvia asked.

'I really don't know. But the murder of Rebecca had a huge impact on Stephen's life. It needs to be considered if only to eliminate that aspect from the inquiry.'

'You heard what Dad said. Stephen didn't kill Rebecca. The last time we spoke he said that he was going to clear his name.'

'Did he tell you how he was going to do it?'

'No, he didn't elaborate.'

Tara nodded and drank her coffee.

'Stephen just wanted to make it as a footballer,' said Sylvia. 'He had no interest in anything else.'

'How did he and Rebecca meet?'

'He got friendly with her brother Freddie. I assume they met around town, although I don't see how they ever had anything in common.'

'How long had Stephen and Freddie known each other?'

'For about two months before Rebecca died.'

'How did she fit into the scene?'

'Stephen told me she was a feisty girl. He really seemed to like her, though, but he'd only met her once. That was on the day she died. He said that she was cheerful and witty.'

'What was Stephen's version of the story?'

Sylvia shook her head, then stared earnestly at Tara.

'Stephen had no idea what happened to Rebecca. He was more disappointed by Freddie's reaction. Refused to speak to him. Right from the start, he blamed Stephen for killing his sister. But I know that wasn't true, Inspector. Rebecca was alive when Stephen last saw her. Freddie had invited Stephen for lunch on Christmas Eve, but when he got to the house Freddie wasn't there. His mother met Stephen outside the door. She thought it was funny that he had a wasted journey.'

Tara thanked Sylvia for being so candid and promised to keep her informed of progress in the investigation. The issue of Lloyd's murder conviction was not going to leave her. Until she could find evidence that his death was down to a random attack, homophobic or otherwise, it would remain in her thinking.

CHAPTER 19

Tara had an appointment with Assistant Chief Constable Ted Havers who occupied an office in the headquarters building of Greater Manchester Police. She drove into a car park set amongst ultra-modern buildings off the Oldham Road. She couldn't help looking around her, a vision of commerce and enterprise to the north-east of Manchester city centre. But the location was of little concern. She had an uneasy sensation in her tummy, always nervous about meeting a senior officer.

After a five-minute wait in reception, she was collected rather than greeted by a secretary. The sandy-haired woman in her forties with a freckled face and a businesslike smile chatted about the weather as she accompanied Tara to the second floor. But the small talk didn't settle her nerves. They entered an outer office and Tara expected another wait. To her surprise, she was shown directly into the office of ACC Ted Havers.

'DI Grogan, a pleasure to meet you, especially a colleague of Harold Tweedy's. How's he doing these days?'

Havers had a broad smile, a trim face and thick combed-back hair. He was fit-looking and suited the white police shirt and dark tie. 'Please, have a seat,' he said, his voice cheerful with an essence of Merseyside.

'He's fine, sir,' Tara replied, sitting on one of the two cushioned chairs opposite Havers. 'Sends his regards,' she lied.

Tweedy had never mentioned any relationship he'd had with Havers, aside from serving in the same force in neighbouring stations. She had asked Tweedy's permission before arranging the meeting, but Tara felt her boss was rather cool to the idea. Tara had explained that she wanted to get the facts of the old case straight in her mind. It might be the only way to move on from that aspect of the Stephen Lloyd investigation.

Havers hadn't stood to greet her, nor had he shaken Tara's hand. He sat behind his desk and moved his keyboard aside as if to suggest that he'd been working hard before Tara showed up.

'So, how can I help you this morning?'

'Well, sir, I'm investigating the murder of Stephen Lloyd in Liverpool a few days ago.'

'Should I know the name?' Havers had his fingers pressed together as if in thoughtful prayer. For a second, she was reminded of Tweedy.

'He was convicted of the murder of Rebecca Winters. You were…'

'Ah yes, of course. How could I forget? I put him away.'

'Yes, sir.'

Tara, neatly dressed in trousers and matching dark jacket, felt the nerves in her voice as though she was at a job interview.

'What do you want to know?' he asked, opening his hands wider as if to welcome her question.

'I've been reading Lloyd's file on his conviction and noted that the murder of Rebecca Winters was regarded as sexually motivated.'

Havers listened but allowed Tara to continue.

'It is not mentioned that Stephen Lloyd was gay. I just wondered why.'

Havers smiled confidently.

'I have no idea. Irrelevant perhaps.'

'Did you know when he was arrested that he was gay? Did he tell you?'

The ACC shook his head doubtfully.

'I really don't recall that kind of detail, DI Grogan. How do you think it relates to Lloyd's death?'

'Just trying to piece things together, sir. We are working on the possibility that Lloyd was murdered in a homophobic attack. I suppose I am interested to know how a gay man could have had a sexual motive for the murder of a young woman.'

'From what I do recall, I don't think it simply came down to sex. There was a rather intense relationship between Lloyd and the Winters girl.'

'I see.'

'If there's nothing further I can help you with, DI Grogan, you'll appreciate that I have a busy day ahead.'

'Yes, sir, thank you for your time.'

Feeling dismissed, Tara rose to leave. Havers was already moving to the door to see her out. She suddenly thought she might not get another chance with this man and decided to air another doubt she'd been harbouring.

'Sir, one more question about the Rebecca Winters investigation.'

'Go ahead.'

'Was there any particular reason why you were appointed SIO on the case? I mean, you weren't based at the nearest main station. It was more likely to have been an officer at St Anne Street rather than Admiral Street.'

'Availability, DI Grogan. You should know how it is. I imagine I was free at the time, that's all.'

He opened the door and waited for Tara to leave. She smiled thinly but ventured a final question knowing it was likely to irritate the senior police officer.

'Did you find it strange, sir, that no other suspects were ever questioned over the murder?'

'Not at all. It was a very safe conviction. Lloyd waited on a country lane on Christmas Eve for Rebecca Winters to come home. When she rejected him, he pushed her from the first-floor window of a derelict farmhouse. She was pregnant, did you know that?'

'Yes, I read that.'

'As callous a murder as you can get, DI Grogan. I have no sympathy for Stephen Lloyd. Nice to have met you, though. Good luck with your investigation.'

Tara strolled to the lift pondering what had just happened. Ted Havers had been reasonably courteous, polite and he answered her questions, but why did she not feel convinced by the man? One reason was that he had not immediately recognised the name Stephen Lloyd. The murder of Rebecca Winters had been a high-profile case, arguably the highest that Havers ever had to deal with. You'd think the name would have instantly registered. Surely, he would have heard about Lloyd's murder. And how did Stephen Lloyd have an intense relationship with Rebecca Winters? According to Stephen's sister Sylvia, he and Rebecca had only met once.

CHAPTER 20

They had warned each other to be careful. Andy was not pleased that Tyrone had even come to see him. Too dangerous. It would only take one of those screw bastards to decide they were up to something, and he would get another late-night visit to his cell.

'We can't go to the bizzies,' Andy whispered harshly to his mate. 'They don't give two shits about the likes of us.'

'But they're looking into Stephen's murder,' said Tyrone. 'We can tell them that he'd been threatened in here. That I've been threatened and you're still in danger. We can give them the names of the screws, Benson and the others.'

'No, mate. Too risky. We have to sit tight until after the complaints against him have been dealt with. He doesn't know that we're behind them. If we go to the bizzies about

Stephen, then Benson will know it's us gunning for him. I'm still in here, remember. If the complaints don't stick, then when I get out, we'll sort him for good. Don't worry, Benson will get what he deserves. Then we'll take the rest of them one by one.'

'Can't see our complaints scaring the likes of Benson. It will all be swept under the carpet. No one cares about abuse in this place. But we have a chance to get him for murder.'

Andy shook his head, no.

'How are we going to prove it was Benson who killed Stephen?' he said.

Tyrone left the prison discouraged by Andy's view. Surely, getting Benson for murder would put an end to his band of evil screws. Why couldn't Andy see that? He realised, though, as he boarded a city-bound bus that Andy was a sitting duck in prison. But he supposed that once he'd been released, he would exact his revenge on the prison staff.

Tyrone wasn't sure if he was happy about that. Andy was capable of all sorts of nasty stuff. Getting Benson and his cronies was one thing, but innocent people would get hurt. The families of the screws didn't deserve to come to harm. He worried that Andy wouldn't know when to stop.

* * *

Graham Benson watched the CCTV recording of the prison's visiting room where former inmate Tyrone Cunningham had just had an intense conversation with Andy Greengates. Benson didn't like it. They were getting too clever. He should have sorted Cunningham before he was freed, but it hadn't seemed necessary at the time. There was no talk of an inquiry then. Yes, he'd been reprimanded by his manager but so what? If things ever got hairy, he could simply claim stress and take a few months off. Some of these inmates, total filth they were, didn't deserve a warm cell and three meals a day. That was no punishment for the things they had done. They should be taught a proper lesson. They needed something to remember of this place when they were freed. Maybe things got out of hand with that twat Lloyd, but he never imagined that it would go as far as senior management. None of the scum had ever taken the official route before now. They just took their punishment and left when their time was up. But Lloyd and his mates had other ideas.

Benson's thoughts were interrupted by Lydia Jennings entering his office. Her appearance was deceptive. She had a slight build and a soft face, but she was fit, and accomplished in self-defence, a first dan in jiu jitsu. Benson would not hesitate in bedding her if she gave him the chance.

'You looking at porn again?' She quipped, leaning her body across him to reach her coffee mug. He smelled her scent and savoured the touch of her hand on his shoulder. 'The IT people monitor what we look at on that computer, you know.'

'I'm just watching those two having a cosy chat.' He showed Jennings the two men seated opposite each other in the visiting room.

'Cunningham! What a waste of space. You're not bothered by the likes of him, are you?'

'Not usually, but don't you think it's strange that he shows up here after Lloyd's dead and he's talking to Greengates?'

'You're getting paranoid in your old age.' Jennings squeezed Benson's shoulder. 'They don't have anything on you. They haven't two brain cells to rub together. Lloyd was the only one with any sense, and he's been sorted for good.'

'I suppose you're right. I'm just nervous about this inquiry.'

'Nothing to worry about there either. They won't find anything. As long as the scum keep their gobs shut. We just have to make sure they do.'

Jennings slid her hand from his shoulder down Benson's chest and squeezed. 'Don't worry, mate. We've got your back. Now, what do you want to do about that new bloke?'

Benson swivelled on his chair, watching Jennings as she filled her mug with coffee. She had a lovely ass, no doubt about that.

'Just make sure he has a nice shower before bedtime.'

CHAPTER 21

They were the original victims in the Stephen Lloyd story. Tara realised she was probably taking a step too far, but she really wanted to meet the Winters family. It would be interesting to get their views on the man who had been convicted of murdering Rebecca. The problem for Tara was how to justify such a meeting to her superiors and to the Winters family. Rebecca's murder was neither an open case nor could it yet be proved that it was connected to Lloyd's death. But Tara could not discount it.

It was late in the afternoon, a miserably damp day outside her office window and she was searching for words that would at least satisfy Harold Tweedy. Might a member of the Winters family have waited for Lloyd's release from prison to exact their revenge for Rebecca's murder? She could put that question to Tweedy, but would it be enough to sway him? She doubted it.

Wilson brought her some news that raised even more questions.

'Ma'am, we've continued to look at CCTV in the city centre on the night that Lloyd was attacked.'

'And?' She almost glared at her colleague as if he was interfering rather than adding to her day.

'If you want to take a look.'

She followed him to a desk on the other side of the office where Bleasdale was scrolling through video recordings.

'So, what have you found?' Tara asked, wanting to be impressed but not feeling confident about it.

'One of the vehicles we noticed stopping when Lloyd ran across the road from St John's Garden,' said Wilson. 'We still don't have a registration, but a similar vehicle was picked up by cameras earlier in the evening around Cheapside.'

Bleasdale retrieved the footage Tara had seen before, showing a car at the junction of Dale Street with Byrom Street.

'The brake lights come on,' said Bleasdale, 'and the car remains stationary for twenty-eight seconds then moves away. We've found what we believe is the same vehicle on three occasions earlier in the evening.'

Bleasdale navigated to another portion of the recording.

'This shows the traffic lights at the London Road-Lime Street junction, close to the Empire. There are roadworks here, but you can see a similar vehicle passing through. The time is 7.42 p.m.'

'Are you sure it's the same car?' Tara asked, sounding peeved. 'Do we even know the make and model?'

'From this portion,' said Wilson, 'it's a Jaguar, metallic blue. But this next piece might be more convincing.'

Bleasdale revealed a still picture of a metallic blue Jaguar parked on a single yellow line.

'The time is 9.23 p.m.,' she stated.

'Where is this?' Tara asked.

'It's at the junction of Dale Street with Cheapside.'

'That's only fifty yards from The Docker's Rest,' said Wilson. 'And that's at a time when Stephen Lloyd would have been inside the bar.'

'I've compared the rear light pattern of Jaguar models to the pattern of the car seen at the Dale Street-Byrom Street junction at the time of the attack on Lloyd,' said Bleasdale. 'It matches a Jaguar F-Pace SUV.'

'I've checked the Jaguar website,' said Wilson. 'There are twenty different models available.'

Tara glared in frustration at her DS.

'But you can't pin it down to one model, and you don't have the registration?'

'Not yet, ma'am,' Wilson sighed.

Aware that she may have sounded too negative about the discovery and the hard work it had involved, Tara changed her tone.

'It certainly casts doubt on the opportunist robbery or homophobic attack theory,' she said. 'Good work, folks. So, there may have been someone loitering in the area on the night Lloyd was murdered. We just have to find out who and why.'

* * *

'Good night, DI Grogan,' said the desk sergeant, Dave McLachlan, in a cheery tone. Dark-haired and fit, McLachlan exuded a friendly manner but, seemingly, reserved it for the attractive women at St Anne Street station.

'Night, Dave. Have a good one,' Tara replied as she made for the exit. McLachlan's eye lingered on the DI until she exited the building. On her drive home Tara answered two phone calls.

CHAPTER 22

Dark nights were the worst. Elizabeth's agitation bubbled over when the care worker drew the curtains in her room, her prison. Bedtime came early, at just six thirty. She was left alone as the demons seeped from the walls and swirled around her cot, goading and mocking her with threats of damnation. There was always one that hovered close to her face. Its breath was ice-cold, with the stench of a putrid swamp, its fangs snarling, and its piercing eyes like black holes, where only hatred and malice lurked. Elizabeth pulled the duvet over her head. Just as quickly, Marni, one of her carers, slipped it back.

'You mustn't do that, Elizabeth,' Marni scolded. 'You will suffocate.'

'They're here again,' Elizabeth muttered. 'Please get them out of here.'

Marni, a forty-year-old immigrant worker from southern India, smiled and gently stroked Elizabeth's forehead.

'No one here but you and me, Elizabeth. Try to sleep. All will be well in the morning.'

Suddenly, she was alone again with them clawing at her body. She didn't dare move for fear they would rape her or drag her away to hell. She pulled the duvet back over her head.

'Go away! I'll call the police! Fuck off! Fuck off!'

The mantra was repeated until finally Elizabeth drifted into sleep. But even in sleep evil bodies slithered around her, groping her, slipping their bony hands into her intimate places, pushing into her mouth until she choked, then gripping her neck and squeezing hard. Amid this mayhem a young girl sailed on a breeze, looking down on her and smiling. Elizabeth reached for the beautiful creature, but she could never get a hold. Something pinned her to the bed. Then those bloody demons returned. Night-time was the worst for Elizabeth.

'Fuck off!'

The night staff in the nursing home knew to ignore her cries.

'They were here last night,' she said to her husband the following morning.

'Were they, dear?' Jack replied, offering a spoonful of orange jelly.

'My baby daughter too.'

'Well, that was nice for you.'

CHAPTER 23

Tyrone Cunningham sat uncomfortably in interview room two at St Anne Street station. He had a nervous tick that caused his left cheek to twitch. He was conscious of it, and each time it happened he followed it up by wiping a sleeve across his mouth. Since the age of seventeen the now forty-two-year-old had known freedom periodically for a total of just eight years. It wasn't the first time he'd sat in a police interview room. Wasn't even the first occasion he'd sat in St Anne Street's.

'Why am I here?' He demanded to know as Tara sat down next to Wilson. Informed of the news that Tyrone Cunningham had been brought to St Anne Street, Tara, on her way home, had turned around and headed back to the station.

'You tell us, Mr Cunningham,' Tara replied.

'What the hell does that mean? You brought me here.'

Stella Ramsey had been swift in alerting the police when she next saw Tyrone Cunningham enter The Docker's Rest. A patrol car had been despatched and two uniforms had escorted Cunningham without fuss from the bar to St Anne Street station. Tyrone, despite his bolshy question, knew exactly why he'd been brought to the nick.

'I haven't done nothing.'

'I haven't accused you of anything,' said Tara with a forced smile. 'Tell me about Stephen Lloyd?'

'Don't know him.'

'Come on, Tyrone,' said Wilson. 'Don't mess us about. We know that the two of you were buddies in Liverpool Prison.'

'So?'

'And we know that you met him in The Docker's Rest on Friday, 8 September.'

'So what?'

'Stephen was murdered later that night,' Tara put in. 'Do you want to tell us about that?'

'Fuck off! I don't know nothing about no murder.' Cunningham's cheek twitched and he wiped his sleeve across his mouth. Tara had decided that a worried expression was the default for Tyrone Cunningham. He had a pimpled complexion, watery blue eyes and untidy mousey hair. It was understandable to regard him as shifty.

'Tell us why you met with Stephen at The Docker's Rest,' Tara asked.

'Like you said. We were mates. He'd just got out of prison, and we met up for a pint.'

'That's all?'

Cunningham shrugged dismissively, twitched and wiped his mouth.

'What did you talk about?' Wilson asked.

'Don't remember, football, beer, fuck knows.'

'What time did you leave Mr Lloyd?' Tara asked.

Cunningham shrugged again.

'Don't know, about nine, half-nine, something like that.'

'And Lloyd was still there?'

'Yes.'

'Had he met anyone else before you left? Another friend, perhaps?'

'He said he was going to have another pint and then head home. He was on his own when I left.'

'And did you see him later that night?' Tara asked.

'No! I went home.'

'Any thoughts on who might have wanted to kill him?' Wilson asked.

For a moment Cunningham looked stunned as if Wilson's question had suddenly hit a nerve. He shook his head. This was not the time to tell the bizzies anything. Andy had warned him to keep quiet. Tara had noticed the hesitation as Cunningham wiped his mouth.

'OK, Mr Cunningham. That will be all for now. If you think of anything that might be of help, no matter how trivial, please get in touch.' Tara gave him her card.

Cunningham wasted no time in getting out of St Anne Street station. Such places gave him the creeps.

'Good night, again,' said Dave McLachlan.

Tara smiled.

'I hope this is it,' she replied.

As she drove home to Wapping Dock, Tara reflected on the other phone call she'd taken earlier in the evening. Mandy Wetton from Clark's Estate Agents had called with the news that her offer on the property in Hoylake had been accepted.

CHAPTER 24

'That's brilliant, Tara.'

'I know, I'm really excited about it.'

'Adele and I can't wait to see it,' said Kate. 'Beside the beach, you said?'

'Yes. It's just a few yards along the road.'

The two friends had snatched a few moments for coffee before heading into work. Tara could hardly wait to share her news. She had come to realise that Kate was especially worried about her since Aisling's death, and more so since she had resumed her job for Merseyside Police.

'All we need now,' said Kate, 'is for you to find a new career to go with the new house.'

'If I'm to afford the new house I'll be working as a cop for a long time to come.'

Kate, fresh-faced and as usual sporting a daring hair colour – this morning a silvery pink – looked disappointed by Tara's remark. She and Aisling had always worried about Tara and the hazards she faced in her job.

'Well, cheers for making a fresh start.' Kate raised her latte and Tara sipped her Americano.

'Talking of fresh starts,' said Tara, 'how have you been getting on?' She wanted to ask, "how have you been getting on since Aisling's death?" but she couldn't bring herself to say her friend's name.

'I'm fine. Adam and I have finally decided to call it a day, so no more back and forth to each other's flats.'

'I'm so sorry.'

Kate smiled wistfully.

'I'm not. At last, I can get on with things. Adele is settled into school and I'm trying to get a better shift at the hospital. Things are looking up for me too.'

'You're welcome to come and live with me in Hoylake. It's such a big house. I don't need all the space and I would love the company.'

Tears emerged in Kate's eyes and, embarrassed, she attempted to wipe them away with her fingertips.

'Sorry,' she said. 'Told myself that I mustn't get upset every time we meet up. My crying won't bring Aisling back.'

Tara now had to soak up her own tears. She placed her hand on Kate's.

'Think about it. Hoylake would be a wonderful place for Adele. Good schools, plenty to do and the air is fresher than the city.'

'Do you think we're always going to be on our own, Tara? That neither of us will ever find a good man to love?'

Tara knew the answer for herself. She didn't want to think the same for her best friend.

* * *

It was as peaceful an area as one could ever wish for. Firs Lane lay between Aughton and Ormskirk as far off the beaten track as it was possible to get in this part of the world. Tara and Bleasdale parked several yards from the entrance to the lane. They strolled past the first houses, a trio of converted farm labourers' cottages on the right-hand side, and a hundred yards further along a single detached cottage resplendent in white. There was nothing more for half a mile until they reached a pair of stone gate posts, ornate brass lanterns perched on each one. There was a badly tarnished plate on one post with the name Briarwood Manor still visible. The wrought-iron gates were closed and secured with a rusting chain and padlock. Tara gazed at the grey-stone house at the end of a sweeping and weed-strewn driveway. The architecture was Victorian gothic with bay windows and pitched roof, although there was a modern extension that included a sunroom on the south-side. It wasn't derelict but it didn't look as though it had been inhabited for years. Bleasdale located a spot to the left of the gates.

'Might be able to get through here, ma'am,' she said, tramping dock weed and nettles into the ground with her foot. The two officers managed to scale a low barbed-wire fence, stepping into a patch of soft mud before reaching the driveway.

'Glad we're not wearing heels,' said Tara. 'You never know when you might have to traipse through ground like this.'

On reaching the house, they noticed that the doors, front and back, had been sealed with metal grills and the ground-floor windows had been bricked up.

Tara looked up at the first floor.

'It's a fantastic building. Must have been a super family home until the tragedy.'

'There was a book written about the murder,' said Bleasdale. 'I came across it when you mentioned the connection between Lloyd and Winters. I picked up a copy in Waterstones. It's supposedly a true account of what happened.'

'I wouldn't mind having a look at that.'

Tara rattled the grill fixed across the front door of the house.

'We may as well head back, we're not going to find much here.'

'We can have a look at the spot where Rebecca's body was found,' Bleasdale suggested.

They re-traced their steps along the drive, negotiated the mud and fence then stood again on Firs Lane. The next building, a quarter of a mile further down the lane, stood only a few feet off the road and was derelict, a stone shell with some of its roof intact. Bleasdale checked her notebook.

'Rebecca was discovered below a first-floor window to the side of the building,' she read.

They located the spot where the young woman had been found by a police patrol on Christmas Eve nearly nineteen years ago.

'Less than five minutes' walk from her home,' said Tara.

'According to the investigation file, Lloyd attacked her on the first floor then pushed her from the window. She broke her neck from the fall and probably died instantly.'

'But why bring her here?' said Tara.

'I think you should read the book, ma'am. All those questions are raised by the author.'

'What's it called?'

'*Road to Nowhere.*'

CHAPTER 25

Tara had intended to review the evidence gathered so far on Lloyd's murder. Her most likely suspect was the person with whom he'd left The Docker's Rest. But Tara believed it would be difficult to identify this individual. While she sat at her desk thumbing through the pages of *Road to Nowhere*, two of her team waded through yet more CCTV recordings from the night of the murder. Gradually, Tara was drawn into the text of the paperback. The cover was a muted blue image of a country lane resembling the one she and Bleasdale had visited earlier in the day. She noted the tagline beneath the book title: "a harrowing tale crying out for the truth."

Tara read the brief profile of the author Anthony Sawyer on the first page. Sawyer was an investigative reporter, originally from Manchester – a Cambridge graduate who had worked on several newspapers in the northwest and then had become a freelance journalist and author. She noted his three titles published since *Road to Nowhere,* each of them dealing with mysterious true crime stories in the north of England. *Road to Nowhere* had been published three years after Rebecca Winters' murder.

It wasn't long before Tara was engrossed in Sawyer's telling of the events surrounding the murder. Deciding that she would be more comfortable at home, she bid goodnight to the five members of the squad still working on Lloyd's case.

With a lasagne ready meal inside her, she settled down on the sofa with a glass of chardonnay and the paperback. The TV was on, but the sound was muted, a reality show playing where young attractive people were holed up in a country estate attempting to solve a fictional murder. Tara had no interest; it was purely background. Alone in her flat, at least the pictures on the TV imbued a feeling of company. She longed for the home she hoped to buy now that her offer had been accepted. There was added hope that Kate would decide to move in with her.

As with many such true crime books, the author began with several chapters on the family background.

The Winters family had moved into the house, Briarwood Manor on Firs Lane, when Rebecca was just fifteen months old. Prior to the move and flourishing careers and salaries, the family had lived in a terraced house in Woolton. Both parents worked full-time and could afford to employ a housemaid, and a nanny for their children. The kids attended private schools and were quite active, Rebecca participating in a local pony club and her brother playing rugby. It was soon apparent, however, that the boy, to his father's dismay, showed little interest in such a brutal pursuit. Consequently, in place of rugby, he was enrolled in a drama academy in the city and was moderately successful in several local film and television roles.

Rebecca developed into a rather bookish young lady, who sailed through school and opted for study at university. Only during her sixth-form years, and her subsequent first year as a student, did she emerge from her books and become outgoing and indeed quite daring.

Tara felt that Sawyer had demonstrated a liking of the Winters children. His scorn, Tara got the impression, was reserved for the parents. The father was described as a bulk of a man. A former university rugby player, he was an imposing figure and possessed a rather antagonistic attitude to go with the physique. Tara read that he had been a successful financial director in the Liverpool office of a global bank. His wife, at the time of Rebecca's murder, had been the serving chief constable of Merseyside Police.

Several glasses of wine consumed and late into the night, Tara continued to read the account of the Rebecca Winters' murder. She noted with interest how Stephen Lloyd had been portrayed by the author. It was clear that Sawyer had contempt for the man convicted of the killing. Lloyd was described as a dull-witted youth, and as someone who had ingratiated himself with the Winters children. He had played on his prospects of becoming a professional footballer with a top club and had mixed with those people who had an interest in courting celebrity. Sawyer stated that Lloyd had latched onto Freddie Winters after several meetings at night clubs in the city. Having befriended Freddie, he then pushed for an introduction to his attractive sister Rebecca. This had been his undoing, Sawyer had stated. Rebecca Winters was intellectually far superior to a state-educated man with little interest in the world beyond a football pitch. The cliché "could have had him for breakfast" sprang to Tara's mind. While Lloyd proceeded to chase after the affections of Rebecca, according to the author, she had led him a merry dance that turned to horrific tragedy on the night when Lloyd finally cracked and put an end to her life.

Tara wondered where the mystery lay in this story if Sawyer, from the outset, was fitting Lloyd as the murderer. Before reading, she had assumed the book to be an account of a miscarriage of justice. It seemed not. Sawyer, despite posing many unanswered questions and highlighting shortcomings in the police investigation, did not contradict the guilty verdict for Stephen Lloyd.

By the time she finally tossed the paperback to the side and moseyed off to bed, Tara realised that there were many unanswered questions regarding the murder of Rebecca Winters. But more importantly, she wondered if finding those answers would lead her to Stephen Lloyd's killer.

CHAPTER 26

Before going on duty at Liverpool Prison for his two-to-ten shift, Graham Benson opened a letter he'd lifted from his dining table. His wife, Nikki, had discarded it with a pile of junk mail and it had nearly been missed when he'd gathered the bundle of envelopes to dump in the recycling bin.

Nervously, he glanced over his shoulder to an empty living room. Nikki was already at work and the kids were at school. No one else in his family were ever to know what was stated in the letter. It would destroy his marriage, never mind his career. Instead of the news that he hoped would arrive confirming his promotion to the highest band in his prison officer role, he was informed of a disciplinary hearing he was required to attend. There were no details of the charges against him. It merely stated that this was a preliminary hearing after which a decision would be taken on whether to progress to a full disciplinary tribunal. Benson's hands shook as he read. He realised that those slimy no-hopers on his wing had had the balls to go to the prison senior management with their allegations of abuse. Sod them! Lydia was right. They had no proof. His team would remain tight-lipped. Say nothing and they could prove nothing.

Closing his front door and stepping to his pride and joy, his gleaming car, he realised that the meeting between Greengates and Cunningham had been far from innocent. The pair of them had been scheming. But he would ensure that they got what they deserved. Reversing from his driveway, he gazed at the cracked glass of his lounge window, thinking also that he had something of a defence for his disciplinary hearing. Someone had been stalking him and had thrown a brick at his home. Nikki and the kids had been traumatised. A clear case of a prison officer subjected to abuse simply for doing his job.

But his unease was compounded when he attempted to enter the staff car park at the prison. Waiting by the security gate to meet him was senior manager Desmond Robertson. He was a pleasant-looking man of forty-five with greying hair and a businesslike smile. He would perform this unpleasant task by the book. Standing next to him was an admin assistant who'd come to act as a witness.

Benson lowered his window.

'Good afternoon, Graham.'

'What's going on?' Benson asked, looking confused from Robertson to his companion whose name he couldn't recall. Maureen, he thought, was her first name. The woman, with short blond hair and a pudgy nose, didn't acknowledge Prison Officer Benson. She was present merely to witness the proceedings. She stood as close to Robertson's burly shoulder as she could get.

'I am here to inform you that pending your disciplinary hearing next month, you are suspended from duty on full pay, effective immediately. Please surrender your photo ID and electronic pass to Miss Russell and leave. You are not permitted to enter any location within the prison.'

Benson couldn't summon words. He wanted to swear at the supercilious bastard, tell him he was wrong, but he knew it was pointless. What he really wanted to know was whether any of his colleagues had been dealt the same fate. It was clear from Robertson's stance that he was not prepared to say anything further. Benson pulled his lanyard over his head and handed it to Maureen. With that done, Robertson instructed Benson to turn his car around and leave.

On the drive home, he thought about how to get back at Cunningham and Greengates before they did any more damage. He thought also of what he was going to tell Nikki. She would not be happy.

His reluctance to go home became too much, and instead he drove to Crosby beach, parked the car by the sea wall and began making calls to the people who, he considered, needed to know what was happening to him. By the time he'd spoken with his closest colleagues, he knew that for now he was on his own as far as disciplinary hearings were concerned. No one else on his team had been suspended. Then suddenly Benson understood what was happening. He was being set up to take the blame. He was the senior officer on his wing. Management was intending to make an example of him.

He sat for more than two hours, gazing over wide, open sands and the strip of grey sea in the distance. A car pulled in next to his, and he smiled at the driver. She had come to see if he was all right. The woman left her own vehicle and climbed into the passenger seat next to Benson.

'So sorry, mate,' said Jennings. 'We're on your side. You know that, don't you?' She leaned over to give him a hug, but in seconds they were kissing passionately. Benson would have more than the news of his suspension to hide from Nikki.

When they had cooled their passion, Jennings posed several questions for her supervisor. She lay across his lap, Benson stroking her hair and face.

'Is there anything you need me to do?'

'Keep an eye on Greengates, make his life difficult but don't overdo it. We don't need any more complaints.'

'No problem. What are you going to do?'

'Cunningham needs sorting. I don't know how but I have to make sure he is not going to be a witness at any hearing against me.'

'I can help with that.'

'How? I don't want you or any of the others getting dragged down with me.'

'It won't come to that, Graham. No one in the team is going to speak out. Meantime, I can help you sort Cunningham.'

'I think he's the guy who threw a brick at my front window. Maybe I should just play the victim here?'

'You can do both,' she said. 'Sort Cunningham and Greengates *and* make it seem like they've been coming after you.'

'Clever girl.' He ran his fingers through her hair as she opened his fly.

CHAPTER 27

Tara hoped a meeting with Anthony Sawyer would be a discreet way of learning about the Winters family. Maybe then she could set aside this angle to the Lloyd murder and get on with the search for his killer. Bleasdale, through the author's publisher, had managed to set up an afternoon appointment for Tara with Sawyer at a coffee shop in Liverpool One. Tara spent her morning revising by rereading salient extracts from *Road to Nowhere* and compiling a list of questions to ask the author. Most were related to the points Sawyer had raised in the concluding chapters of the book.

Approaching two o'clock and feeling peculiarly nervous, she made her way to Caffè Nero in Lord Street. Glancing around the interior, she didn't see anyone who she imagined could be Anthony Sawyer, so she bought a cappuccino and chose a table away from those occupied by shoppers on a break from their retail pursuits. Eventually, at 2.45, a tallish man wearing a brown sports jacket and dark jeans entered the shop, gazing around him. He had dark wavy hair, designer stubble or perhaps was merely unshaven, a dimpled chin and crows' feet developing around his eyes. Immediately, Tara concluded that this stranger was her appointment, Anthony Sawyer, arriving fifteen minutes late. When he looked in her direction it seemed that he had made a similar assumption. He bounded towards her.

'Hello, I'm Anthony Sawyer, might you be DI Grogan?'

Tara stood and held out her hand, smiling broadly.

'That's me,' she said more coyly and less professionally than she'd intended.

'Just a sec, I'll grab a coffee,' he said, making for the counter. 'Can I get you anything?' he called.

'No, thanks, I'm fine.'

While she waited, Tara was conscious of straightening her blouse and running her fingers through her short hair. If she'd had a mirror to hand, she would have been checking her make-up.

'Thanks for agreeing to meet me,' she said when Sawyer at last joined her and slipped off his jacket.

'No problem. Always happy to help the police. Being a journalist, I'm also intrigued by your request. How can I be of help?'

'I've just finished reading your book on the Rebecca Winters murder. It was very interesting, very interesting indeed.'

'Thank you. I assume you're not working on the case. I hadn't heard that it was reopened.'

'No, you're right, it hasn't. I'm investigating the murder of Stephen Lloyd.'

'Ah yes, of course. I'd heard about that. And you want to know if someone connected with Rebecca Winters could be involved in his killing?'

Tara was slightly unnerved by the speed at which the conversation was going. She was used to asking the questions, but so far Sawyer had asked more than she had.

'I'm considering the possibility,' she replied. 'When I read your book, I realised that there are still questions to be answered regarding the Winters murder, despite the fact that Lloyd had been convicted and served his sentence.'

Sawyer slurped his flat white.

'OK,' he said. 'But I'm not sure that I can help you. I haven't found any more answers since I posed the questions in the book. Haven't looked, to be honest. It's been a few years since it was published. I can't think of any developments in that time.'

'Apart from the murder of Stephen Lloyd.'

'Yes, of course.'

'Since Rebecca's case is closed, we don't think it appropriate to approach the family directly to ask about Lloyd, at least not without some justification.'

Tara wondered if the author was already tiring of the conversation. He was gazing around the shop. Suddenly, he was out of his seat and approaching the counter again.

'Can I get you anything to eat?' he asked over his shoulder. Tara declined the offer. Several minutes later, the man resumed his seat and tucked into a ham and brie croissant.

'Sorry, I haven't had lunch, or breakfast come to think of it.'

Tara was frustrated. They were fifteen minutes into a meeting where so far, she had learned nothing except that Anthony Sawyer appeared to be a man distracted. She moved what she had intended to be her final question to the top of her list.

'Do you think any of the Winters family would be capable of killing Stephen Lloyd in revenge for Rebecca?'

Sawyer, mouth full of food, shook his head.

'Don't think so,' he managed. 'My impression of the father when I met him was that he just wanted it all to go away. He was relieved that the police convicted Lloyd so quickly. In my dealings with him for the book he was never keen to comment on the murder. Once Lloyd's trial was over, I reckon he consigned all of it to the past and moved on.'

'What about the mother?'

'A different kettle of fish. She was chief constable on Merseyside at the time. It was no secret and completely understandable that she pushed hard for a swift conclusion to the case. Although she had to be seen to be impartial, she exerted her influence to make certain that Lloyd was charged with the murder.'

'Do you believe he was guilty?'

'I said so in the book. Although I have no doubts that Rebecca gave him plenty of motive. She goaded him, teased him, promised him things, sex obviously. She played him, Inspector, and he was the type to be sucked in. It was your typical Greek tragedy.'

'I'd heard from Lloyd's family that he'd only met Rebecca on one occasion, the day she was killed.'

Sawyer shook his head dismissively.

'I don't believe that was the case. Even if it were true, it only takes one meeting for someone to commit a murder.'

'You also raised questions about the mother.'

'Yes. I must admit, I didn't like her. Too glib. I asked questions about details of the case, forensics, timing and stuff but she dismissed all of them and me for that matter. She did not approve of my writing the book. Tried but failed to block publication.'

Tara knew of the doubts raised by Sawyer in his book, but she wanted a first-hand account of them.

'What was the problem with the forensics?' she asked.

'Mainly the lack of forensic detail presented in court. I'm sure plenty of evidence was gathered at the scene but very little was mentioned during Lloyd's trial. For example, nothing was ever presented regarding sexual assault having taken place and yet that was the motive expressed by the prosecution for Lloyd killing Rebecca. She rejected him, and he lost his rag.'

'Anything else?'

'Rebecca's body was found beneath a first-floor window as if she had fallen or had been pushed, but the forensic report suggested that the body could have been placed in that position. Yes, her neck was broken, consistent with a fall, but the shape of the body on the ground didn't support the injury being incurred at that location.'

'You suspect Rebecca was killed elsewhere and her body moved?'

'Exactly.'

'But who?'

'I still believe it was Lloyd, but I think he killed her in the family home and then he carried her outside to make it look like she'd had an accident.'

'Do you believe that the chief constable suppressed that aspect of the investigation?'

'I think she was determined not to involve her family or her home in the murder inquiry. She had her own reputation to protect. She would not have wanted scores of detectives and forensics people going through her private life. It's bound to be the reason why her home was never searched, not even the garden and grounds.'

'You mentioned the timing of the murder,' said Tara.

'Yes. The family account, Lloyd's account in his statement, and the recorded time of death did not tally at all. From what the chief constable told investigating detectives, Rebecca went missing in late afternoon. Lloyd stated that he visited the house around lunchtime on Christmas Eve. That's also consistent with witness statements of the two people who noticed him on Firs Lane. Rebecca wasn't reported missing to police until the evening, shortly after seven. Her body was discovered later, close to midnight. The temperature was at least -2°C and time of death was estimated between five and six that evening. That puts Lloyd inside the Winters' home or at least in the area at tea-time. Witness statements suggest that Lloyd departed Firs Lane before two in the afternoon. These discrepancies were never presented in court. When I asked the chief constable to clarify she became defensive and bluntly directed me to the police report.'

'Seems as though I should attempt to meet the former chief constable, although I doubt that I'd get permission.'

'You'd be wasting your time anyway,' said Sawyer.

'Why is that?'

'Elizabeth Winters suffers from early-onset dementia. She's spent the past year in a nursing home.'

CHAPTER 28

'The only family member we haven't talked about is Freddie Winters,' said Tara, sipping at another cappuccino. Sawyer was enjoying a second flat white.

'Of all the family, he is the one person I was most suspicious of.'

'In what way?'

'I think if there was any conspiracy by the family to hide something then Elizabeth and Freddie were at the centre of it. Many of my requests for information from the family were denied, I suspect, to protect Freddie and not Rebecca's reputation. He was Mummy's little pet. She saw no wrong in her son.'

'Any chance that he was responsible for his sister's death?'

Sawyer frowned.

'It is plausible, but the timeline doesn't fit. According to the family, Freddie was not at Briarwood Manor during that day or the early evening. Of course, this testimony may not be truthful.'

'But Freddie had invited Lloyd to the house for lunch,' Tara remarked.

Again, Sawyer shook his head dismissively.

'I think Freddie, the little shit, genuinely forgot about his invitation to Lloyd. I can't believe that Freddie would have wanted Lloyd to show up at his family home when he wasn't going to be there. Too risky for Freddie's new friend to meet his mother without him. I reckon he made the invitation when he was off his head on some illegal substance, or he was plain drunk. He would never have invited Lloyd intentionally.'

'Why on earth would Lloyd go chasing after Rebecca if he was gay?'

'When I interviewed him in prison, Lloyd told me that at that time he had not come out regarding his sexuality. He was frightened about revealing he was gay. He was intending to become a professional footballer and back then being gay would have hindered his career.'

'What about Freddie?'

'I think he was experimenting. Unsure of how he felt sexually. He refused my requests for an interview. But I think he was under Mummy's orders.'

'Did Lloyd and Freddie have a sexual relationship?'

'Lloyd told me they did, but he said that Freddie was the one who insisted upon secrecy. There was no way Freddie wanted his mother to find out. Lloyd claimed that Rebecca knew of her brother's sexual preference, and she was the type to have taunted him. That had always been their sibling relationship, teasing each other until one or the other cracked. It's possible that Rebecca threatened to out her brother, and he lost his temper and killed her. Of course, the circumstantial evidence doesn't support the theory.'

'But if it were true, it would give Freddie a motive for murdering Lloyd.'

'Yes,' Sawyer agreed. 'Especially if Lloyd was determined to clear his name and was in possession of evidence that proved Freddie was the killer.'

'Do you think that Lloyd had such information?'

The author shrugged.

'If he did, he didn't mention it when I interviewed him.'

'Whatever happened to Freddie Winters?'

'He skipped the country a couple of years after the murder. He is a financial wizard for an American bank. He's been married twice, has four kids and lives in Hawaii.'

'Not gay after all?'

'Apparently not.'

Following a short pause during which Sawyer eyed the food counter again, Tara studied the writer. His eyes suggested that he was quite a jolly man. She enjoyed how he looked at her as if they were on a first date. He'd been forthcoming, but a little hyper. There was perhaps a lot more going on in his day than a conversation with a police detective about one of his books. When she again had his attention, she posed a question that had niggled her since she'd first read the book.

'You didn't refer to Rebecca's pregnancy. Why was that?'

He grinned wryly.

'Elizabeth Winters threatened to sue my ass off if I mentioned it.'

'Why did that stop you? It was cited during the trial, and it was established that Lloyd was not the father.'

'At the time of writing I got the feeling that a lawsuit was not the only thing that the bold Elizabeth would use against me.'

'You mean she threatened violence?'

Sawyer gave a redolent shrug.

'Look, Inspector Grogan, I really must get on. It was a pleasure to meet you. I hope you're successful in finding Stephen Lloyd's killer.'

Sawyer got to his feet and slipped on his jacket. Tara was taken aback by his sudden need to get away.

'Here is my number,' he said, handing her his card. 'Call me.'

'Thanks for sparing the time,' she said. 'It was very helpful.'

He smiled again, revealing perfect white teeth.

'Call me,' he repeated. His gaze lingered on her for a moment longer than was comfortable, but she matched his smile before he turned away.

CHAPTER 29

The sun descended to a haze that hung over the Irish Sea, creating a vermilion stain across the western sky. The sea lapped gently to shore as Adele trotted joyfully over muddy sand in bright yellow wellies and matching raincoat. She was perfectly equipped for splashing in puddles and a half-expected rebuke from her mother did not come. Tara and Kate meandered along the beach savouring the tranquillity, each asking questions of the other about the plans for Tara's new home.

'Please, say you'll move in with me?' Tara begged, aware that she sounded desperate. 'It makes perfect sense, Kate. We're both on our own, and Adele would get so much from living here. Look at her.' The six-year-old trailed a thick ribbon of seaweed behind her, intrigued by the lines it made on the sand.

'But what if you suddenly find Mr Right?' said Kate. 'I'd be out on my ear!'

'You know I'd never throw you out. Besides, that's very unlikely to ever happen. Finding a man is not high on my list of priorities. And if you found someone, our living arrangements can always be changed. Just tell me that you want to live here with me, for now, and we can start to plan the rooms.'

Kate laughed nervously.

'What the hell! Let's do it.'

The two best friends hugged, and Adele skipped over the beach to join in.

* * *

Back in the flat at Wapping Dock, Tara browsed Anthony Sawyer's book, hoping for some tiny clue that would shed light on her present case. Several things mentioned by Sawyer when they had met still troubled her. He believed that there had been a slapdash approach to gathering the evidence used to convict Lloyd. The forensic report had been largely ignored and may even have been altered or sections deleted. For instance, where were the details of Rebecca's post-mortem examination relating to whether intercourse had taken place prior to her death? If there had been evidence to suggest that the body had been moved after death and placed below the window of the derelict farmhouse, where were the details of a subsequent search to prove it? At the very least the grounds of Briarwood Manor should have been searched. There was no record of this having been done. The timeline didn't stack up either. Sawyer's view was that the entire trial hinged on the testimony of the Winters family, particularly Elizabeth, and the finding of Lloyd's DNA in Rebecca's car.

Tara sipped her wine, wondering how on earth Lloyd had ever been found guilty of the murder. She'd learned that meeting Elizabeth would be futile, and with Freddie living abroad that left the husband Jack Winters. Perhaps he would agree to a meeting. The only other person of interest was the SIO of the investigation. She wished she'd read Sawyer's book prior to her meeting with Ted Havers. Now she would have to bother him a second time and imagined that he would not be forthcoming. No professional police officer cares to have their integrity challenged.

CHAPTER 30

Tyrone and Angie had gone to the pub for a few drinks after the cinema. Angie enjoyed herself, a romcom was her kind of movie, but Tyrone could not relax. He'd heard that the screw Benson had been suspended from duty at the prison. That meant things were moving. Maybe they would finally expose what the bastard had been up to for years and they would get justice for Stephen. Andy had warned him to be careful. If they were named as witnesses, then Benson and his mates would come after them. Andy was in the most danger. The rogue screws, those that did Benson's bidding, could easily get to him. Andy had instructed him to go to the papers if he was threatened. Get the story in the news and the screws could do nothing but wait for the disciplinary. He wondered which of them had killed Stephen. Surely Benson would have avoided getting his hands dirty. That bitch screw Lydia Jennings would do anything for old Graham. Ex-army, Jennings could certainly handle herself. She'd knocked him to the floor more than once. Jennings could easily have killed Stephen on her own. Had she been waiting for him that night when he left The Docker's Rest?

Angie, a cheerful forty-five-year-old, three years Tyrone's senior, slipped her arm through his as they left their local on Queen's Drive. She seldom wore flat shoes on a night out because she enjoyed the sensation of walking in heels. She clipped along the damp pavement in stilettos and slim jeans. Fortunately, they had only to walk half a mile to reach home. The road, even after ten o'clock, was busy with traffic. Tyrone listened as Angie regaled him of the machinations of her family, her two sisters, their fellas and their problems travelling home from Greece with cancelled flights and airport strikes. He was glad they had turned down the invite to go with them. A holiday was not something they could afford right now. Angie was sensible in that respect. She knew there would be better days ahead. Several times she had told him that she was happy just to have a man to love her and treat her nice. She didn't need the world, only his love and company. Once he got settled into a job they could think about a holiday. He realised that Angie was perfect for him. When all this bother with Stephen's death and prison screws was finished, he could get his head together and really have a go at making a better life for himself.

They strolled along East Prescot Road passing Alder Hey Children's Hospital, oblivious to a car slowing down behind them. When they turned into Woodbourne Road, the car followed. A few yards on, they reached an alley that ran behind a row of shops, and briefly were caught in the glare of the car's headlights. This was a dead-end street, a quiet neighbourhood, only Tyrone had reason to believe they were in danger. Suddenly the car cut across them, and two darkened figures jumped out. Tyrone had little time to react.

'Run, Angie!'

He pushed her away, but she struggled to run, hampered by her shoes, squealing as she went.

Tyrone stood ready to take them on, his fists clenched. A broad figure in a woollen mask and hooded anorak bounded towards him wielding a claw hammer.

'You know what this is about, don't you?' said a deep voice. He swiped his arm wildly and the hammer thumped against Tyrone's shoulder. He yelled in pain but avoided his attacker's next blow. Then he saw Angie. His distraction was costly. Pain shot through his face as the hammer cracked his jaw and blood spilled from his mouth. He toppled over, crying out for his girlfriend.

The other assailant had pursued her. Angie managed only baby steps on her high heels. It was just a few more yards to her house. She squealed. The swipe of a heavy wrench caught her on the side of the head. Her lifeless body slumped to the ground.

'Leave it the fuck alone, or you'll get worse,' that same deep voice shouted.

Tyrone couldn't imagine anything worse. Oblivious to his attackers speeding away, he crawled along the pavement to help Angie.

CHAPTER 31

'How was the honeymoon?' Tara asked. 'And I don't need lurid details.'

Murray smirked. Marriage hadn't cured his lewd sense of humour.

'Great,' he replied. 'I can recommend the Maldives.'

'I'll keep it in mind.'

'So, what have I missed?'

Murray threw himself into the chair at Tara's desk. He was in great spirits, and she wasn't about to burst his bubble. Instead, she perched herself on the edge of the neighbouring desk, her legs dangling over the side. She told him about the Stephen Lloyd murder and was describing what she believed to be an important connection with the death of Rebecca Winters, when DS Wilson approached.

'Ma'am, sorry to interrupt but there's something of interest I came across this morning.'

'It's OK, John. I was just bringing Alan up to speed. What's happened?'

'The lads in Huyton attended the scene of a street attack on Saturday night off East Prescot Road. A couple were assaulted on their way home from the pub.'

'Someone we know?'

'Well, the female was dead at the scene. Her name is Angela Campbell, forty-five from Knotty Ash. Her companion was injured and he's in hospital. It's Tyrone Cunningham.'

Tara puffed air through pursed lips. Murray looked on eagerly, waiting for an explanation.

'I recognised the name in the report,' said Wilson.

'We'd better have a word with Tyrone,' said Tara. 'Can you find out if he is well enough to be seen by us?'

'Ma'am.'

As Wilson went to check on their chances of visiting Cunningham, Tara continued explaining her present case to Murray. She was pleased to have her main assistant back from honeymoon. She'd missed him. As she spoke, however, it dawned on her that an attack on Tyrone Cunningham, if connected to the murder of Stephen Lloyd, would have little to do with the death of Rebecca Winters nineteen years ago. The more she explained the connection between Lloyd and Cunningham, the more the relevance of the old case diminished. Now she felt rather foolish. Had she wasted two weeks going down a blind alley? To quote Anthony Sawyer, a road to nowhere.

* * *

The news from Aintree Hospital was that Cunningham was not fit to be interviewed by police. He was unable to speak; during surgery several small plates held together with screws had been fitted to repair multiple fractures of his lower jaw. A meeting with the ex-offender would have to wait. Tara had to settle for whatever information she could get via Wilson from police in Huyton. So far, no witnesses had come forward other than neighbours who had found the victims immediately after the attack. Frustratingly, no motive had yet been established. Perhaps it was a completely random assault, although there was no mention of robbery. Tara knew little about Tyrone Cunningham. He'd met Stephen Lloyd in The Docker's Rest on the night he was murdered, and they knew each other from their time spent in Liverpool Prison. The attackers might be linked to drugs or gangs with a score to settle. But it was Cunningham's girlfriend who was dead, and he had survived.

Tara had to rethink her entire strategy as far as finding Lloyd's killer was concerned. Over coffee in the canteen, she finished telling Murray about Lloyd.

'Until this morning when I heard about Tyrone Cunningham, I'd convinced myself that the answer was linked to Rebecca Winters.'

'And now?'

Murray's eating habits had resumed after his pre-wedding diet. He scoffed a jam doughnut, while Tara sipped her coffee.

'If the attack on Cunningham is linked to Lloyd's murder, then it makes no sense to consider the Winters killing any further. But at least we know that Lloyd's death was never a random assault.'

Despite her logical evaluation, Tara continued to run her thoughts past Murray on Rebecca Winters' murder. At least it made interesting conversation on his first day back to work.

'The police investigation was riddled with holes. A lack of procedure, poor record keeping and possibly suppression of evidence. And then there's the fact that the victim was the daughter of the then serving chief constable. Was everything wrapped up quickly just to spare the family?'

Murray listened to Tara's recounting of the investigation but said nothing.

'Aside from evidence being suppressed and forensics perhaps destroyed or ignored, there's a whole raft of issues still bugging me. For instance, why were police already searching for Rebecca less than an hour after her being reported missing? Was it merely because her mother was chief constable? And why was a patrol car from Admiral Street despatched to search the area? The local bizzies would have come from Southport, Marsh Lane, Walton Lane or even here at St Anne Street. It doesn't make sense.'

'It was Christmas Eve,' said Murray. 'Maybe it was the only patrol available.'

'Maybe.' Tara gazed at him. Something had just pricked at her thinking.

'Anyway,' she continued, 'I met Anthony Sawyer, a journalist who wrote a book about the Winters murder. Although he's convinced that Lloyd was the killer, he has questioned a lot of the police investigation and, more interestingly, the role the other family members played in the episode. I really want to speak with the family.'

'You want to question the former chief constable?'

Tara shook her head. 'Not possible. She has dementia and lives in a nursing home. No, I would settle for meeting the father, Jack Winters.'

Murray gathered his coffee cup and the paper plate from his doughnut and prepared to stand. He looked as though he'd heard enough of this story and Tara's theorising.

'We should concentrate on the link between Lloyd and Cunningham,' he said.

'I suppose you're right. I was just bouncing my thinking off you, bringing you up to date. I've probably been wasting my time.' Suddenly, as Tara rose from her seat to follow Murray from the canteen, she was struck by the reason for her unease a few minutes earlier.

'Alan? How did you know it was Christmas Eve?'

'Sorry, ma'am, not with you.'

'When I mentioned the patrol car having come all the way from Admiral Street, you said it was because it was Christmas Eve, and it may have been the only available unit. I never mentioned it being Christmas Eve. How did you know?'

'I read about the case years ago. It must have stuck in my head.'

'You should have said you were already familiar with the story. I wouldn't have rambled on for so long.'

'No problem, ma'am.'

CHAPTER 32

Andy Greengates awoke to the clatter of the Judas window on his cell door sliding open. He knew it was a bastard screw, who else? He couldn't care less. Maybe it was his turn. His time. They'd sorted Stephen and Tyrone. It was a relief to hear that his mate was going to live, although it was bad about his girlfriend. Maybe Tyrone would be able to identify the culprits, and Benson and his lackeys would get done after all. Then a sudden fear engulfed him. If Tyrone could identify his attacker, then he was now in even more danger. They couldn't let him live. And that meant that he too was in danger inside the prison. If Tyrone had now been frightened off, then he was the only one left. He had to speak with his mate, convince him not to give up. Benson had already been suspended. Surely, even a hint that the screw was associated with the attack on Tyrone would end his career.

His attention returned to the eyes peering into his cell. No talk, just eyes watching him lie on his bed, his arm resting on his forehead. Had to be one of Benson's cronies. He had counted six who he was convinced did the bidding of the supervisor. Lydia Jennings was a definite, then there was Irvine, Warwick, Mawdsley, Murphy and one other female, although he had doubts about her. Steph Paige was a recent arrival on his wing. She didn't display the same degree of intolerance to him or any other inmate. She went about her duties in a quieter fashion, although they say it's the quiet ones you have to watch.

For now, though, he had to be careful around Jennings. In the absence of Benson, she was acting supervisor. Andy had no doubt that she reported every little thing to the suspended screw. And she could dish out punishment of her own. His balls still throbbed from her kick as he returned to his cell the night before. Bitch had chuckled to herself as if some bloke had tickled her armpit.

'Just a reminder that normal service has been resumed,' she had said through the flap on his door.

'Night, Andy; night, grandpa; night, John-boy,' she giggled as the flap was slammed shut.

* * *

Benson wasn't feeling at all easy.

'What the hell happened?'

The person on the phone was doing nothing to relieve his fears. A morning that had begun badly was quickly turning to shit. He'd had to finally own up to Nikki that he'd been suspended from duty. All weekend he'd tried to find the courage to tell her, but it never seemed to be the right moment. On Saturday they'd gone shopping for new bedroom furniture. Couldn't tell her when they were wandering around IKEA. Saturday night they'd visited Nikki's sister and her boyfriend for dinner. Not then. Nikki would have spouted it in front of Karen, and she was a woman whose wrath was to be avoided. The two sisters formed a scary duo. At home in bed, having sex was more important to him. They'd been making an effort recently to make love instead of watching TV late into the night.

He never did find the right time, but this morning it all came out over breakfast.

'I thought you were on earlies this week?' Nikki inquired, as she packed lunches for the kids.

Benson winced at his gaff. Since his suspension he'd put all thoughts of his shifts out of his head. If he was going to keep it a secret from Nikki, he should have pretended to leave for work two hours ago. Now he was busted.

Nikki continued to fuss in her kitchen. Even without her husband's reply she looked unusually stressed. She was thirty-nine and took care of her appearance, looking ten years younger. Her fair hair was gathered in a ponytail, and she looked ready for her workout at the gym. Before leaving home, though, she awaited a response from her husband.

'Not going in today,' he mumbled. Within a few seconds the entire story was out there for Nikki to deal with. Her immediate reaction was to say, "Fuck you, Graham," and hurry from the house to drive the kids to school.

His response was to crack open a bottle of single malt and flop into the sofa, breakfast news reporting the death of a woman from Knotty Ash following an attack on Saturday night.

CHAPTER 33

At a pinch, Tara had decided, she could afford the move. She'd spent her lunch break with a financial advisor, arranging a mortgage to buy the house in Hoylake. And there was good news. She had accepted an offer on her apartment at Wapping Dock. Now there was no going back. She was overjoyed that Kate and Adele would join her in Hoylake. A new beginning for all of them.

At St Anne Street her team were researching Tyrone Cunningham's background and looking for information on how he and Lloyd had become friends.

'Got anything for me?' she asked when she returned from her meeting. It was likely that Wilson would be first to respond. Tara glanced over at Murray. He had his head down. She thought that he'd been subdued since his return from honeymoon. She assumed it was Monday blues after a great holiday; he'd seemed in poor form when they'd spoken earlier.

'Nothing much, ma'am,' Wilson replied on cue, coming over to her desk.

'Let's have what you've got then,' she replied. She pulled off her jacket and sat down.

'Tyrone Cunningham, as we know, served time with Lloyd. He's been a small-time thief and burglar since his teens. No convictions for violence. I contacted Liverpool Prison. Here's the interesting bit. Cunningham, Lloyd and a current inmate, Andrew Greengates, are, among others, the alleged victims of abuse at the prison. A senior prison officer has been suspended pending an investigation.'

'Good luck to proving there's been abuse in a prison,' Murray chirped. 'Isn't that one of the perks of putting criminals away? Inside, they get what they deserve.'

Tara glared at Murray. Something was definitely up with him. She turned to Wilson.

'Set up a visit with Mr Greengates. Let's see if he's willing to talk about what's been going on.'

'Yes, ma'am,' Wilson replied and made to walk away.

'Oh, and let's speak with the prison management too.'

'Ma'am.'

Tara looked over to Murray who had his head down once again, presumably dealing with a long list of emails amassed while he'd been on honeymoon. She decided to leave him alone and get on with her own work.

Until she could meet with Greengates or the injured Cunningham, there was little she could do regarding that angle of the investigation. Officers were continuing to sift through hours of CCTV recordings trying to identify the person who'd left The Docker's Rest with Stephen Lloyd and searching for evidence of the part a Jaguar SUV may have played in the murder.

Her mind could not dismiss the issue of Rebecca Winters. But the investigation had become two separate cases: one, the murder of Lloyd, and two, the murder of Rebecca Winters and Lloyd's dubious conviction for the crime. She was conscious, of course, that she was tasked only with finding Lloyd's killer. Rebecca Winters was an old case and officially solved.

She realised that Tweedy would not be pleased to learn of her preoccupation with the old case.

Nevertheless, the remainder of the day passed with her study of the murder timeline, the police investigation, and the forensic and post-mortem reports for Rebecca. She read the statements given by the Winters family.

According to Elizabeth Winters, her daughter had returned from Cambridge for Christmas on 15 December. From that date, until her death, she'd spent her days meeting with friends from school and her evenings at home and mainly in her bedroom. On Christmas Eve, Rebecca had been out of the house from early morning, supposedly shopping and then lunching with friends. Tara could not find statements from any of Rebecca's friends to corroborate this. Strangely, it appeared that none of the friends who had spent that Christmas Eve with Rebecca had been interviewed or even identified.

Elizabeth, after a morning spent shopping in the city, arrived home at around three o'clock accompanied by two friends who stayed for coffee and left before five. Again, Tara was surprised to discover that neither of these companions had been interviewed or even identified in the police files. Aside from the statement from Elizabeth, there was no record that she had ever been interviewed by investigating officers. Had her status as chief constable rendered her exempt from questioning?

Next, she read the statements provided by Jack and Freddie Winters. It seemed to Tara that the men had merely provided an alibi for each other. The pair had lunched together in the city and returned to their respective offices to join in Christmas parties. Again, there were no recorded witnesses to both men spending the afternoon and evening at their places of work. Tara recalled that Freddie had invited Lloyd to Briarwood Manor for lunch. This was denounced by the prosecution team during Lloyd's trial. According to Freddie's statement, he did not arrive home until after Rebecca had been reported missing and the search for her had commenced. Jack Winters arrived home at 7.25, having been summoned by his wife and informed that their daughter was missing.

There was nothing more, as far as the Winters family was concerned. Freddie had not been interviewed regarding his friendship with Stephen Lloyd. There was no information recorded as to how Rebecca would have come to know the man who was convicted of her murder. So, the question remained for Tara. Where was the opportunity or the motive for Lloyd to have killed Rebecca?

CHAPTER 34

The next day, Tara and Murray were shown into the visitors' room at the prison, a space with fixed tables and chairs, and bare walls except for a few informational posters on visitor behaviour and fire safety. They sat down at a table furthest from the door through which Andy Greengates appeared, a minute later. He had a slender frame and limped towards the police detectives. His face was drawn and serious, his lower teeth crooked and discoloured. He said nothing as he sat, ignoring Tara's friendly greeting. Tara was not intimidated. She had just endured two minutes' frank discussion with prison governor, Malcolm Hollingdale, who had flatly refused to engage with her and curtly stated His Majesty's Prisons' procedure. He would not discuss the upcoming disciplinary hearing regarding one of his officers. She was not impressed by Hollingdale.

'I gather that you are friends with Tyrone Cunningham and that you also knew Stephen Lloyd?'

Greengates shrugged a so-what.

'We're trying to find Stephen's killer. Anything you tell us might be of help.' Tara observed Greengates, scanning the empty room, save for one officer who had remained by the door.

'Do you feel safe to talk?' Tara asked him.

Another shrug.

'I understand that together with Cunningham and Lloyd you have lodged a complaint about your treatment in here. Is that correct?'

'Not talking to bizzies about that. You're all the fucking same. Besides, I'm not the one to ask.'

'And who should we be asking?' Murray put in, sounding unimpressed.

'The fucking screws! You should be investigating them. They're the ones what caused all this.' He glanced nervously over his shoulder. 'Stephen is dead and now Tyrone's girl is dead and if I tell you anything I'll be joining them. So, piss off and do your fucking job.'

* * *

'That didn't get us far,' said Murray on the drive back to St Anne Street.

But Tara had already dismissed the meetings in the prison from her thoughts. She had something else troubling her since the previous evening as she'd continued to study the Rebecca Winters case. Alone with Murray, she could now address the problem.

'Are you finding it hard to settle back to work after your nuptials?'

'Never easy, ma'am, returning to work after a holiday. How have you been coping since coming back?'

'Difficult, to say the least. But I suppose you just have to get on with things.'

'Absolutely.'

'Pull over,' she said, abruptly. 'There's something we need to discuss.'

Looking startled, Murray pulled into a lay-by and switched off the engine. Tara turned in her seat to face him. He waited expectantly.

'You know that I've been looking at this old murder case of Rebecca Winters and how it may have a bearing on the Lloyd killing?'

'Flogging a dead horse, if you ask me, ma'am.'

'That's as maybe, Alan. But you know me, I don't let things go if I believe they might produce results.'

'Yes, ma'am.'

'I spent most of yesterday going through the case files on Rebecca Winters. There's a lot of stuff in there that troubles me. Most of it has to do with Lloyd's conviction. And I'm still wondering if there is something arising from the case that led to Lloyd's murder.'

'Doesn't explain the attack on Cunningham or why Greengates is living in fear at Liverpool Prison.'

'Yes, thank you, Alan. I realise that, but I have something else that troubles me.'

'Fire away, ma'am,' Murray retorted. Tara studied his face. She was already angry with him; she didn't want to lose her temper.

'I read the police reports for the day that Rebecca Winters disappeared, and it still didn't make sense. So, I went over it all again, in case I'd missed something. And lo and behold, what do I find?' Her eyes widened as her anger rose. Her tone became accusatory. 'Well, we know that Elizabeth Winters was chief constable at the time so, I suppose, she got pretty swift service from her own officers. She reported Rebecca missing from home at 7.15 p.m. on Christmas Eve despite revealing that her daughter had not returned from her afternoon in the city centre. So, at that time Rebecca might have been simply enjoying a Christmas drink with friends and was only a couple of hours late returning home. But Elizabeth also expressed her concern that a prowler had been seen on Firs Lane during the day. So, a patrol car was despatched to the area, and sharpish. It did not, however, come from any of the local stations. No, it came all the way from Admiral Street.'

Murray attempted to speak, but Tara raised a hand to stop him.

'I know what you're going to say, Alan. It was down to availability, it being Christmas Eve. But that's what's bugged me since yesterday. How did you know it was

Christmas Eve when I hadn't told you? So, I found the report made by the senior officer in the patrol car that came all the way to Firs Lane on a freezing cold night. The officers in that car, several hours later, discovered the body of Rebecca Winters at the derelict house. The officer in charge was Constable Anne Farnham, but the driver of the patrol car was none other than Constable Alan Murray. Why didn't you tell me, Alan?'

CHAPTER 35

'The GP called to see her this morning. It's believed that she's suffered a TIA, a mini stroke.'

Jack looked at his wife in the bed as the nurse related the events of the early morning. He saw that Elizabeth's face looked strangely different since his previous visit. Her mouth drooped slightly to the left and so far, she had said nothing.

'Shouldn't she be in hospital?'

'We're keeping a close eye on her, Mr Winters. Any signs that she's deteriorating, we'll send for an ambulance. The GP thinks she is over the worst of it, and it was a very mild attack.'

'Will she recover? Will she be able to speak again?'

'She has been talking to us already this morning. She's been telling us about the police.'

'Really?' Jack wondered what his wife might have said.

'Yes,' the nurse replied. 'She was very concerned that their siren was on when they came to see her.'

Jack smiled with some relief.

'She used to be chief constable of Merseyside Police,' he explained, sounding quite proud of his wife.

'Wow! That must have been a challenging job.'

'And now look at her.'

'It's a terrible disease, Mr Winters. It takes your mind before anything else. The most we can hope for is that Elizabeth remains as comfortable as possible. It makes a big difference too when a dementia patient has family close by. Some of our residents, once they stop engaging, are left alone. Their families don't see the point in visiting.'

'Elizabeth only has me. Our son lives in Hawaii. Our daughter died nineteen years ago.'

'But your son *has* visited recently.'

Jack looked startled by the remark. Surely, the nurse was mistaken. He hadn't been aware of Freddie returning to Liverpool. They had rarely spoken since he had gone to America. When he did come back to England, it was either on business or to visit his in-laws. He'd kept in touch with Elizabeth until her mind had slipped and she was eventually moved to the nursing home. But Jack was not aware that his son had ever visited his mother here.

'Yes, of course,' he lied.

When the nurse had left, Jack studied his wife's face. Her eyes held a peculiar stare, and he believed it was for his benefit. If he didn't know better, he'd swear that she had understood every word of his conversation with the nurse. That she'd enjoyed seeing him shocked to learn that Freddie had visited her. Elizabeth, he thought, was relishing his discomfort.

Suddenly, she raised her right hand, moving it towards him. Her distorted smile was defined only by the glint of her eyes. When he took her hand, she squeezed it tightly. The sound she made was impossible to decipher, but she persisted. Eventually, he heard it clearly.

'Freddie.'

CHAPTER 36

Murray apologised but hadn't offered an explanation why he'd stayed quiet at the outset. Tara seethed all day, and most of the night at home, was unable to sleep, resorting to wine and the enigmatic book *Road to Nowhere*. With each passage she read, a fresh set of questions popped into her head, but she realised that it was difficult to justify this line of inquiry in the face of what had happened to Tyrone Cunningham and his girlfriend. Whatever miscarriage of justice, if any, had occurred when Lloyd was convicted of murder was not for her to put right. She had to focus on finding Lloyd's killer, who most likely had also killed Angela Campbell. Such thoughts, however, would not stop her from challenging Murray over his involvement in the Rebecca Winters investigation when he was a uniformed constable.

The following morning, she invited him for coffee in the canteen. He was not one to refuse if it meant filling his face with a fry-up or a jam doughnut.

'I want you to tell me what happened the night you were called to Firs Lane.'

Behind a busy mouth full of sausage and egg, her DS still managed to look sheepish. His large eyes seemed to plead for clemency. Quickly, he swallowed his food and rushed to his second apology.

'I'm sorry, ma'am. I should have told you.'

'Spare it, Alan. Just tell me what happened.'

He explained about receiving the order to search the area around Firs Lane for a suspected prowler. The issue of there ever having been a prowler was another mysterious aspect to the case that irked Tara.

'She was standing in the middle of the bloody road in her dressing gown,' he said, incredulously. 'I damn near ran her over. The road was very slippery with black ice. She told us that she was searching for her daughter, but we thought it wise to get her indoors.'

'So, at that stage you hadn't begun looking for Rebecca?'

'No, ma'am. Our instructions had been to keep an eye out for a prowler in the area. But it was hardly the kind of place for a prowler to be operating. There were only a few houses, and it was a freezing Christmas Eve.'

'Yes, you've mentioned already that it was Christmas Eve.'

Murray looked admonished yet again by his boss. He returned to his food before Tara posed her next question.

'When did you actually begin searching for Rebecca?' she asked, sipping her overly strong coffee.

'We escorted the woman into her house. Nice place it was, too. Beautiful Christmas tree.'

'Was there anyone else inside?'

'She told us that her son and husband had just arrived home. Didn't see the son but we met the husband briefly in the hall. There were plenty of lights on in other rooms, but we never got any further than the entrance hall. Once we were standing in the light, Anne recognised her straight away. Chief constable. I nearly shat myself. I was only three months into the job. The thought of me dealing with the chief constable, seeing her in a flimsy dressing gown and nightie, and almost running her over.'

'What happened next?'

'Anne did all the kowtowing, ma'am this and ma'am that. Winters had calmed down a little bit by then. She basically ordered us from the house to search for her daughter. Her husband led her away, and we left.'

'And that was all?' Tara's eyes widened in surprise.

'Yes, ma'am. We drove up and down the lanes in the area for two hours. Later, when we were back on Firs

Lane, Anne suggested that we search an old farmhouse, so we got out to look around.'

'Why there?'

'Anne said that we'd already driven past it twice. That we may as well have a look and discount it from the search. And that's where we found the body. We called it in.'

'And what did you think?'

'I was seriously spooked. It was my first dead body. Anne was in charge until the circus showed up. I just did as I was told.'

'Did anything seem strange to you? Like something wasn't right?'

Murray shook his head as he continued to eat. 'It was all new to me. I didn't think anything other than there being a young woman lying dead on Christmas Eve and only a few yards from her home.'

'And what about your prowler?'

'I'm sure if there was one, he scarpered when all the blue lights showed up. We never saw anyone suspicious.'

When Tara eventually allowed Murray to enjoy the remainder of his late breakfast, she held one final question back until they were walking to their office.

'Did you have any further involvement in the investigation?'

'No, ma'am, not really.'

'What do you mean, not really?' Here was Murray again at his most reticent, Tara thought. Sometimes speaking to him was worse than interviewing a suspect. He stopped in the corridor and seemed to choose his words carefully.

'I was only a junior constable, ma'am. I wasn't involved in the murder inquiry.'

'But?' said Tara, her blue eyes wide in expectation and looking up at Murray.

'Anne Farnham and I were brought into an office in Admiral Street a few days after Christmas. The SIO of the case was there and the chief constable. She thanked us for our work on the night her daughter was found and then she left. Then the SIO said he wanted to go through our report on the incident. He said there were a few points that were not relevant to the investigation and should be deleted.'

CHAPTER 37

Harold Tweedy looked pensive. He sat at his desk and having listened to the reasoning of DI Tara Grogan, considered his response. Tara was conscious of sounding desperate. Despite her resolve of the night before to set aside the old case, here she was trying to convince her boss that she was on the right path.

'Tara,' Tweedy began. 'I understand your thinking over this old case, but you haven't explained how this will bring us closer to finding the killer of Mr Lloyd and indeed this latest victim Ms Campbell.'

'I can't explain its relevance to the attack on Tyrone Cunningham and Angela Campbell, sir, but there are anomalies in the investigation of the Winters murder and therefore the conviction of Stephen Lloyd. I believe that his murder could be linked to the events of nineteen years ago.'

'Your finding of shortcomings in that case does not convince me that someone involved back then has, nineteen years later, sought out and killed Lloyd. You've already spent too much time on this. I would prefer that you concentrate on the connection with the abuse allegations from Liverpool Prison. And you have not yet exhausted the possibility of a homophobic attack on Lloyd.'

'Sir, I'm simply requesting permission to speak with Jack Winters about the time his daughter was killed. I might get a feel perhaps that a family member is capable of exacting revenge for Rebecca's murder.'

Tweedy was already shaking his head.

'No, Tara. Please leave this line of investigation for now. It would not go down well to raise the murder of Rebecca with the Winters family. It's long in the past but no doubt still painful for those affected. I had allowed you time to study the Winters case simply as background to Stephen Lloyd. I did not intend for you to reopen what was a successful investigation. Concentrate on the points I've mentioned. We can meet in a day or so and review progress.'

'Yes, sir.'

Tara left the super's office feeling the weight of a reprimand. The sickening feeling in her stomach was exacerbated by a lack of food and her overindulgence in chardonnay the night before. She felt alone in her consideration of this murder investigation. None of her colleagues agreed, even those who had to carry out her orders seemed bemused by the direction she was taking. And Murray was still licking his wounds after she'd told him off for something that he'd decided was irrelevant. She hadn't really settled properly into her job since her lay-off. Was this investigation one too many for her? Could this be the point where she must finally decide to get out of this career? Heaven knows, it had never been an easy path. The number of times when she'd considered it. Had even written out her resignation to give to Tweedy. Kate and Aisling had always said that policing wasn't right for her. Too meek a soul, they'd said. It was her damn job that killed Aisling, her dalliance with a serial killer. She should have died at his hands, not her beautiful friend.

She flopped into the chair at her desk, longing for a cool glass of wine and maybe she would try those damn tablets the police doctor had prescribed after Aisling died.

Suddenly paranoid, eyes all around scolding her for her incompetence, her fixations, she had no idea what to do next. Before anyone got to her, even uttered a word, she jumped to her feet, slipped on her jacket, hung her bag over her shoulder and stomped from the office.

* * *

The wind was stronger today than on her previous visit with Kate and Adele. Waves were high too, the tide running close to shore. She ambled from Stanley Road around the point at Red Rocks feeling that this was already her new home, even though she had to await completion of the purchase and that was also dependent upon the sale of her Wapping Dock apartment. But this was now her happy place, if happy was the right word. Safe, maybe. Or slightly relaxing place. The entire feeling was diluted at every attempt to describe it. She tried to plan. What she would do with the lounge and the kitchen, with Kate's input, of course. That was the most important factor in her move. She had someone close to share in her joy.

Her feet sank in the softer sand. Heeled boots were not appropriate on the beach, but she hadn't come prepared. She just needed to get out of that damned station. As she walked and breathed fresh air an adventurous thought sprang to mind. Could she disobey Harold Tweedy? With that came an idea. She retraced her steps, and once out of the wind and seated in her car she searched her handbag for the number. She dialled on her mobile and waited for him to answer.

'Hi, there. It's DI Grogan. I have a favour to ask.'

CHAPTER 38

Jack Winters placed a tray of china cups and a coffee pot on the table. It appeared an awkward operation. He was such a large man, and the table was low. His stoop seemed to cause discomfort and he breathed uneasily. Tara was surprised that he'd struck her as a friendly man. She'd imagined a bitter soul without patience and no time for small talk. But he'd nattered away about the weather, the latest from Westminster and expressed his hope to go on a Caribbean holiday quite soon. They were seated in a compact yet serene lounge in a modern apartment block on Grosvenor Road in Birkdale, near Southport, as leafy a suburb as you could wish to live. It was another district for her to have considered for her move.

'You have a lovely home,' she said, gazing at several family pictures on the walls and admiring the man's taste in furnishings and matching colours.

'All my Elizabeth's doing,' he replied, reaching a cup filled with coffee to Tara. 'We moved here about five years ago, before she became ill. Downsizing they call it nowadays. It was her last project, I suppose. Now she's just around the corner, in more ways than one you could say. A life of blissful ignorance they call it.'

Tara smiled sympathetically. Winters spoke with a smooth bass voice, although she got the feeling that underneath he was strong and determined. His insistence that they should have coffee at his home rather than meeting in public had been forcefully stated. Tara didn't think that Winters was a man to be trifled with.

'It's good of you to spare the time, Jack,' said Anthony Sawyer helping himself to a slice of fruit cake. 'I'm writing an update on the story, and I wanted to get your opinion on the murder of Stephen Lloyd. Tara is helping me.'

A feeling of sheepishness washed over her. For a moment, she couldn't look at either man. The meeting was a scam, and she was the instigator. She was off-duty and off-piste. No need for Winters to know that she was a cop. This morning, she was merely assisting an author friend with his writing project. Sawyer was pleased to help her and within an hour had set up the appointment. Tara had primed him with questions she would like asked of Winters. It would be a step too far for her to conduct an interview, considering that Tweedy had forbidden it.

Winters, silver-haired and clean-shaven, sat in a studded wing-back chair opposite Tara. He hadn't bothered with the coffee. His eyes were firmly set on the attractive woman in his living room.

'How did you feel when you heard that Stephen Lloyd had been murdered?' Sawyer asked, already on a second slice of cake.

'Can't say I felt much,' Winters replied, rubbing his double chin. 'No sympathy for the man who destroyed our lives. I know he served his time, but he was released way too soon. My family is still serving their sentence. When we lost Rebecca, it completely dismantled our family life. Freddie moved away, and Elizabeth was never the same. I'm convinced that Rebecca's murder brought on her illness. She was only sixty-three when she started showing signs: mislaying things in the flat, confused at the shops and getting lost on her way home. No, I didn't feel anything when I heard about Lloyd.'

'What would you say to the suggestion that his murder is linked to Rebecca's death?'

Tara saw his anger rise instantly. Sawyer had cut beneath the surface, and Tara thought Winters was about to leap from his chair and throttle the author.

'How very dare you!' Winters snapped. 'I know exactly what you're implying, Sawyer. That someone in my family went after Lloyd. And tell me, just who do you think that could have been? Me? I told you I'd hardly given a thought to Lloyd in eighteen years. I didn't even know that he'd been released from prison until I read of his death. Maybe you're thinking it was Elizabeth? That she nipped out of the nursing home, killed the man who'd ruined her life and was back in time for the afternoon singsong in the residents' lounge? And if you're thinking about Freddie, he doesn't even live in this country.'

Winters fumed. Tara glanced at Sawyer, wondering if he was brave enough to ask him her next question. Then she noticed Winters staring right at her.

'You're very quiet, Miss Grogan,' he said. 'Are assistants not permitted to voice an opinion?'

It was sarcastic and aggressive. On duty she would have cut the man down, but she had embarked upon the role of passive companion to Sawyer and must remain so.

'I'm not so familiar with the case, Mr Winters,' she said.

'Case? You sound like the police. Did you know that Elizabeth is a former chief constable?'

'I did know that.'

Winters seemed content with his verbal assault and switched his attention back to the author.

'Anything else you want to know, Sawyer? Haven't got all day.'

Sawyer swiped a hand across his hair, clearing it from his eyes. He glanced briefly at Tara as if to glean the courage to put another question to Winters.

'Jack, you know what went into the book about Rebecca and the time she was killed. Have you ever had any doubts about Lloyd's guilt? Were you happy with the original investigation?'

Winters, this time remaining calm, seemed to think carefully before answering.

'Why are you asking me that question now? Should have asked it when you started writing that bloody book of yours. I was so cut up about Rebecca I never paid much attention to the police investigation. Besides, Elizabeth was better placed to take an interest in getting justice for our daughter.'

'What about your son?' Tara asked the question, barely realising that she'd jumped into the discussion. She cursed herself for the gaffe. Winters grinned.

'The lady speaks!'

Tara couldn't prevent her blush. She was seething.

'What about my son?' Winters retaliated. It sounded like a challenge. Say the wrong thing, Tara, and this man will have you by the throat.

'Did he take an interest in proceedings after Rebecca's death?' she asked.

'Freddie only thought about himself, Miss Grogan. He never really engaged with his family. He and Rebecca bickered their entire childhood. And it didn't stop when she went off to Cambridge. He never cared much about me, but Elizabeth still thought the sun shone from his ass. Such was our loving family. After Rebecca's death, he simply took off and started a new life in the United States. Do you know, he was back in England from Hawaii recently, and he visited his mother? Didn't tell me, didn't make any contact. He turned up at the nursing home, stayed for half an hour and left. That's Freddie all over.'

'When was that?' Tara asked. She didn't care any longer that she sounded like a cop. She needed the answer.

'Sometime earlier this month,' Winters replied, looking warily at her.

At that point the conversation ran aground. Sawyer seemed reluctant to ask further questions. Tara would only give herself away if she took charge. She'd said enough. Perhaps, she'd heard enough too. The revelation that Freddie Winters had been in Liverpool, possibly around the time of Lloyd's murder had set her thinking on edge. She would check with Elizabeth's nursing home for the exact date the son had visited his mother.

They thanked Winters for his hospitality and rose to leave. Winters looked puzzled by the episode, and he laid his thick hand on Tara's shoulder after helping with her jacket. He squeezed hard as if to deliberately inflict pain.

'Very nice to meet you, Miss Grogan. I hope I was of some help this morning.'

'Indeed, Mr Winters, thank you.' She edged from his grasp and looked him sternly in the eyes. His touch was at best rude. She couldn't figure out his returned gaze. It was either flirtatious or malicious.

* * *

Jack Winters stood by his lounge window overlooking the gardens of the apartment complex and the path leading to the car park. He watched as Tara climbed into the driver's seat of her Ford Focus. When he'd seen them drive away, he went to a table in his hall and retrieved a soft-bound address book from the drawer. He found the number and dialled on his landline telephone.

'May I speak to Ted Havers, please?'

CHAPTER 39

'Bit early for me, Mr Benson,' said Tara.

She and Murray looked on as the prison officer filled a glass tumbler with a flavoured gin. He took a drink before speaking again. He wore a fleece bathrobe, but Tara suspected there was little underneath and Benson made no effort to keep himself covered. The lounge held the odour of burnt toast and the remnants of breakfast were scattered on the coffee table.

'I didn't think the police would be interested in this fiasco,' he said, his back turned to them and gazing through his lounge window.

'What fiasco is that?' Tara asked.

Benson scoffed.

'My disciplinary. I'm supposed to attend a hearing and respond to the allegations. Didn't think management had called in the bizzies.'

'That's not exactly why we are here,' said Tara. 'We have some questions to ask you, that's all.'

Benson spun round, barely keeping the gin within his glass.

'About what?'

'Can you tell us of your whereabouts on the evening of Friday, 8 September?'

'Why do you want to know?'

'If you could answer my question, Mr Benson?' said Tara.

Benson smirked at Murray.

'Is she always like this?'

Murray didn't respond.

'Like that is it? Are you her lapdog?' He took another gulp of gin.

'Your whereabouts please, Mr Benson,' Tara persisted.

'I have no idea, love. Need to check my rota. If I wasn't working, I was most likely here with the wife. I'll have to ask her when she comes home.'

'Check your rota please.'

'What's so bloody important about 8 September anyway?'

Benson lifted his phone from the coffee table and searched for the information.

'OK, I wasn't working, so I was probably here. Nikki can vouch for that.'

'When did you last see Stephen Lloyd?' Murray asked.

Benson paused as if he was retrieving more information from his phone. He shook his head.

'Don't remember when I last saw the toad. Probably around the time he was released. I had little to do with him.'

'Surprising,' said Murray, 'since he is one of the alleged victims in the abuse inquiry for which you've been suspended.'

'Proves how daft the whole thing is.'

'What about Saturday, 23 September?' Tara asked.

'What about it?' He grinned facetiously at the woman seated on his sofa. Tara maintained a cold stare for the man she already detested. A misogynist with a hefty dose of self-importance and now playing the victim.

'If you're asking about Cunningham,' he said, 'I was nowhere near him. Hadn't seen him since he was on the wing with Lloyd.'

'Again, Mr Benson, if you can tell me where you were on that date.'

'Oh yes. I remember that one. We were at my sister-in-law's house for dinner.'

'Where exactly was that?' Tara asked.

Benson looked on the verge of a tantrum.

'For fuck's sake. She lives in Little Crosby. Nowhere near Knotty Ash.'

'Knotty Ash?'

'I know what you're trying to say. That I had something to do with Cunningham getting thumped.'

'It was more than a thump. He is still in hospital. His girlfriend died in the attack. It was murder, Mr Benson.'

Tara had had enough of this beast. She rose to leave. They would check his supposed alibis, but she realised she needed proof to go with a motive that Benson was implicated in the murders.

'I've been attacked too, you know.' He pointed to the crack on his lounge window. 'Somebody threw a brick at it. My kids were here. They could have been injured.'

'I hope you reported it,' said Tara, dryly. 'Thanks for your time. I'll let you get back to your breakfast.'

Benson showed the detectives to his front door. His car, gleaming in the morning sun, was parked on the driveway close against the garden wall. He watched with concern as Tara and Murray had to squeeze by.

On the drive from Litherland back to St Anne Street, Tara asked Murray what he thought of their meeting with the prison officer.

'He certainly has motive and an attitude to go with it,' said Murray. 'Doesn't have much of an alibi for either murder, only his family to vouch for him.'

'If he is our killer, do you think he acted alone?'

'The reports for both attacks suggest there was more than one perpetrator. Maybe there's a whole squad from the prison on disciplinary charges.'

'We need Cunningham, when he is able, to tell us what went on inside that jail.'

'Neither Greengates nor Cunningham seem willing to share what they know.'

'We'll just have to convince them that it would be wise to help us before anyone else gets hurt.'

Murray, with some confidence restored, posed his next question to Tara.

'I take it you've parked the idea of finding a link between Lloyd's murder and the Winters family?'

Tara glared at him as he drove the car. She was still peeved at him for keeping his part in the Winters case from her. What had been his reason for it? He had yet to tell her. She couldn't understand it.

'I've been ordered to,' she replied.

'And you're going to obey the order?'

'Of course.'

Murray couldn't help his wry grin.

CHAPTER 40

Bleasdale waited for Tara to reach her desk. There were times when it felt good to be greeted by another female in the office. The males on her team, even Wilson, sometimes had a gung-ho manner in their delivery of news. A slap on the face rather than a gentle tap on the shoulder. Either that or it was an effort to squeeze information out of them.

'Stella Ramsey from The Docker's Rest called earlier,' said Bleasdale. 'She thinks she may have come across the guy who left the bar with Lloyd on the night he was killed.'

'How so?'

'No details, but Stella will be at work later this afternoon, if we want to speak to her.'

'Let's do it. Fancy lunch on the way?'

'OK, ma'am. I'll grab my coat.'

The two women waved goodbye to Murray seated at his desk. He looked puzzled that Tara was off somewhere without him.

They ate lunch in a twee café in Whitechapel then walked to Cheapside. The Docker's Rest was devoid of clientele when they stepped inside. Stella wiped down tables in the gloom. The din of cheap pop music gave the impression that the place was jumping. But Stella was the only person to be seen.

'Hiya!' she chirped. 'With you in a sec.'

Tara and Bleasdale stood at the bar watching as Stella flitted around several tables with a cloth and disinfectant spray.

'Can I get you anything to drink, while you're here?'

Tara requested an orange juice and Bleasdale a tonic water. When she'd served the drinks, Stella leaned on the bar.

'So,' she began, sounding conspiratorial. 'You want to know about this guy?'

Tara smiled.

'Yes, please,' she replied as if to join in some juicy gossip.

'If you ask me, I think he's a male prostitute,' said Stella. 'He was in here last night with a crowd of mates. They all got rat-arsed, really pissed. Half of them were dressed like *RuPaul's Drag Race*, and this one lad was chattering away. You know what I mean? Drink loosening his tongue. I was standing at this very spot, and I heard him mention the name Stephen Lloyd. I hung around to hear the rest. He was boasting to his mates that he'd been paid three hundred quid to show Lloyd a good time.'

'Who paid him?' Bleasdale asked.

Stella shook her head.

'No idea. He didn't mention any other names.'

'Did he say that it happened on Friday, 8 September?' Tara asked.

'No mention of when. He was just telling his mates that he'd been with some guy, and he'd heard later that he was murdered.'

'You know what I'm going to ask next, Stella,' said Tara.

'CCTV. I've already had a peek. I'll show you.'

In a cramped office behind the bar, Tara and Bleasdale were shown the recording of the previous evening on a laptop. As before, it was merely footage from the bar's entrance. Stella froze the images of seven people as they filed inside. Five of them were in drag.

'This is the guy.' Stella pointed to the second person in the line stepping through the door. The figure had long straight, silver-blond locks, and wore a white biker-style jacket and a white mini-dress.

'Any chance that you could identify this person in the footage from 8 September?' Tara asked Stella.

'Might be able to, although I don't remember anyone in drag from that night. He would look totally different without the make-up.'

Tara and Bleasdale finished their drinks and enjoyed a casual chat with Stella. She was a very affable woman and, Tara imagined, would be great fun on a girlie night out. The very thought of it reminded her of Aisling. She wondered, sadly, if her partying days were over. It concerned her that lately she didn't feel inclined to even attempt such things.

'Do you think we have found our killer, ma'am?' Bleasdale asked on their way back to the station. Tara shook her head.

'I don't think so. The killer is not likely to shoot his mouth off like that. If this lad was paid to show Lloyd a good time and it happened on 8 September, then the person who hired him is likely to be our killer. Makes it seem that the murder was well planned. It wasn't a random street attack.'

'It might be difficult to find the guy that Stella came across in the bar.'

'Poor Wilson. He's going to have another session of scouring CCTV for this crowd who were out on the town last night.'

* * *

Tara had another appointment with her financial advisor in late afternoon. It felt exciting to be doing something to change her life, even just a little.

She cleared her desk, bid her colleagues goodnight and headed downstairs.

Dave McLachlan lifted his head and smiled broadly.

'Enjoy your evening, ma'am.'

'Thanks, Dave, you too.'

He maintained his smile and kept his eyes on her as she left. Tara thought the desk sergeant was friendly but didn't know him terribly well. He hadn't been at St Anne Street for long. Wasn't bad looking, though.

When Tara had left, McLachlan called a number on his mobile.

CHAPTER 41

It was all very painless. Sign a few forms, present ID and details of her current mortgage, and she would hear in a few days on whether her application had been accepted. Her financial advisor did not foresee any problems.

Back in her car, the remainder of the early evening was devoted to heavy traffic. There was little movement on Strand Street, which was frustrating since she was only a quarter of a mile from Wapping Dock. Traffic news referred to a heavy goods vehicle that had shed its load causing lanes in both directions to be closed.

Her thoughts returned to her work. It seemed clearer now. The likely scenario was that Benson and accomplices were responsible for killing Lloyd and Campbell. With Stephen Lloyd it had involved, possibly, the hiring of a man to lure him to his death. This individual may or may not have been complicit in the murder. As for Angela Campbell and Tyrone Cunningham, the killers, it seemed, had been more upfront, simply pulling over by the roadside to carry out the attack. Tara realised she still needed hard evidence to link Benson with the killings, and she had to identify the person who may have led Stephen Lloyd to his death. But, as the traffic at last crawled forward, Tara asked herself why she remained uneasy about the events of nineteen years ago. She wondered about Jack Winters and his son. She still had to contact Elizabeth's nursing home to confirm the date when Freddie had visited his mother. Murray's attitude to the case infuriated her. Why had he been so reluctant to discuss his role in finding the body of Rebecca Winters? She doubted the entire record of the murder investigation. Even Anthony Sawyer's book had set her thinking on edge. Tara doubted every little thing.

Despite a meal of breaded cod, oven chips and peas, and nursing her essential glass of chardonnay, Tara could not relax. She craved activity. The net result was her making several phone calls, the first to identify the nursing home in Birkdale where Elizabeth Winters was a resident. It took three attempts to find the correct establishment. She spoke with a senior nurse at the Summer Breeze Residential and Nursing Home and asked for information regarding a visit by Freddie Winters to his mother Elizabeth. The nurse, eventually convinced that Tara was indeed a police officer, informed her that Freddie had visited his mother on the afternoon of Sunday, 10 September. That was just over a day after Lloyd had been murdered. Jack Winters had commented that his son's visit was a surprise to him. Apparently, Freddie had not been home to Liverpool in years. Tara pondered the reason for the recent visit. Was it to inform his mother, despite her mental state that he had put an end to the family trouble, that Stephen Lloyd had finally got what he deserved? Or did Freddie Winters have another motive beyond revenge? Did Lloyd have information that would have implicated Freddie in his sister's murder? After nineteen years it would seem strange for Freddie to have become concerned. For him to travel all the way from Hawaii to silence Lloyd, it must have been crucially important.

'Hello, sorry to bother you,' Tara said.

'No problem,' Sawyer replied. 'Nice to hear from you again.'

Tara was conscious of sounding too formal. She wanted to be casual. She was not proposing a date, but she did intend it to be a friendly invitation to dinner.

'I keep returning to this issue of Rebecca Winters despite everything pointing to a different scenario for Lloyd's killing. If you're free, maybe we can have dinner and I can ask a few more questions?'

'I'm up for dinner. Not one to refuse a good meal.'

The phone calls had quenched her evening's anxiety. She ended the night with several glasses of chardonnay and a spy movie on Netflix.

By the following morning, Tara was lucky to still be a serving police officer.

CHAPTER 42

See me. The Post-it was stuck to her monitor. Tara gazed around the office. No one was paying her any attention. She guessed the message had come from Tweedy although it wasn't his style. The two words jumped at her throat. Threatening, abrupt, angry, rude, all of those, she couldn't decide.

She slipped off her jacket, draping it over the back of the chair and placed her handbag in the bottom drawer of the desk. Stalling. She removed the note and switched on her computer. All the while, she hoped for someone to enlighten her. Finally, she called out to Bleasdale who was browsing news online.

'Any idea who left this on my screen?' She brandished the Post-it in the air.

Bleasdale shook her head.

'No, ma'am.'

Resigned to her assumption that it was Tweedy, she headed for his office and knocked on the window of the door.

He looked up then nodded for her to enter.

'Morning, sir. Did you want to see me?'

'Take a seat, Tara,' he said without greeting her. Already, she knew this wasn't right. This was not his way.

'I'll get straight to the point, shall I?' His voice was louder than she'd ever heard him speak. 'Seldom, in over thirty years of policing, have I had to hold a conversation such as this.'

Tara was dumbstruck. What had happened? What had she done?

'I've just spoken with Assistant Chief Constable Havers in Manchester. It seems he had been contacted by Jack Winters.'

Tweedy glared icily at her.

'The man spoke to Havers because he suspected he had just been hoodwinked by a police detective asking questions about the murder of his daughter. Can you confirm if this was you, Tara?'

'Yes, sir.' Tara felt her relationship with the man who had trained her, protected her and mentored her collapse before her eyes. In that moment, the trust that Tweedy held for her had slid away. Ashamed, she dropped her head.

'Give me one good reason why I should not suspend you? You disobeyed a direct order not to interview members of the Winters family. I had also instructed you to set aside the link to Rebecca Winters in this investigation and to concentrate on the connection between Lloyd and Cunningham. Isn't that correct?'

'Yes, sir.'

'I am disappointed that you have defied me to such an extent.' His eyes pierced hers. She dropped her gaze as tears began to well.

A silence ensued. Tweedy switched his attention to his mobile, while Tara wished she'd brought a tissue. She struggled to choose words in her defence. Her pain lay in seeing the anger of a man she respected more than any other. A man who had patience on a biblical scale but was now on the verge of losing his cool with her.

Tweedy had used the pause in the discussion, seemingly, to regain his composure. When he next spoke, his tone had returned to that which Tara knew well. There was empathy within it.

'Take this as a verbal warning, Tara. I will suspend you if there are any further breaches of my direct instructions. Is that clear?'

'Absolutely, sir.'

'Good. Now give me an update on the case.'

Tara looked in surprise at her boss. Maybe his trust in her was still there. It was sufficient to ease her nerves as she summarised the evidence they had been considering.

'We're trying to identify an individual who apparently was paid to have sex with Stephen Lloyd. We don't know if this took place on the night Lloyd was killed.'

'Any luck?' Tweedy asked.

'We're trawling CCTV from the night of Monday the twenty-seventh. That's when Stella Ramsey overheard this person speak of their involvement.'

Tweedy nodded acknowledgement then surprised her with his next question.

'Despite my annoyance at your behaviour, I know you well enough to believe that you wouldn't have ignored my orders unless you thought you would get a result. So, tell me, did you learn anything from meeting Winters?'

Tara related the story of Freddie Winters having visited his mother around the time of Lloyd's murder.

'There were so many things wrong about the Rebecca Winters investigation, sir. If Lloyd, after his release from prison, was attempting to clear his name, perhaps someone had a reason to stop him.'

'But none of this explains the attack on Cunningham and Campbell.'

'I realise that, but I'm finding it difficult to ignore the link to Rebecca Winters.'

Tweedy thought for a moment, his fingers pressed together as if in prayer.

'OK, you may resume this strand of your enquiries but under no circumstances will you approach the Winters family or Assistant Chief Constable Havers. Is that clear?'

'Yes, sir. I understand.'

'Tread carefully, please.'

Tara left Tweedy's office feeling as though she'd just endured the full gambit of human emotion in a ten-minute spell. Her objectives seemed clear but how to achieve them remained a whirlpool of doubt and mystery.

CHAPTER 43

Tara had arranged to meet Sawyer at a Thai restaurant in the Albert Dock after work. She was able to walk from her apartment and it meant she could enjoy a drink or two, especially if the evening were to drag.

'I haven't even asked if you are married,' she said as they clinked wine glasses. Sawyer was dressed in chinos and a casual blue shirt, but his thick hair was still a mess. Tara, wearing jeans and a navy tunic, didn't feel that she looked attractive.

'Divorced,' he replied. 'Twice.'

She was intrigued by his answer. What do you say to a man who's failed twice in marriage? He spoke again before she could respond.

'And you?'

'Not married. Never been married.'

'I find that hard to believe.'

Tara cocked her head to the side. Then she gave her recently adopted stock answer.

'Relationships are difficult when you have a job like mine.'

'But you're not opposed to it?'

She shrugged indifference. Time to get off this dodgy subject. She moved on to the reason for the meeting, or as Sawyer might have been viewing it, their date.

'Jack Winters contacted Ted Havers after we'd been to see him,' she said. 'Seems that I was not convincing as your assistant.'

'Really?' He said with raised brow. Tara noted the surprised look on his face.

'Havers spoke to my boss. Neither one was pleased with me.'

'He wasn't at all co-operative when I interviewed him for the book. Went on the defensive from the get-go.'

'Did you glean anything interesting?'

'Depends on how you look at it. I asked about several aspects of the investigation. Mostly, he directed me to the reported evidence and wasn't prepared to discuss details of timelines, forensics or suspects. I didn't get much out of him that I could use for the book.'

'When I met him,' said Tara, 'he had no doubts that Lloyd killed Rebecca. Did you ask him why he, based at Admiral Street, was put in charge of the investigation?'

A wry grin enveloped Sawyer's face.

'What?' Tara asked.

'I have no proof, so I wasn't allowed to include it in the book. Might have only been a rumour.'

'What? Spit it out, Anthony.'

'Well,' he said, hesitantly, 'as you know, Elizabeth was chief constable at the time of her daughter's murder. Ted Havers was a detective superintendent.'

'So?'

'Eighteen months before the murder, Elizabeth was an assistant chief constable. Prior to that she was a chief inspector based at Admiral Street station. She jumped several grades to make assistant chief. At the time it was viewed as a very political appointment. She was the most suitable high-ranking female, and the force wanted to be seen to advance the fortunes of women. It left several officers who might have expected to get the job with their noses out of joint. It was salt in the wounds when she very swiftly made it to chief constable.'

'Did that include Havers? Was he aggrieved by her rise to the top? But wasn't she responsible for appointing him SIO on her daughter's murder investigation?'

'Yes, to both,' Sawyer replied with a smirk. 'But Elizabeth may have needed to reward certain officers.'

Tara looked puzzled. She attempted to eat some of her green curry.

'Reward them for what?' she asked.

'For their continued support *and* their discretion.'

'I'm losing you.'

Sawyer smiled glibly.

'It is merely rumour, and there was no way I could ever refer to it in the book, but Elizabeth, whilst serving at Admiral Street, had acquired a reputation.'

'A reputation for what?'

Sawyer's eyes widened at Tara's apparent naivety, but he didn't elucidate. Then it suddenly hit her.

'You mean, she slept her way to the top?'

'Not so much. I think the modern term is cougar.'

CHAPTER 44

Sawyer accompanied Tara back to her building. They continued to discuss the mysteries extant from Rebecca Winters' murder.

'Did you interview the officers who came to Firs Lane on the night of the murder?' Tara asked. 'There were two who found the body.'

'No. I worked from the police reports for that night. Again, Elizabeth Winters was not happy for me to go snooping through her nice clean police force. Why do you ask?'

'I am curious as to why a patrol came all the way from Admiral Street rather than a local station.'

'I imagine that when Elizabeth called the police to report that Rebecca was missing, she actually rang one of her pals at Admiral Street, and they sent a patrol to the area.'

'Sounds plausible. My DS, Alan Murray was the driver of that car. He's been quite cagey in talking about that night. It's not like him.'

'You think he's hiding something?'

'Possibly.'

Tara was content to bid him goodnight on the ground floor of her building, but Sawyer insisted on seeing her to her door. She got the feeling he was angling for more than a goodnight, or even a goodnight kiss.

'This is me,' she said without unlocking her door. She looked up at the twinkling eyes smiling back at her. But he seemed unsure about what to do or say next. Tara helped him. 'Thanks for meeting me again. I've managed to get some things straight in my head.'

Sawyer stepped closer, attempting a kiss. Instinctively, Tara turned her head, and it became a peck on the cheek. She had plans. A new home, a life to be shared with her closest friend and her goddaughter. She didn't need romantic complication. Although Sawyer was not a suspect in her investigations, he was still a part of it. She didn't need his amorous intentions. Fortunately, he took the hint.

'Good night, Tara. Thanks for dinner.' He started on his way as she fumbled nervously in her bag for her key, relieved that he was leaving.

It was close to eleven, but she didn't feel like going to bed. With a glass of wine poured and Classic FM playing, she got comfortable on her sofa. The book that had occupied the last few hours lay beside her, but her thoughts centred on what she'd learned from its author. Maybe she was old fashioned, or simply naïve, but she couldn't help feeling shocked on hearing of Elizabeth Winters' alleged reputation for sleeping with younger colleagues. She was intrigued by the woman who had so quickly risen to the rank of chief constable. Aside from her high-profile career, Elizabeth, it appeared, had led a frenetic lifestyle. Tara wondered if Jack Winters had also strayed from the marital bed. On that thought, she returned to the chapter in the book where Sawyer outlined what life had been like within the Winters family. It certainly did not read as straightforward. Sawyer never used the terms close, devoted or happy when describing this family. Tara wondered to what extent Sawyer had been censored in his telling of the story.

She drank the last of her wine, but before closing the book, reread the author profile inside the cover. Although they had now met several times, she had learned very little about Anthony Sawyer. But at this late hour, something registered that she found interesting. The author, she read, was a graduate of Cambridge University. She recalled that Rebecca Winters, had also been a student there.

CHAPTER 45

Nikki was still pissed with him for getting suspended. Benson couldn't tolerate the huffy atmosphere in the house and went for a drive, firstly to a garage to check tyre pressures and buy petrol then out to Crosby beach. He sat in his car overlooking the sands, the Gormley statues guarding the coastline, and scrolled through several apps on his phone. He browsed local news items hoping yet fearing that he would encounter a piece about himself. He was interested, however, in discovering how far the bizzies had got with investigating the deaths of Lloyd and of Cunningham's bird. There were multiple references to Angela Campbell on social media sites. Most were tributes to a kind and gentle woman who had worked hard and was cruelly taken at such a young age. Benson found more unsavoury comments in deference to the rumours circulating about Campbell's death being a gang killing. One or two individuals had only negative things to say about the woman who had been shacked up with a seasoned criminal.

He navigated to his contacts and called a number.

'Fancy a chat?' he asked when she answered the call.

Within twenty minutes, Lydia Jennings sat next to him in his SUV. Her long hair was wet and hung loose, she had just come out of the shower when her phone rang. As soon as she'd entered the car she leaned across and kissed him. He stopped her hand as it slipped to his crotch.

'Not now,' he said coldly without looking at her. She dropped back into her seat.

'What's up with you?'

'Nothing. I've been thinking that's all.'

'Oh yeah?'

'We need to cool things.'

'What do you mean cool things? We've hardly done anything, Graham. I want you. You know that, don't you?'

Benson glared with irritation. He had no real feelings for this woman. She was simply his relief when he and Nikki were annoying each other.

'I'm not talking about us. I mean we need to be more careful dealing with Greengates and Cunningham. The bizzies are sniffing around.'

'Don't worry about it. You're not even at work right now. They can't blame anything on you.'

'What's been going on at work?'

Jennings smirked.

'Not much. We gave Greengates a nice treat in the shower the other night. I think he knows now that it wouldn't be safe for him to go chatting to the tribunal. Without his evidence your disciplinary hearing will collapse, and you'll be back at work before you know it.'

'What about Cunningham?'

'I've heard he can't say anything, literally can't say anything.' Jennings giggled at her joke. 'Besides, the bizzies think the attack is down to a gang that Cunningham has crossed. Says so online.'

'No more for now, Lydia. Understand? Leave them alone until this blows over.'

'Are you going to go all broody or are you going to fuck me?'

Benson made no attempt to touch her. Reassured or not by her news, he wanted to get home. His car needed washing.

'Not now,' he said. 'I have to get back. Nikki will be wondering where I've got to.'

Jennings stood forlorn in a chilling wind and watched as his car sped away.

CHAPTER 46

By the end of the week, she would be the owner of a house, away from the city in a quiet suburb. She compiled a list of things to be done in preparation for the move. Next, she jotted down ideas for decorating and choosing furniture. Kate must be consulted, of course. It was to be her home too. Several WhatsApp calls between them were scattered across her Sunday afternoon, each one an excuse to fill a glass with wine. But it was a fun and exciting day. If all went well with the survey and mortgage application, they could visit furniture showrooms next weekend.

Monday morning, and still mulling over paint colours, she entered Tweedy's office hoping to find him in a receptive mood. She was armed with fresh information about the Winters family that she believed was worth discussing.

She began by retelling what she had learned from Anthony Sawyer regarding the private life of a former chief constable. Tweedy never appeared comfortable in discussing matters of adultery. His Christian faith, Tara supposed, and of course the love for his wife meant that he'd probably never given succour to the idea of having an affair. Consequently, he always looked disheartened by news of it occurring with others, particularly those he knew.

'Sir, I wanted to ask what you know of Elizabeth Winters.'

His eyes widened and Tara hurried to elucidate.

'You would have served while she was chief constable. How well did you know her?'

'There's not much to tell. Our paths crossed obviously. I had to submit several reports on cases to her during her time in charge. I was a DCI back then. Elizabeth Winters was a very direct woman. Confident. I suppose she had to be. She liked to get to the bare bones of an issue but wasn't one for sticking to protocol.'

'Was she friendly?'

'To me, always professional. I met her once at a conference. She was more relaxed in that environment. We chatted about family and holidays and how a police career interfered with both. My impression was that she relished her role as chief constable and the attention she received from it. She was good PR for Merseyside Police and had a healthy relationship with the media. Always willing to be interviewed.'

Except, Tara thought, when it came to the murder of her daughter and the subsequent investigation.

'How about Assistant Chief Constable Havers? Did you have dealings with him when he was at Admiral Street?'

'Very little. I was in CID here at St Anne Street, our jobs crossed at the edges. He seemed professional enough, if a tad cocky.'

'What about his investigation into Rebecca's murder?'

Tweedy shook his head.

'Can't help you there. Havers appeared to wrap things up swiftly. Once Lloyd had been convicted the story went away.'

'Were you aware of Winters' reputation for having extra-marital affairs?'

'No. I never heard any rumours either. Elizabeth Winters resigned from Merseyside Police about two years after her daughter's death. Understandable, I suppose.'

Tara returned to her desk relieved not to have upset Tweedy by raising the subject again of Elizabeth Winters. The meeting had not, however, provided her with any fresh information or ideas on how to proceed. But she had little time to dwell on the subject. Wilson, as was his habit, was suddenly standing over her.

'Morning, ma'am.'

'Ah, good morning, John. How was your weekend?'

'Great, ma'am, except for the result.'

'Result?'

There was a loud scoff from Murray on the far side of the office. Tara looked towards him, smiling.

'Tell us the score, John?' Murray called, jovially.

'Four one.'

'Can't hear you, John. What was that? Four one, was it?'

'Just ignore him,' said Tara. 'Liverpool didn't fare much better.'

'An away draw is definitely better than a home defeat,' Murray jibed.

Tara returned to Wilson.

'What do you have for me?'

'We might have an ID for the person who was shooting his mouth off in The Docker's Rest last week.'

'Might have?'

'Yes, ma'am. Stella Ramsey, off her own bat, asked some questions of a group who came into the bar on Saturday night. She spoke to a friend of the person who'd been talking about Lloyd.'

'I'm beginning to think Stella is wasting her talents working in a bar. We'll have to send her an application form for Merseyside Police.'

Wilson handed her a slip of paper.

'That's the name she got from the guy.'

'Josh Yarnly,' she read. 'Any address?'

'Not for Yarnly, ma'am, but Stella got the address of the bloke she'd spoken to. I have a note of it. Seems like student accommodation. Chances are, this Josh Yarnly might live there too.'

'I'd better get over there,' said Tara, rising from her chair. 'Alan! Let's go.'

Murray jumped to attention. Tara was conscious that she had sidelined him the previous week. It still rankled that he had not been forthcoming in revealing his connection to the Rebecca Winters case. She knew it would please him that they were steering away from that angle of the investigation.

CHAPTER 47

'It's all right, Kevin, calm down, you haven't done anything wrong.'

Kevin Roberts was, to say the least, effeminate. He'd greeted his callers wearing a white mesh T-shirt and blue flowery-patterned shorts. His blond hair was slicked back exposing a high forehead. His hands flapped wildly in all directions, flustered in the extreme that the bizzies had reason to speak with him.

'Then why are you here?' he said in a Yorkshire accent. The young man looked close to tears. Tara smiled sympathetically. Murray grinned his amusement.

'We understand you are friends with Josh Yarnly. We want to have a word with him.'

'OMG! What's he done? Is he OK?'

'Can you tell us where we can find him?'

The lad's face was ashen. He gripped at the flesh beneath his smooth chin.

'The floor below me, 17a. But he'll be in class this morning.'

'And where would that be?'

* * *

They made their way from the student accommodation building on Grove Street to the City College of Art and

Design on Duke Street. Inquiring at the reception desk, they were directed to a first-floor room where a dozen students were at work on various projects associated with fashion. Scanning the room through the window of the door, Tara saw just two males present. She guessed which one would be Yarnly. A gangly youth in a striped T-shirt and moussed black hair was taking a pair of scissors to a piece of red jacquard cloth. A woman in her thirties, presumably the lecturer in charge of the class, came to the door. She was casually dressed, her long brown hair held in place with a colourful band.

'Can I help you?'

Tara introduced herself and Murray; it was sufficient to wipe the warm smile from the woman's face.

'We would like to speak with Josh Yarnly,' said Tara.

'Yes, of course,' the woman replied, uneasily. She turned around and called out for Josh.

To Tara's surprise, the youth that she had discounted as Yarnly looked over from a bench by the window. The young man, with shaven head and smooth features, suddenly looked uncomfortable when he noticed the strangers by the door. He left two girls who were placing a dress on a mannequin and strode towards them. He wore slim jeans, an oversized T-shirt and canvas pumps. As he approached, Tara noticed that he also wore full make-up.

'Thank you,' Tara said to the lecturer. 'We can take it from here.'

The woman backed away, and Tara introduced herself to Yarnly.

'Is there somewhere we can talk, Josh? How about a coffee?'

Yarnly had not uttered a word and merely walked ahead of the two detectives. He led them to a ground-floor refectory where Murray organised the purchase of three coffees and several tray-bakes.

'What's this about?' Yarnly at last uttered.

'Oh, I think you know exactly what this is about, Josh,' Tara replied.

'I didn't have anything to do with it, honest to God. I didn't know what they were going to do. I–'

'Hold on, Josh. Calm down. Let's start at the beginning.'

Murray arrived with the coffee and sat next to Tara.

Yarnly wiped a tear away with the tip of his manicured finger. Murray handed him a napkin.

'Tell me about yourself,' said Tara. 'Where are you from?'

'Chester.'

'And you're a student here in Liverpool?'

'Fashion design. I'm in my second year.'

'Enjoying your course?'

'Yeah. It's great.'

'And what do you want to do afterwards?'

'First, I want to get a place in a good design house, in London. For the experience. Eventually, I want to have my own business in dress design.'

With the youth slightly more relaxed, Tara raised the subject of The Docker's Rest.

'So, last Wednesday night you were in The Docker's Rest with some friends?'

Yarnly looked confused by the question.

'How do you know?' he asked.

'Not important for now. Do you remember what you said that night? The story you shared with your mates?'

'Not really. I'd been drinking vodka shots. My head was buzzing. We were out to celebrate my friend getting a job.'

'Am I right in saying that several of you were in drag?'

'So?'

'I'm not judging you, Josh. It's just to confirm that I am speaking to the right person. If you can't recall what you said that night, then tell me what you were doing on Friday, 8 September.'

Tara watched the tears rolling down Yarnly's face. He gazed to a point beyond her then dabbed at his eyes with the napkin.

'I was in The Docker's Rest.'

'Were you alone?'

'Yes, to start with, then I met this fella.'

'Take a step back,' said Tara. 'Why did you go to The Docker's Rest?'

'Are you going to arrest me?'

'Depends on what you have to tell us,' Murray chipped in.

Tara glared at him. Countless times he'd weighed in without considering the delicate nature of the situation. It was vital to keep Yarnly talking. Threaten him and he would simply clam up.

'You're not in any trouble, Josh, but it would help if you can tell us what happened that night. You do know that a man was murdered?'

Yarnly sniffed back tears then blew his nose. Murray gave him another napkin.

'I got a booking from some guy.'

'What do you mean, a booking?'

'Online.'

'A dating site?' Murray asked.

'Kind of. More like an agency. You can list your profile and people, guys, can hire you, like, as an escort or for a date.'

'And you get paid for this?' Murray continued.

'Hell yeah. My student loan isn't enough to live on. I need to earn.'

'OK,' said Tara, wanting to calm the issues arising in Murray's head. 'Tell me about the guy who made the booking.'

Yarnly shrugged.

'Usually, I meet a client at a pub and then we go somewhere, his place mainly. But this fella arranged to meet me in a car park at Liverpool One. Didn't even get out of his car.'

'Do you know his name?' Tara asked.

'Said to call him Bill. That's all I had. When I met him in the car park, he told me I was to pick up this fella in The Docker's Rest and then give him a good time.'

'OK, OK,' said Tara. 'Slow down, please. How did you find this man? Were you given his name?'

'No. I was told to go to The Docker's Rest and someone there would point him out to me. Then, if I got off with him, I was to lead him to St John's Garden and do whatever to keep him sweet. Bill gave me a hundred and fifty quid and told me I'd get another hundred and fifty if I did a good job.'

'Were you told anything about the man you were going to have sex with?' Tara asked.

Yarnly shook his head and dropped his gaze.

'The man you met in the car park, can you describe him?'

'Looked normal, a regular fella, but I couldn't really see his face properly. He wore a baseball cap and sunglasses. I mean, who wears shades at night in a multi-storey car park?'

'Would you recognise him if you saw him again?'

'No chance. That bloke didn't want to be remembered.'

'What about his car?' Murray asked.

'It was very nice. Big and fancy.'

'Make?'

'I don't know about motors. It was a lovely blue, tinted windows. Expensive.'

CHAPTER 48

It was slow going but Tara thought that they were finally making progress. Josh Yarnly was proving helpful. The youth hadn't touched his coffee as Murray went to fetch a second for himself.

'Tell me about the person in The Docker's Rest who directed you to Stephen Lloyd,' said Tara.

'When I went inside, a man grabbed my arm and squeezed it hard. Really hurt me. I thought he was a bouncer. All he did was point at Stephen and he asked me if I understood. Then he sort of pushed me away and left.'

'Can you describe him?'

'Big, quite old. He wore a baseball cap too, but it wasn't Bill. He wore a donkey jacket. That's all I can remember. He made sure I didn't see much of his face.'

'Tell me what happened with Stephen.'

Tara's question induced further tears from Yarnly, and he lowered his head when Murray returned to his seat. It seemed that he found the burly detective an intimidating presence and was more at ease when speaking only with Tara.

'He was alone,' he continued. 'I checked before I went anywhere near him. I didn't want to get into anything weird. Bill told me that Stephen would be up for it, but that I was to make it seem like a chance meeting and not a paid-for date.'

'Did you know anything about Stephen before you spoke to him?'

'Not really. Bill told me that he was Stephen's mate. He hadn't seen him for a long time, and he wanted to give him a nice surprise. I just sat next to Stephen and smiled. He smiled back. It was easy. And I liked him. Would have spent the night with him for free.'

'What did you talk about?'

'He asked what I did, and I did the same. He said that he'd been away for a while and had recently come home. We just talked and maybe flirted a bit. He bought me a drink and then I bought the next round. We sat close and kissed a couple of times.'

'Did he tell you that he'd been in prison?' Murray asked. Tara glared again at her colleague.

Yarnly's face paled and he raised a hand to his mouth.

'OMG! I didn't know.'

'He'd served eighteen years for murdering a young woman,' said Murray. Tara looked incredulously at her DS.

Yarnly's hand remained over his mouth. He looked on the verge of throwing up. He rushed away, while Tara fumed at Murray.

'Really, Alan. Can't you see how fragile he is?'

'Wish to hell he'd just get on with it. We're having to squeeze every word out of him.'

'Sometimes, Alan, I wonder about you.'

'I know. You're still miffed with me about Rebecca Winters.'

'At least you've sussed that much. You have yet to explain why you didn't share the information.'

Murray cleared his throat and adjusted his tie. Stalling, Tara reckoned.

'No reason,' he said.

'Why do I not believe you?'

Yarnly reappeared looking nervous and drawn. His lipstick and some foundation had been wiped off.

'Feeling better?' Tara asked.

Yarnly shrugged indifferently.

'Maybe you can tell us what happened after you left The Docker's Rest,' she said.

'That night, was it the actual night that Stephen was killed?'

'Yes, I'm afraid so, Josh.'

For a while, it didn't seem that Yarnly could finish the story of his involvement with Stephen Lloyd. He laid his head in his arms on the table and sobbed. Tara waited. Murray wasn't impressed.

'Josh?' Tara said after a couple of minutes. 'We really need you to tell us what happened.'

Slowly, Yarnly raised his head. He looked as though he'd been asleep.

'Please try, Josh,' she said.

'I suggested we go somewhere,' he began with a sniff. 'Stephen was up for it. I knew where I was supposed to go, and he didn't seem to mind me taking him by the hand. I led him to St John's Garden. We sat on a bench close to the big statue in the middle. We kissed a bit then I started to suck him off–'

Again, Yarnly broke down in tears. Tara waited in silence. She hoped that Murray could do the same.

'What happened, Josh?' she asked after a reasonable period.

'Somebody grabbed me. I heard Stephen shouting, and there was a scuffle. I think it was Bill who dragged me away. "Here's your money, now fuck off," he said. Another man was beating Stephen with a stick or something. I was really scared. I just ran off.'

CHAPTER 49

Back at St Anne Street, Tara arranged to have Graham Benson invited to the station for questioning. Before that took place, however, Bleasdale approached with news for her.

'Ma'am, I checked with Aintree Hospital. Tyrone Cunningham is now well enough to be interviewed.'

Tara had not reached her desk. Murray had sloped off somewhere, probably to the canteen. He never missed an opportunity, despite having just had coffee at the art college. Wilson, strangely, was not at his desk engrossed in evidence gathering.

'Can you come along, Paula? Best not to waste the opportunity.'

'Yes, ma'am.'

'I want to run a few ideas past you on the way.'

'Ma'am.'

Bleasdale drove the unmarked Ford, while Tara unburdened herself of the crazy notions swirling in her head. She felt foolish for not realising sooner.

'Everything points to Graham Benson. Can't believe I missed it.'

'Ma'am?'

'His car. Murray and I had to squeeze past it on his driveway. It's a blue SUV.'

'Like the one we noticed on CCTV at Dale Street the night Lloyd was murdered?'

'Yes. Josh Yarnly told us that the man who paid him to meet Lloyd in The Docker's Rest was driving an expensive-looking blue car.'

'Then it's all beginning to fit.'

'Yes. I hope Tyrone Cunningham is willing to tell us about the attack on him and his partner.'

* * *

Cunningham, looking desolate and alone, lay in a private room. He'd lost the only person who cared for him, and the news of Angie's death had sapped any desire to continue with his own life. The arrival of two bizzies was not likely to improve his state of mind.

'Fuck off, will ya,' he managed to say, despite the pain darting across his face.

'I realise this is difficult for you, Tyrone,' said Tara, trying to sound sympathetic to the man's situation, 'but if we're to find Angela's killer we really need your help.'

'Benson.'

'The night you were attacked, did you recognise any of them?'

Cunningham rolled his head from side to side in frustration. It merely exacerbated his discomfort.

'You were walking home; did they get out of a car?'

'Yeah.'

'Can you describe it for me.'

'Big, like a Range Rover. Don't know the make.'

'How about the colour?'

'Don't remember. Grey or black, maybe.'

Tara pulled a chair close to the bed and sat down. She spoke with a gentle tone.

'What did you and Stephen know about Benson that would cause him to harm you? I'm aware he's under investigation for abuse at the prison.'

'Can't tell you.'

'Why not? We need to get this guy if he's responsible for Angela's and Stephen's death.'

'Andy is still inside. They'll kill him too.'

'Benson has been suspended. He's not working at the prison.'

'There are others. Benson's lackeys can get to Andy. He's not safe.'

Tara took Cunningham's hand and gently squeezed. The man looked startled by the gesture, but he didn't pull away.

'We can get him moved,' she said. 'Is Benson frightened by what will come out at his disciplinary hearing? Has he been trying to silence you?'

'You don't know the half of it, cop.'

'Then you have to tell me, Tyrone. It's the only way I can help you.'

He snatched his hand away.

'Imran Fadel.'

'Who's he? Where can I find him?'

'He's fucking dead. Now leave me alone.'

CHAPTER 50

On the drive back to St Anne Street, Tara tried to get information on Imran Fadel. All she had to go on was the name and a possible connection with Tyrone Cunningham and perhaps Graham Benson. She had Wilson on the phone, while he conducted a search on the Police National Computer Database for the name. It did not take long to strike gold.

'Fadel was an inmate at Liverpool,' Wilson read. 'Twenty-three years old, from Fazakerley. Serving two years for robbery with assault. He was found dead in his cell on 17 July this year. Investigation ongoing.'

'Great, John. Thank you.'

Tara could hardly wait to confront Graham Benson. If he had been involved in the death of a prisoner under his care, then he had motive to silence those who perhaps knew the truth about what happened. Tyrone Cunningham was certainly frightened.

'He's all ready for you, ma'am,' said Sergeant Dave McLachlan when Tara walked through reception. She noticed the desk sergeant's beaming smile and wondered if it was entirely for her alone. Then she noticed Paula blush as she smiled back at the man.

To Tara's chagrin, Benson had brought his solicitor along. She could not recall the presence of a brief ever helping her during an interview. She didn't expect any now, as she sat opposite the solicitor who, despite his churlish grin, appeared nervous.

She had brought Wilson to the interview room instead of Murray. Tara still did not feel confident in Murray's current attitude. Something was off with him, and she believed it concerned this investigation. Wilson sat opposite Benson's solicitor from the prison officers' association – a man named Charles Smith – his face creating as little impression as the name.

Tara advised Benson that he was not under arrest and was free to leave at any time.

'What is this about, Inspector Grogan?' Smith asked. 'My client is at a loss for any reason you may have to question him.'

Tara smiled her acknowledgement but did not care to explain herself. Instead, she put her first question to Benson.

'Tell me about Imran Fadel.'

Benson unfolded his arms and looked at Smith for guidance.

'What is your interest, Inspector?' Smith asked.

'Mr Fadel was an inmate on a wing of Liverpool prison, one for which you are responsible, Mr Benson. Is that correct?'

Smith whispered in his client's ear.

'No comment,' said Benson with a smirk. Tara returned the smirk and continued.

'He was found dead in his cell on 17 July.'

'Right, that's enough,' said Smith. 'The death of Imran Fadel is already the subject of an investigation by the appropriate authorities. You have no right to interfere by asking these questions of Mr Benson. I think we're done here.'

'As I have already stated,' said Tara, 'Mr Benson is free to leave at any time. But we do appreciate his willingness to help with our inquiries.'

'He will not be discussing Imran Fadel,' Smith said bluntly. 'I suggest you move on.'

'What make of car do you drive?' Wilson asked.

Benson looked startled by the change of subject, but Smith was still inclined to whisper his instructions.

'Jaguar, why?'

Wilson placed three photographs extracted from CCTV recordings on the table. Each one showed a blue Jaguar SUV.

'Is this your vehicle?'

Benson had a cursory look at the prints.

'Might be,' he said with a shrug. 'I'm not the only bloke to drive a Jag.'

'These were taken in Liverpool city centre on Friday, 8 September.'

'So?'

'That was the night that Stephen Lloyd was murdered. This one' – Wilson placed his finger on the picture showing the side view of a blue Jaguar – 'was taken in Dale Street, close to the junction with Cheapside.'

Benson shrugged a so-what.

'Stephen Lloyd, at that time of the evening, was drinking in The Docker's Rest bar only forty yards from there. Do you know anything about that?'

'No comment.'

'Enough!' Smith got to his feet. 'This is harassment. You have no purpose here, it seems, other than to upset my client. First you ask about an incident in his place of employment and then you move on to something entirely unconnected. You're fishing and you're wasting our time. We're leaving now.'

'Thanks for your time, gentlemen,' said Tara. 'Sorry to have touched a nerve. Rest assured we will speak again as new evidence emerges. I'm sure it won't be long.'

* * *

Dismayed at how her meeting with Benson had gone, Tara realised they had nothing concrete on the prison officer. Before retiring to her desk, she noticed Murray. He looked bored with his task of trawling CCTV data for more information on what happened the night Stephen Lloyd was murdered.

'Fancy a coffee, DS Murray?'

His head shot up. Tara stood by the office door, smiling.

'Yes, ma'am.' Murray followed her out.

Over coffee and the essential fruit scone for Murray, Tara brought him up to date with the investigation. She felt guilty about excluding him from much of the day's activity and, admittedly, missed his input despite his ham-fisted approach at times. When Tara had finished speaking, Murray set down his cup and pushed his half-eaten scone away.

'Ma'am, since you seem to have things progressing with Lloyd, I think I should apologise for not explaining myself about the Winters case.'

'Go on,' Tara said, looking sternly at her DS. She wasn't about to make it easy for him.

'The truth is, I didn't think I had anything important to tell you that would have helped your investigation.'

'I should have been the judge of that, don't you think? Are you telling me now that you deliberately withheld evidence?'

Murray's eyes widened in horror.

'No, ma'am. I really don't think I had anything useful.'

'You've just said that, Alan.' Tara's face reddened. 'But there's something you're still not telling me now. It's come between us. I don't think I can go on working with you like this. I can't trust you. Either share with me, or I'll arrange for us to go our separate ways. And you know what that means?'

He rubbed his face with both hands while Tara fumed. Murray was a man in crisis. She did not enjoy seeing him in that state, but she still felt hurt.

'Come on, Alan,' she tried softly, placing her hand on his. 'I'm your friend as well as your boss. You know me better than anyone. I love you, for goodness' sake!'

Murray looked at her with bulging eyes.

'You know what I mean. We've been through so much. You've saved my life more than once. It shouldn't be like this between us.'

'I was ordered not to,' he blurted.

'Not to what?'

'Tell you about the Winters case.'

'Ordered? Do you mean by Tweedy?'

'No. Don't be daft.'

'Spit it out, Alan. You said ordered. That means someone above you told you not to discuss Winters with me. Who was it?'

Murray looked defeated and resigned to an unknown fate. He shook his head as he answered.

'Ted Havers.'

CHAPTER 51

Tara was perturbed by the information she'd just received about the death of Imran Fadel. The young man had been found hanging in his cell, an apparent suicide. The ongoing investigation, however, was centred on the prisoner's state of mind in the days before he died. There were claims that he had been mentally and physically abused by prison staff. A second allegation concerned the failure by prison officers to check on Fadel. According to initial reports from prison inspectors, he was supposed to have been on suicide watch. Thirdly, witnesses, fellow inmates, suggested that Fadel might have been saved if staff had responded quickly when the alarm was raised. Nearly twenty minutes elapsed before Fadel's cell was unlocked and attempts made to resuscitate him.

But as she tried to concentrate on reading the reports, Tara's thoughts turned repeatedly to what Murray had revealed in the station canteen. The name Ted Havers had so far been an unwelcome aspect of her investigation of Stephen Lloyd's murder. When she'd met him, Tara had found Havers indifferent to her objectives. He cropped up again when he'd complained to Tweedy about her interviewing Jack Winters. Then she'd learned that he might have been one of the former chief constable's sexual interests when they had served at Admiral Street. And now Murray had told her that Havers ordered him not to divulge anything of his involvement in the discovery of Rebecca's body. To her frustration, Murray, in revealing Havers' instruction, still had said nothing about the events of that Christmas Eve.

* * *

The evening was still but cool. Perfect conditions for a run. She hadn't even contemplated it for months, not since her life had been in danger from a serial killer. Tonight, though, she relished the idea of fresh air after a day spent asking questions of dubious characters. It saddened her to think that Murray was included in that list.

Before the notion left her, she changed into running gear and made her way outside. Green Day blared through earphones as she increased her pace, the cool air rasping her throat as she breathed harder. She wasn't fit. She tried to flush her mind of work and even thoughts of her move to a new home. Blank the world.

It worked to a small extent. As she jogged by the Albert Dock, she failed to notice a car, forty yards behind moving slowly on the inside lane. It stayed with her for a minute or so until frustrated motorists blared their horns as they drove around the slow-moving SUV.

Tara's pace was slowing too, she felt badly out of condition. She veered off the main thoroughfare and on Gower Street headed towards the river. She wasn't attentive to her running in the middle of the road but there was no traffic around here at this time of the evening. Suddenly, from behind, the SUV sped towards her. She heard nothing but *Dirty Rotten Bastards* through her earphones. Only the sudden glare of headlights alerted her to any danger, and she glanced behind. The car veered, narrowly missing her legs as she dived to her right, landing on a bench within a bus shelter. She saw the car negotiate the turning circle at the end of the road and come towards her again. Scrambling to her feet, she took refuge behind the shelter. But the car stopped. Her first instinct was to run, but she wanted to see who was in the vehicle. The driver's window lowered halfway. She couldn't see the face clearly, but it was male.

'Keep your nose out, Grogan.'

She didn't manage a reply before the window was closed again. The car roared off and soon merged with traffic on Strand Street. Leaning against the bus shelter, Tara bent double sucking in the night air.

CHAPTER 52

'Did you get the car reg?' Murray asked.

'No, Alan. I was trying to pick myself out of the dirt at the time.'

'But you say it was an SUV?'

'Yes, but I don't think it was Benson. I couldn't see his face clearly, but it didn't sound like him. Besides, the car wasn't blue.'

Tara sat at her desk surrounded by Murray, Wilson and Bleasdale, all eager to hear her story. She was sorry she'd opened her mouth. None of them were helping with their questions. She was certain the encounter was connected to her present case, but she couldn't help thinking of the last time she'd felt threatened while out running, and that had not ended well.

Her colleagues were convinced that the man who'd threatened her had done so at the behest of Graham Benson. Tara wasn't so sure, but she didn't have long to dwell upon it. Wilson had more irritating news to impart.

'Ma'am, a message from Tweedy. We've been ordered not to interfere with the present enquiry at Liverpool Prison.'

'Why ever not?'

'The death of Imran Fadel is already under review by prison authorities. It's felt that a police investigation at this stage might hamper that work. The powers that be have already spoken to Tweedy about it.'

Tara shook her head.

'I'm fed up with this. First, I get zero cooperation from the prison regarding Benson and now we're not allowed to ask about Fadel. On top of that, I'm told to stay clear of the Winters family. What is the point?'

'Ma'am,' said Bleasdale, 'I've got a list of prison staff who work under Benson. Might be of interest.' She placed an A4 sheet on Tara's desk.

'Thanks,' she replied, taking a cursory look down the list of twelve names. 'At this stage they don't mean anything and since we're not allowed to pursue our inquiries, we'll have to leave them.'

'Ma'am, before we were ordered to steer clear I got the duty rota for Benson's squad at the prison.' Bleasdale handed Tara another sheet of A4. 'This is a list of officers who were on duty the night Imran Fadel died.' She handed Tara a third sheet. 'And this is a list of those working on Friday, 8 September and Saturday, 23 September, the days when Lloyd and Campbell were murdered. More significantly, perhaps, it indicates who *was not* working on those nights.'

Tara's interest was suddenly heightened as she studied the list. She lifted a pen and marked the names of prison officers who were off duty on the nights when the murders occurred. She had to underline only two names.

'So,' she said, 'it seems that officers Ivan Warwick and Lydia Jennings were off duty on those nights.'

'And,' said Bleasdale, 'those two *were* on duty at the time of Imran Fadel's death.'

'Should we bring the pair of them in for a chat?' Murray asked.

'No, we'll make a couple of house calls. And we'll discuss only the murders of Lloyd and Campbell. They might be too close to this damn prison review. We don't want to interfere with that now, do we?'

The group dispersed and Tara was left to consider her next steps. Her eyes followed Murray as he retreated to his desk. His recent behaviour still irked her, but she realised she'd gone too far the day before. She should not have threatened him with a transfer out of her squad. Besides, it was Tweedy and not her who made such decisions. When relative quiet had descended in the office, she wandered over to her DS.

'Fancy a coffee?'

Murray looked at her astonished.

'Another one? Getting to be a habit, ma'am, people will talk.'

Tara winced more than smiled. At times she endured rather than appreciated his humour.

'We need to talk,' she said, already moving towards the door.

In the canteen, noisy with several groups enjoying their morning break, Tara paid for two coffees and two fruit scones. If Murray needed more, it could wait until they'd finished their conversation.

'What exactly did Ted Havers say to you?'

'When, ma'am?'

'Whenever he ordered you not to discuss the Winters case.'

Murray looked surprised by her question as if they had not discussed the subject before.

'It wasn't about you, ma'am. At least, not the first time.'

'I don't understand, Alan.'

'At the time of Rebecca Winters' murder, Havers spoke to all the officers involved in the investigation.'

'I'm sure he did. That's what an SIO should do.'

'Yes, ma'am, but as I mentioned before, a couple of days after we'd found Rebecca's body, he summoned Anne Farnham and me to his office. He told us that under no circumstances were we to discuss our part in the case with anyone. Anne believed it was because the mother of the victim was the serving chief constable. I never thought much about it. I hadn't been a cop for long. I just reckoned that sort of thing happened all the time.'

'You said about it being the first time Havers spoke to you?'

Murray cleared his throat.

'Yes, ma'am. Second time was when I got back from honeymoon.'

Tara's eyes widened; her mouth dropped open.

'You mean to say Havers spoke to you just last week?'

'He called me, he said, just to remind me that even after all this time I was not to divulge any information or discuss with anyone what happened on the night of the Winters' murder.'

'What did you say to that?'

'I told him that the old case was being considered because of the murder of Stephen Lloyd. He said he was aware of that and then he mentioned you.'

'Me?'

'Yes, ma'am. He ordered me not to discuss the matter with you.'

'But he can't order you to do anything! He doesn't work for Merseyside Police.'

'Well, he suggested that it would not be wise for me to share information with you. He said it would only confuse your investigation.'

Tara was aghast. She could scarcely believe the utterances from Murray. Then something occurred to her.

'Havers must have checked me out after I'd gone to see him,' she said. It was a thought that she had spoken aloud by accident. 'How else would he know that we work together?'

Murray shrugged.

CHAPTER 53

Tara fumed all afternoon. The investigation was stymied at every turn. Her thoughts were interrupted by Wilson who told her they had obtained the home addresses for Warwick and Jennings. She was grateful for the activity and called out to Murray.

'Let's go, Alan. Can't sit there moping all day.'

* * *

Warwick was older than Tara had envisaged. He looked at least fifty, mostly bald, his remaining hair cut short, and he sported a well-maintained beer gut. He appeared mystified by the two detectives on his doorstep.

'If you have a few minutes, Mr Warwick, we'd like to ask you some questions,' said Tara.

'About what?'

'May we come in?'

Warwick stood back, allowing Tara and Murray to enter the bungalow in a pleasant cul-de-sac in Hightown. It seemed quite a lavish home for a mere prison officer, but perhaps the man had other interests. They were shown into a bright lounge with a plush corner sofa and a huge wall-mounted TV. Tara sat at one end and Murray at the other.

'You need to be quick,' said Warwick. 'I go on duty in an hour.'

'OK,' said Tara. 'Can you tell us of your whereabouts on the night of Friday, 8 September?'

The man's pudgy shoulders lifted in a shrug. His face contorted with it.

'I was probably working.'

'We already know you weren't on duty that night,' said Murray.

Warwick had not sat down. He seemed perturbed by the police having such knowledge.

'Then I don't remember,' he said, hesitantly. 'I don't go out much, so I was most likely here.'

'And the evening of Saturday, 23 September? Again, you were not on duty?' Tara said.

'What's this about? I can't remember what I was doing and I'm not answering any more questions until you tell me what's going on.'

'Those were the dates when Stephen Lloyd and then Angela Campbell were murdered,' Tara replied, observing the man's reactions.

'What?' he said, alarmed. 'You think I did that? You people have some neck on you.'

Tara simply waited. It wasn't unknown for killers to condemn themselves from their own mouths.

'I know nothing about Lloyd since he got out of jail, and I've never even heard of this other person.'

'Campbell was the partner of Tyrone Cunningham.'

'Can't help you.'

* * *

Lydia Jennings, in running pants and vest, giggled at Tara's question of her whereabouts on 8 September. They stood in the kitchen of her semi on Moss Lane in Litherland.

'I wasn't working that night,' she said. She leaned against her sink, filled with dirty dishes, as if to hide them from her visitors. Her kitchen was far from tidy.

'We know, Ms Jennings,' said Tara. 'It would help us if you could recall where you were on that date.'

Another shrugging prison officer, thought Tara, as the woman displayed a cheeky smile.

'I was here all night,' she said at last.

'You're certain about that?'

'Yes.' Jennings fiddled with her hair clip.

'Is there anyone who can vouch for that?'

'No. I live alone.'

Tara then asked about 23 September.

'At home all night,' she answered briskly. Tara didn't care for the woman's attitude and was surprised that, unlike Warwick, she had yet to ask the reason for their questions. Perhaps Warwick had already notified her of his meeting with them.

'Is that your vehicle in the driveway?' Murray asked. It was a dark grey Vauxhall Grandland.

'Yes, why?'

'And your whereabouts last night?' he asked.

Tara realised that Murray was suggesting that the Vauxhall was the car she'd encountered near the Albert Dock.

'I was here all night,' Jennings replied. 'Finished work at six and came home with a takeaway.' She indicated the foil trays on the kitchen bench and, folding her arms, stared confidently at Tara.

'How did you get on with Stephen Lloyd?' Tara asked.

'What do you mean?'

'He was a prisoner under your care, how well did you know him?'

'Just another inmate to me. Don't fraternise with them.'

'And Graham Benson?'

'Graham?'

Tara noted the sudden change in tone.

'He's my supervisor. We get on fine.'

Tara left the house thinking that little had been gained, although she had found Lydia Jennings to be rather smug.

'She never asked why we were there, Alan. Is that not strange to you?'

'She probably thought it concerned Imran Fadel until you asked about Lloyd.'

'Yes, but her answers about those dates were so dismissive. She was prepared for those questions. And did you see the look on her face when I mentioned Benson? Her eyes lit up.'

'You don't think she and Benson are an item?'

'It's possible. Or Warwick and Jennings are closing ranks to protect their boss.'

CHAPTER 54

Tara awoke at six, immediately frustrated by her lack of progress in finding Stephen Lloyd's killer. She reminded herself that the death of a young woman and the murder nineteen years later of the man convicted of her killing were separate cases, but something about that story still bothered her.

Over a breakfast of cornflakes and orange juice, another thought resurfaced regarding her case. Something she should have checked out before now. It had little to do with prison officers or the deaths of Imran Fadel and Angela Campbell but might just be connected to Stephen Lloyd. She could hardly contain herself on the drive to St Anne Street. Before anyone in the office came looking for her, armed with information or questions and before

Tweedy called her to his office for an update on her lack of progress, she made one telephone call. It took less than five minutes to have her thoughts confirmed.

Soon, however, the elation she'd felt after her call was swept aside. Tweedy, as she had expected, summoned her to his office.

'Good morning, Tara,' he said. 'I have been invited to a meeting with the SIO on the Angela Campbell investigation. He wants to compare notes, since you have made the connection with Stephen Lloyd. I think you should come along with me.'

'Yes, sir.'

'Ten thirty, at Eaton Road station. I'll drive.'

* * *

They spent the morning discussing the murders of Lloyd and Campbell, but it felt as though she had shared a lot of information with the Campbell investigation team but gained little in return. Several times she'd had to stop herself from referring to Rebecca Winters, knowing that it would only have confused matters for the Eaton Road detectives. Only Tweedy would have understood but he would not have been pleased. Still, the more she listened and the more she said, the more she was drawn back to the old case. If there was an idea simmering in her mind, then Tara could never rest until she had acted upon it. Her success in detective work had come with that attitude. On many occasions, however, it had brought her reprimand. It had also brought danger.

* * *

Sawyer was delighted to see her again. He had tidied himself for the occasion with a haircut, a neat striped shirt and black jeans. He kissed her on the cheek, and they entered a pizza restaurant in Old Hall Street.

Tara felt a tad guilty about the meeting. She wondered if Sawyer regarded her invitation as another date. But romance was the furthest thing from her mind. Unlike Sawyer's tidy appearance, Tara was still in work clothes. She'd touched up her make-up in the car but that was all.

If things went to plan, then her ulterior motive would get her some answers but probably raise even more questions. As they browsed the menu and made small talk, she struggled to find a tactful way to ask her questions. Fortunately, Sawyer helped the matter along.

'How's your investigation going? Still think Lloyd's death is linked to Rebecca Winters?'

'You know that I can't discuss the case unless I'm asking you questions in your capacity as a person with an insight into the Winters family.'

'Ooh! Sounds like you have your police hat on tonight. I thought I was in for a romantic evening.'

He beamed at her, and it made her blush. She didn't reply, but the author was persistent.

'And do you?' he asked, still smiling at least.

'Do I what?' she replied coyly, trying to suppress a serious tone.

'Do you have questions for me in my capacity as a person with insight into the Winters family?'

Bless, she had her way in, but still she felt awkward.

'I noted from your book that you went to Cambridge,' she began, watching for his reaction. 'I reckon you are about the same age as Rebecca would have been now. Hell, Anthony, this morning I checked with the university. You and Rebecca were students at the same time. At the same college. Did you know her?'

His smile seemed frozen on his face, his eyes sparkling yet boring into Tara's. He paused before answering.

'Yes.'

'And you never thought to tell me? You didn't even state it in your book.'

'My business only. Besides, it wasn't relevant to the mystery of her murder.'

'You think?' All pretence of romance had fluttered off. Tara was every inch a detective now.

'How well did you know her?' Tara glared at the face grinning back, his expression all the answers she needed.

'Oh my God! Rebecca and you,' she said. Sawyer looked like a naughty politician suddenly exposed to the world. Tara gasped. 'Were you the father of her unborn child?'

CHAPTER 55

'You can't do this, Tara,' Murray warned.

'Yes, I can, and it's ma'am to you,' Tara snapped back. 'Let's get down there.'

'Tweedy will go apeshit when he hears about it. He told you to stay away from the Winters murder.'

The pair were on the stairs to the ground floor, both failing to lower their volume.

'Just where exactly am I supposed to go with this case, Alan? Don't bother the Winters family, steer clear of the prison enquiries, don't upset anyone. Two people have been murdered and someone is trying to stop me from doing my job.'

Sergeant McLachlan smiled weakly as Tara and Murray passed by his desk heading for the interview room. Before going in, Tara turned and spoke quietly to her DS.

'This guy has motive, Alan. At least for killing Rebecca. If Stephen Lloyd knew something about that, then Sawyer had motive for killing him too.'

'And what about Angela Campbell and Tyrone Cunningham?'

'Well, Lloyd may have shared his knowledge with Cunningham.'

Murray's eyes widened in disbelief.

'I don't know, Alan. OK? It's possible. Just humour me.'

Tara threw open the door and bounded in, Murray following less enthusiastically. Seated behind a table was Anthony Sawyer, arms folded, looking smug and wearing the same clothes as the night before. Their evening had ended prematurely after Tara had requested that Sawyer attend St Anne Street station to answer questions.

Next to Sawyer sat a pale-faced solicitor wearing dark-framed glasses looking down her bony nose to a notepad on the table. Her name was Emma Mercer. Evidently, she was not intent on allowing Tara to sit or to make any introductions.

'My client is happy to help with your inquiries but is greatly offended by the suggestion that he is a suspect in your case,' she stated.

The woman, in her mid-thirties, Tara supposed, had that shrill pitch of a true scouser despite her obvious education. She got the impression that the solicitor had only been engaged by Sawyer as late as that morning, chosen perhaps at random from an online search. Solicitors R Us, she mused. Tara ignored Mercer's comment and sat down opposite Sawyer. Proceeding with her introductions and explanation of what was to happen, she then hit the author with her first question.

'Is this your book, Mr Sawyer, *Road to Nowhere*?' Tara set the paperback in front of him. Mercer took a note of the title.

'Yes, Tara. You already know this,' Sawyer replied.

She ignored his referring to her as Tara.

'Why did you write it?'

Immediately, the solicitor whispered in her client's ear. Sawyer smiled at Tara as she waited. At least, she thought, Mercer was doing her job.

'I'm an investigative journalist, Tara. You know this, also.'

His grin was self-assured. Tara felt her anger rise. But the silence was unnerving. Everyone, Murray included, looked at her for the next question. She returned the smile to Sawyer.

'Why specifically did you choose to write about the case of Rebecca Winters?'

Again, Mercer leaned over to her client and whispered. Tara assumed she was instructing him to make no comment but so far Sawyer was choosing to ignore it.

'It was an interesting story about a prominent family and not without its mystery.'

'Why did you omit your connection to Rebecca?'

'Inspector,' Mercer interjected, 'I'm having difficulty seeing any relevance to the death of Mr Lloyd. Is that not the reason why my client is here this morning? To assist your investigation.'

Tara ignored the solicitor's comments and turned to Murray. He opened a loose-leaf folder, had a cursory look at the pages within, then asked a question.

'Can you tell us of your whereabouts on the night of Friday, 8 September, please?'

Mercer again supplied a whispered instruction.

'I'm not sure,' he replied with a shrug. 'Probably at home.'

'Can anyone confirm that?'

'My partner, I suppose.'

Tara looked at Sawyer in surprise. Another thing he'd failed to share with her.

'And your partner lives at the same address?' Murray continued.

'Yes.'

'Name, please.'

'Chrissie Black.'

Tara's gaze fell to her hands on the table. It was just as well she had not allowed Sawyer to get close to her. He'd seemed keen enough to try. Here was another man for her to distrust. She should compile a catalogue.

Murray continued to ask questions surrounding the dates of the Lloyd and Campbell murders. Sawyer answered them but had no alibis for the dates in question other than being at home with his partner. Mercer attempted to end the meeting, but Tara had one final question. She knew the encounter had gone badly for her. But she couldn't let this man walk away without her giving him something to think about. She had already stopped the recording device in the room.

'Before you leave, Mr Sawyer, I have one more question.'

'Really, Inspector? You're wasting my client's time,' said Mercer.

Tara smiled sardonically at her.

'Go ahead, Tara,' said Sawyer, ignoring his brief.

'At the time of Rebecca's death, were you still in a relationship with her?'

'That's enough, Inspector,' Mercer snapped.

Sawyer's confident smile was unshaken. He paused, slid his hands into his pockets then said, 'No comment.'

CHAPTER 56

'That went well, not!' said Murray on the walk back to their office.

'What was I supposed to do? Tell me that. I'm getting stonewalled by everyone in this case, including you.'

'But you haven't gathered any evidence. You have nothing but a few leads from CCTV.'

'They've taken me down a dead end, if we can't identify the person who paid Josh Yarnly to have sex with Lloyd. I give up!'

Murray rested his bottom on the edge of her desk. For once, he spoke softly, although as usual it was less than tactful.

'Maybe you should, Tara.'

He was back to calling her Tara again. She glared at him, eyes wide and filling with anger.

'Should what?'

'Pack it in. Maybe you were right when you considered resigning after Aisling.'

It was too much for her. Tears welled. She could hardly believe her ears. She hit back.

'You would just love that, wouldn't you, Alan? Stepping into my shoes, taking over, getting the job you think you should have had before me.'

'You're stressed, Tara. You shouldn't be like this. Life's too short, walk away before it kills you.'

'You walk away, DS Murray. You're not helping.'

She wiped her sleeve across her face and sniffed back tears. Murray sloped off to his desk as others dared to look at her. Tara was swamped by an urge to get out, she had to breathe fresh air. Before leaving, however, she handed Murray a task to remind him that she was still his boss.

'Track down this Chrissie Black,' she said with a stern expression. 'See if Sawyer's alibi checks out. And why haven't you got hold of CCTV from the car parks at Liverpool One? We need to identify the car that Josh Yarnly saw.' She dropped a written note of her instruction on his desk. Murray did at least appear chastened.

Tara gathered her bag and coat and marched from the office. Her plans for the remainder of the day had yet to take shape. For now, it was sufficient relief to get the hell out of St Anne Street.

'Off out, ma'am?' McLachlan smiled from his perch behind the reception desk.

Tara smiled weakly but said nothing. Why should that man care what she was up to? Maybe he was the only friendly face left in the station. She breezed out, got into her car and, without much thought of where she was headed, drove from the station car park. She soon found herself on a road leading to the tunnel, struck by a sudden desire to visit her new purchase in Hoylake. Rock music blared from the radio; Tara was unaware of a car following.

She parked across the open driveway of her soon-to-be new home. Her mind filled with ideas of what she would do with the garden. Kate and Adele were prominent in her thinking. The front lawn was in good condition despite the time of year, although it could have done with mowing before winter set in. Tara inspected the flowerbeds; the previous owners must have been attentive gardeners. There were areas devoted to perennials, other spaces to winter and spring bulbs, and she noticed the remnants of perhaps the last bedding plants ever put in place by the elderly couple who had spent many years living here.

Venturing to the rear of the house, she surveyed the wide lawn bordered by laurel and privet hedging but low enough to view the shoreline beyond. For the first time, she noticed a picket gate within the hedgerow. It needed repairing, its hinges rusted, and the bar lock broken. She dragged it open and stepped into a lane overgrown with grass and weeds. To her left, she saw that it led to the beach, but to her right it seemed to merge into thick bushes. Back in the garden, she inspected the rear of the house, something she really should have done before she had agreed to buy the property. But people often spend less time deliberating over buying a house than they do in choosing a pair of shoes. She noticed that some repairs to window frames were needed and maybe a few roof tiles would have to be replaced. The surveyor, she hoped, would highlight such matters in his report.

Refusing to feel downbeat about her fresh start, she returned to the driveway at the front, but her attention switched from the house to a car on the other side of the street. Her blood chilled. She was certain it was the same vehicle she'd encountered when she'd been jogging at the

Albert Dock. Determined to remain strong, she bounded towards it. She saw the driver staring at her. He beamed a smile as she drew closer, and he lowered his window to greet her.

'What are you doing here? What do you want?' Her questions came angrily. The man, clean-shaven and wearing a black baseball cap, merely smirked.

'Free country, love.'

'Who are you?' she demanded.

She'd left her bag in her car and couldn't produce her warrant card.

'I'm DI Grogan, Merseyside Police! Get out of the car, please.'

The window was raised, the engine started, and with a condescending sneer, the man drove away. Tara stood in the road, knowing that the car was headed towards the dead end of the street and would have to turn and pass her by. This time she took a mental note of the registration. The vehicle roared towards her, and she darted to the pavement. The driver laughed and beeped his horn as he drove away.

She was certain it was the same guy who had driven at her when she'd been out running. Now at least she had the registration. Soon, she would know the reason why the brute was stalking her.

CHAPTER 57

'They're not just following me; they're threatening me,' Tara blurted to Tweedy and Murray.

'I checked the reg. They were using false plates. We can't trace them,' said Murray.

Tara looked unimpressed. Her colleagues playing down the incident wasn't helping. It was more than a case of being followed. This man had spoken to her on two occasions. He knew her movements.

'What is he up to?' she asked. 'Has it got something to do with Benson or is it connected to Rebecca Winters?'

Tweedy flinched at her mention of the Winters case.

'We'll have to assume for now that it could be either,' he responded. 'For the time being, Tara, I don't want you to go out alone. You will take Alan or John with you on police business.'

'And what about in my own time, sir? Both incidents happened when I was off duty.'

'Don't go out alone.'

'But, sir!'

'No buts, Tara. You should realise by now that you do a dangerous job, and your safety is paramount. I cannot have a repeat of the last case when we almost lost you.'

Tweedy's stern comment cast an uncomfortable air in the office. Murray looked sympathetically towards his DI, but Tara couldn't maintain eye contact with either man. She was reliving every nightmare she'd suffered from this job. Images flashed in her head of each victim for whom she'd strived for justice. The day's events were replaying over and over. It was broken; she was broken.

'If this threat is connected to the present case,' she mooted, 'just where do we go from here?'

'Go home, Tara,' Tweedy said. 'We'll start afresh tomorrow. This is not the time to discuss the case. You need to relax for a while, clear your head. I'm sure Alan will see that you get home safely.'

Tara stewed. If she didn't know Harold Tweedy better, she'd swear he was patronising her. For the second time in the same day, she craved fresh air away from this damned police station. As she prepared to leave for home, she decided that there would be no rest. She instructed Murray to gather the files on the Lloyd murder investigation.

* * *

'Put those files on the table, I'll make some coffee.' Tara hadn't said as much but she was making it clear that Murray was staying. 'I bought some doughnuts yesterday,' she said, opening her fridge. 'They should be fresh enough. Make yourself at home.'

Murray did as he was told, removing his jacket and draping it on the back of the sofa. He stretched, raising his arms and watching his boss flitting around her kitchen.

'Sit down, for goodness' sake. I'll try not to keep you for too long. I know you have a life to get back to.'

'It's fine, ma'am. I have nowhere special to be. Trudy is in London this week.'

Tara set a tray with two mugs and a plate of doughnuts on her coffee table. She kicked off her boots and sat down opposite Murray who had finally flopped onto the sofa. While he helped himself to the refreshments, Tara sifted through the files they had brought from the station.

'So, what exactly are you hoping to get from this?' Murray dared to ask.

She wanted to scream in his face. She didn't know, did she? But she had to do something. She felt so close to self-destruction, surely this had to help her. It had to make a difference. She was tired, frustrated and scared of all that was going on with this case, or these two cases. Hell, she had no idea why she was doing this.

'Nothing more to lose, Alan,' she replied, stifling tears and slipping papers from a folder.

'Where do we start?'

'You said the car that I saw in Hoylake had false plates?'

'Yep.'

'Seems too well organised for it to be a few prison officers trying to frighten me. Surely, using false plates implies professional.'

'As we said at the station,' said Murray, 'maybe it has sod-all to do with the present investigation. Could be someone from a past case.'

'But the guy told me to keep my nose out. That has to mean the Lloyd murder.'

Murray had no further comeback. He directed Tara's attention to the papers in her hand. 'What have you got there?'

Tara spread them on the coffee table.

'Just some notes I've scribbled over the past few days. The first sheet has a list of suspects for the murder of Lloyd.'

'What about Angela Campbell?'

'Yes, Alan,' she snapped. 'We'll get to that. Please, just work with me for now.'

Murray lifted the page from the table. He read out a name, and Tara responded to it.

'Graham Benson.'

'He has motive but apparently a sound alibi for the night of the murder. Doesn't rule out the possibility that he had others do the job for him.'

'Lydia Jennings?' Murray continued.

'Possibly under the influence of Benson and has no real alibi for 8 September,' Tara replied.

'So, we can't discard her?'

'No, but if she's guilty then I imagine several of her colleagues are too.'

'Ivan Warwick.'

'Same as Jennings. Working under Benson and no firm alibi.'

Murray raised an eye as he read the next name.

'Tyrone Cunningham?'

'I know, I know. It's just that he met with Stephen Lloyd on 8 September. I can't rule him out yet, even though I have no motive for him to have killed his friend.'

'And his partner Angela was also murdered, ma'am.'

'Yes, of course. But we'll keep him on the list for now.'

Tara couldn't help a smile as she watched Murray tuck into a second doughnut. She couldn't even face one and hadn't touched her coffee.

'Next is Josh Yarnly,' Murray mumbled, his mouth full of pastry.

'We'll keep him on the list, but I think he was telling us the truth. Somebody paid him to lure Lloyd to St John's Garden.'

'Maybe we could press him for more information about the guys who hired him?'

'He's too naïve to have paid any more attention to the hand that fed him. All about the money, I think.'

Murray lifted a second sheet of paper from the table.

'That's a list of people associated with Lloyd but also linked to Rebecca Winters,' Tara said. 'Whenever you're ready, Alan.'

Murray set down his coffee and glanced down the list.

'Just start at the top,' said Tara.

'Jack Winters.'

'Definitely has motive. I didn't get an alibi out of him for 8 September. Not allowed to approach him in our official capacity.'

'Freddie Winters,' said Murray.

'Interesting one. As Rebecca's sibling, he also has motive. He lives in the US but visited his mother on 10 September. That means he could have been in Liverpool on the eighth when Lloyd died.'

'Doesn't support any theory that he's your stalker or that he was still in Liverpool when Cunningham and Campbell were attacked.'

Tara glared at Murray. Still fragile, she didn't feel she could handle strong criticism of her thinking.

'Moving on,' she said dryly.

'Anthony Sawyer.'

'Mm. Wrote a book on the Rebecca case. Then I discover that he had been in a relationship with her and quite possibly was the father of her unborn child.'

'He didn't admit to that. Besides, where is the motive to kill Lloyd?'

'I don't know, Alan! Maybe Lloyd knew something about Sawyer that could expose him as Rebecca's killer.'

'But what would Lloyd have known, and why didn't he speak out at his trial or during the original investigation? Why wait nineteen years?'

Tara lost it.

'I don't know! If Sawyer didn't have motive to kill Lloyd, he had a reason to kill Rebecca.'

'Calm down, Tara. I'm trying to help. Devil's advocate and all that shit.'

Tara wiped a tear from her eye, rose from the sofa and went to her kitchen. Coffee wasn't helping. She removed a bottle of chardonnay from the fridge and filled a large glass.

'Next,' she called.

'Ted Havers.'

'Shit.' She gulped her wine.

CHAPTER 58

'Do you realise what time it is, Inspector Grogan?'

Freddie Winters, understandably, was not pleased to be woken up at two thirty in the morning. Tara had little sympathy, and besides she hadn't considered the time difference between Liverpool and Honolulu. She'd asked Wilson to get contact details for Rebecca's brother. There wasn't much wriggle room in this investigation before somebody yelled harassment. Speaking to Freddie Winters might eliminate him as a suspect and she could cross him off her list before Tweedy had the chance to reprimand her again.

'My apologies for the late hour but it is office hours in Liverpool.'

'What do you want?'

Winters had a peculiar sounding accent. Hardly scouse but not completely Americanised, it displayed those annoying inflexions where everything sounded like a question. To be fair, the man had done nothing but ask questions since the conversation began.

She asked him to confirm his recent visit to Liverpool and the meeting with his mother.

'Yes, I was there a few weeks ago,' he said irritably. 'Why are you interested in me?'

'Did you visit your father?' Tara asked.

'My God, I didn't realise it was a criminal offence not to see my father when I went back home.'

'I take it that's a no?'

'No. I had no desire to speak to him. I was in London on business, I visited my in-laws in Surrey and nipped up north to see my mother.'

'You visited your mother's nursing home on Sunday, 10 September?'

'If you say so, Inspector.'

Tara heard Winters yawning.

'Can you please confirm how long you stayed in Liverpool?'

'I caught the train from Euston on the Friday and left Liverpool on Sunday, directly after visiting the nursing home. Now, can you please tell me what this is about, or I will end this call.'

Tara ignored the threat. She reckoned that Winters was intrigued by her calling him and would not put the phone down until he got the reason behind her questions.

'Did you meet with anyone, besides your mother, while you were here?'

'I met a couple of old friends for a drink on the Friday night, and I had dinner with another on Saturday.'

'Their names, please.'

'No way! I'm not telling you anything more until you explain yourself. Does my father know that you're calling me, Inspector?'

Tara ignored the question about Jack Winters. She doubted Freddie would ever call his father to find out.

'Were you aware that Stephen Lloyd had been released from prison in September?'

'At last! The reason for your call. Yes, Inspector, but I heard also that he's been murdered. Good riddance to the animal who killed my sister.'

Winters' accent had suddenly defaulted to Liverpool, not broad scouse but Liverpool, nonetheless.

'Oh my God! You think I did it? That I killed Lloyd? I wish. But whoever did do it, Inspector, I'd love to buy them a drink.'

'If you could provide the names of your friends whom you met while in Liverpool, I won't detain you any longer.'

Tara heard a laboured sigh as Winters retrieved contact details of his friends from, in American parlance, his cell phone.

She ended the call, thanking Freddie Winters for his help. He mumbled something in reply, but she could not make him out.

Summoning Wilson to her desk, she gave him the details of Winters' friends and asked him to confirm their meeting with Freddie.

Murray came over. He looked fresh despite the late night at her flat going through every aspect of the case. She had eventually chucked him out at one o'clock amid his protestations. He'd said that he didn't mind staying for the night as her protector.

'How did it go?' he asked, unwrapping a Snickers bar.

'Well, he wasn't happy about me calling at what was the middle of the night for him. He told me that he'd spent the weekend from 8 September in Liverpool, so he had opportunity to seek out Lloyd. He claims to have spent time catching up with friends, and he came up from London by train. We can check with the railways for dates and times.'

Tara slumped over her desk, head resting on her arms.

'I hope this works, Alan. I think I'll go nuts if we get nothing from it.' Speaking into her arms, she was barely audible, but Murray got the gist of her comment.

'It'll work, ma'am. It's solid policing. We must go through everything again, starting with those who are not currently off-limits. But we will get back to the people at the centre of it eventually. After all, it is a murder investigation.'

'OK. I believe you. Stop talking before you start sounding like the guy from *Line of Duty*. Just tell me what's next on our list?'

'We've been ordered to steer clear of the prison thing, and we can't go anywhere near Havers or Jack Winters, so the next issue to deal with is Tyrone Cunningham.'

Tara sprang from her seat with a joyous smile, though it had a sarcastic taint.

'Right, let's go. The man better have more to say than last time or I might just arrest him as a suspect for murder.'

CHAPTER 59

Cunningham had shared Angela Campbell's home, situated amongst a sprawl of housing off East Prescot Road. The well-maintained semi, like many around it, had a front garden paved over to provide parking. When Cunningham opened his door to be faced with a pair of police detectives, he threw his head back in frustration.

'What do you want now? I've nothing to say to bizzies.'

Despite his protestations, he left the door open and padded in his socks back to the living room. Tara accepted the grudging invitation and stepped inside with Murray following. Cunningham was already seated in a leather reclining armchair facing a TV showing afternoon racing from Haydock Park. He looked frailer than Tara remembered, even when he was in hospital, his face pinched and now with a scar running from his left cheek to below his chin. He massaged his outstretched thigh as Tara spoke.

'How have you been, Tyrone?'

'What's this? You're a fucking social worker now?'

'Just asking, that's all. I realise this has been a difficult time for you.'

Murray remained standing, while Tara perched herself on the arm of a sofa.

'You don't know the half of it, cop.'

'Tell me then,' said Tara softly. 'That's why I'm here.'

Cunningham looked unconvinced by her show of concern.

'Angie's gone and now her family want me out of this place. I've nowhere to go. Can you fix that one for me, love?'

'I'm sure we can help get something sorted out. But we need some help from you, Tyrone.'

'Sure, you do.'

From a cluttered side table, Cunningham lifted a vaporiser and took a long drag from the device, exhaling a plume of scented vapour into the room. Tara couldn't identify the aroma, caramel perhaps.

'Did Stephen Lloyd ever mention anything about his conviction for killing Rebecca Winters?'

'We talked about lots of things. Can't do much else when you're inside.'

'I'm thinking particularly about the days leading up to his death or maybe that last time you spoke at The Docker's Rest.'

'Might have done, can't remember exactly.' He took another hit from the e-cigarette.

'Think, Tyrone. This is very important if you want to help us track down Stephen's killer.'

'And what about Angie? What the hell has Stephen's conviction for killing a girl years ago got to do with Angie? I've told you who killed them. It was those bastard screws trying to cover their asses over Imran Fadel. What are you running around asking questions about ancient history for?'

Tara remained silent for a moment. In her heart, she pitied the man sitting opposite her. He had lost everything, his partner, a friend, and soon it was to be his home. But she needed more from Cunningham.

'Please, Tyrone. Did Stephen tell you anything about what happened to Rebecca Winters? Was he frightened that someone was intent on keeping him silent?'

'I don't know the details or anything, but he was scared of someone.'

'And this wasn't connected to Benson and the others at the prison?'

'He was definitely scared about that, but in The Docker's Rest, he told me that he was going to clear his name for what happened to Rebecca. He told me he'd had eighteen years to piece it all together. Before he got out of the nick, he'd tried to contact the girl's brother to explain it all.'

'Freddie Winters?'

'Could be, don't remember names very well.'

'Why? Had he discovered something, new evidence?'

Cunningham shook his head and finally set the vaporiser back on the table.

'In The Docker's Rest, he told me that he'd got no reply from calls to the brother, but he'd received a warning from your lot.'

'The police? What happened?'

'The day after his release he met some bizzie in the park. The guy warned him to let things drop because he could never prove anything and would only cause the Winters family more distress. He'd caused them enough heartache when he'd killed Rebecca.'

'Did he tell you who this person was?'

'I told you I can't remember names. But Stephen recognised the guy. It was the bizzie who had put him away.'

'Havers?'

Cunningham shrugged indifference to the name.

CHAPTER 60

They sat in silence in their car, still parked outside the home of Tyrone Cunningham. Tara was slowly digesting the revelation about Ted Havers. She had no reason to believe Cunningham was lying, but she needed more than the word of an ex-prisoner and friend of a convicted murderer to act upon it.

'Shall we go, ma'am?' Murray had not only broken the silence; he'd interrupted her train of thought.

'I suppose so.'

'Anthony Sawyer next?'

Tara's thoughts were stuck on Cunningham. She didn't answer.

'Ma'am?'

'Something niggles me about Cunningham,' she said.

'You think he's lying?'

'No, but I think he knows more about Lloyd. For some reason, he's unwilling to share it with us. And how did Ted Havers even know what Lloyd's intentions had been?'

'What do we do about him?'

'I think we'll run this new information past Tweedy. He can decide whether we bring in the assistant chief constable to help with our enquiries.'

* * *

Tara had arranged to meet Sawyer at a Starbuck's in a retail park near Speke. Sawyer had reluctantly agreed to the interview, off the record and without his brief, when Tara had stated the alternative was another session at St Anne Street. She allowed him to choose the location for their meeting. This time also, Tara had brought Murray with her. There would be no pretence of friendship. Sawyer was a suspect like any other in a murder enquiry.

'And what does Merseyside's finest want with me today?' Sawyer chirruped. His face, however, suggested he was nervous. He didn't look as if he'd had any sleep. Tara sat down opposite him, while Murray fetched two coffees. Sawyer was already sipping a latte.

'I appreciate your time, Mr Sawyer, and as agreed this interview will be off the record.'

'What do you want to know?' He seemed surprised at being addressed as Mr and not Anthony.

'I want to know everything that you either decided not to include or were prevented from doing so in your book.'

Sawyer glanced at his watch and chuckled.

'We should have met for breakfast. This could take all bloody day.'

'Let's make a start then, shall we?'

Murray joined them, setting a cappuccino in front of Tara with an Americano for himself. Then a barista arrived with a toasted sandwich and placed it in front of Murray. Tara was not surprised. The man had a bottomless pit for a stomach.

'I have already told you that Elizabeth Winters did not want the details of Rebecca's pregnancy included.'

'And were you the father of her unborn child?'

'Nice try, Inspector,' Sawyer grinned. 'Still no comment.'

'OK. So, what else was omitted?'

'Mostly personal details of the Winters family.'

'Meaning what?'

Sawyer paused to drink some coffee. He seemed unsettled by the intensity of Tara's questioning. In situations such as this, Tara exercised great patience. If necessary, she could wait all day for an answer.

'Well, I was allowed only to write a brief history of each family member: where they were born, schools attended, dates of birth, that kind of thing. I had written detailed accounts of the career histories of Jack and Elizabeth, but they were redacted, supposedly by my editor, although I don't believe that was the case. I think Winters' solicitor insisted they be removed. I attempted the same for the senior investigating officer of the murder enquiry but was told again by my editor that it was irrelevant.'

'Did you have anything controversial to say?' Tara asked.

Sawyer shrugged and sat back in his seat.

'All of it was controversial. Otherwise, why exclude it?'

'Tell us what you wrote about Jack?'

'He was a private sort of man to begin with. During the investigation and trial, he simply wanted the entire episode written off like some kind of tax issue that he was used to dealing with. It didn't seem to matter that it was about his murdered daughter. Many of his friends and associates said the same about him. He was ruthless in business. Cold. From what Rebecca shared with me when we were together, there was little love given to anyone by Jack Winters.'

'And Elizabeth?' Murray asked.

'An even cooler subject. Her mind was focused on her career and once she'd established her family, she expected everything and everyone within it to run smoothly in the background. She laid down the rules in the household. Any affection for her husband and children was overshadowed by her drive for career success. By the time she'd made it to chief constable, the relationships within the family were already damaged beyond repair. That's why I think Rebecca and Freddie were so rebellious. At times, they deliberately set out to upset the parental regime.'

'How so?' Tara asked.

'It was just the usual teenage stuff to begin with – drinking, drugs, mixing in bad company – but by the time Rebecca reached Cambridge, she was in danger of going over the edge. I knew before we ever went out that she'd had a string of, let's say, unconventional relationships. One minute she was sleeping with a much older man, next she was having a lesbian fling with a woman old enough to be her mother. The most bizarre episode was when she started hanging around with a seventy-year-old homeless man in Cambridge. She lived on the streets with him until Jack found out and dragged her home. Whatever he said to her, after that she settled down. Apart from me, everyone she slept with was at least of her parents' age. Her drinking and drug taking threatened to end her studies at Cambridge until she realised that being at university meant that she didn't have to live at home. Getting pregnant, I believe, was just another way to inflict pain on her parents.'

Sawyer was in full flow. He seemed to derive some vindication from at last telling the story he'd been prevented from recounting in his book. Tara didn't get a chance to interrupt with her next question.

'Freddie was a more devious character. Rebecca told me that the two of them played games to outdo one another. Sometimes they went too far. Once they tried swapping places at their respective schools. Rebecca cut her hair short, while Freddie borrowed his sister's clothes. They lasted about thirty minutes one Monday morning. Elizabeth was called to both schools and wasn't pleased to have had her busy day diverted to family issues. The worst story that Rebecca told me involved an incident with their father's secretary. I don't recall her name, but she was a quiet, refined lady and not terribly street smart. Rebecca went to Jack's office and begged this secretary for money to buy lunch. When the woman gave her the money, Rebecca attempted to thank her by coming onto her, lifting her school skirt in front of the poor soul. When she politely refused Rebecca's offer, Freddie suddenly appeared. He then offered himself to the woman, dropping his trousers. Rebecca told me it was brilliant just to see the shock on the secretary's face. She filmed it on her phone and Freddie then threatened to pass it to the police if the woman ever told their father. They were schoolkids and no one would believe that the incident had been their idea. The secretary didn't last another day. She resigned from her job.'

'Can't say I'm surprised that the Winters family didn't allow you to publish that tale,' said Murray. 'Fancy another coffee?'

When Murray went to fetch drinks for Sawyer and himself, Tara continued the conversation.

'It is a horrid story, Anthony,' she said. 'From what you say, it would be hard to like any member of the family. But is there anything that you were barred from publishing that may have had a bearing on Rebecca's murder inquiry? You told me that you believed the case was poorly investigated.'

'I'm convinced of it, Tara,' he replied.

Tara was suddenly aware of how relaxed their meeting had become. Both had reverted to first names. Despite his previous duplicitous attitude, Sawyer was a likeable man.

'The relationship between Rebecca and Freddie got out of hand at times. I believe that it was their mischief with each other that led to Rebecca's death.'

CHAPTER 61

Murray returned with two coffees. Tara hoped to get more from this meeting with the author. The conversation had been interesting but, so far, she had gained little to help her find the killer of Stephen Lloyd. Murray couldn't hide his boredom, but Tara knew that he'd long made up his mind that rogue prison officers were responsible for the murders.

'Elizabeth slapped a court injunction on the book,' Sawyer continued. 'It was only removed after she was given the final say on what was published.'

'What else caused offence?' Tara asked.

'Much of it related to the day of Rebecca's murder and the police investigation thereafter. Some of what I'd written was purely my supposition because the family refused to share their account of that Christmas Eve. Elizabeth did not like any of it.'

Tara couldn't help a sideways glance at Murray. She knew what it was like dealing with someone who withheld information.

'My take on what happened that day is this. Firstly, I believe that Freddie was the only family member who knew that Rebecca was pregnant. Why she'd told him I will never understand. He couldn't be trusted. Around that time, Freddie had become friends with Stephen Lloyd. He was claiming to be gay although only Rebecca was aware of it. He was either experimenting or he was up to mischief again. It's possible the siblings were winding each other up about the pregnancy and being gay. They each had a secret that prior to that Christmas had not been shared with their parents. Lloyd was innocently caught in the middle. When Freddie invited Lloyd to the family home that Christmas Eve, Lloyd might have believed that he and Freddie were going to spend the afternoon together having sex. Freddie wasn't going to be there, but he guessed that Rebecca would be. What he thought would happen is anyone's guess. Maybe he was setting up the opportunity for Rebecca to meet his gay lover, to get her approval, or else, cruelly, he imagined that Rebecca would come onto Lloyd and then be rejected because he had no interest in girls. Or, as I said before, Freddie was probably off his head when he invited Lloyd to his house. But what he didn't realise was that his mother would be there. And she would not be alone.'

'Hold on,' said Tara. 'You're losing me. How do you know who was at home?'

'That's where the police investigation is a little vague. None of this information was committed to the file on Rebecca's murder. It's just my theory, and Elizabeth did not allow any of it to go in the book. The only thing definite for the afternoon of that day was that Lloyd was seen at the house and loitering in Firs Lane. Rebecca's movements are not detailed, except that she returned home at some point in the afternoon and was found dead in the lane later that night. Freddie and his father were apparently in the city until late evening, but there is little detail recorded about Elizabeth and no mention whatsoever of the family's housemaid.'

'Housemaid?' Tara sounded surprised.

'Yes. The Winters employed a woman to clean the house, do the laundry and when the kids were younger, they also employed an au pair.'

'You mentioned a housemaid and an au pair in your book, but I don't recall reading anything about that in the police file.'

Sawyer raised his eyes as a light went on in Tara's head.

'I told you there were gaps in the police investigation. The au pair was long gone obviously. The kids were grown. But as far as I know, the housemaid was never interviewed by detectives.'

'Was she working at Briarwood Manor on the day of the murder?'

'Yes. She'd been asked specifically by Elizabeth to help get the house ready for Christmas.'

'And she was never questioned over what she knew?'

'Not by the investigating team. A uniformed constable took a brief statement from her. It merely confirmed that she had been working at the house on Christmas Eve.'

Tara couldn't get her questions assembled quickly enough.

'Did you interview her for your book?'

'Of course. But all references to her presence at the manor on that day were redacted.'

'What did she tell you?'

'That she'd been working there all morning and into the afternoon on Christmas Eve. At various times during the day, she was aware of Elizabeth and Rebecca coming and going from the house. She remembered Lloyd calling at the front door, but he was confronted by Elizabeth. At no point, she told me, did Lloyd come inside the house.'

'There's nothing in any of that to contradict what's recorded in the police file,' said Murray.

Tara glared at her colleague. Since when had he decided to bolster a shabby investigation, one in which he had played a part?

'So, how was the housemaid's testimony deemed a threat to the Winters family?'

Sawyer smiled, poised to deliver the *coup de grâce*.

'Before leaving that afternoon, the woman took a final stroll around the house, making sure she hadn't missed anything in her Christmas preparations. As she passed the master bedroom, she heard voices inside. She knew that Elizabeth had arrived home a few minutes earlier, but she also heard a male voice within the bedroom. It was clear to her that whoever was inside that bedroom, they were having sex. The housemaid was certain that it was not Jack Winters.'

'Why so sure?'

'Because he had telephoned the house landline an hour earlier. He left a message with the housemaid to say that he would not be home before eight o'clock when the family were supposed to assemble for dinner, prior to attending midnight communion at the parish church.'

'What if it were Rebecca and Lloyd?' Murray suggested.

'Why would they be in Elizabeth's bedroom?' Tara countered. Then she gasped like a schoolgirl who'd just been told a friend's guilty secret. 'You told me that Elizabeth Winters had sexual encounters with younger colleagues at Admiral Street?'

'Allegedly,' Sawyer corrected her. 'And we don't know for sure that she continued to do so after she became chief constable.'

'But you suggested that one of those men could have been Ted Havers,' she said. 'If so, is it possible that Havers was the man in Elizabeth's bedroom? And was he still at the house when Rebecca disappeared? Alan?' Tara looked earnestly at Murray.

'Ma'am?'

'Is that what you have refused to tell me? Was Havers already at the house when you found Elizabeth in the lane and brought her back inside?'

CHAPTER 62

Throughout the weekend, Tara rehearsed what she would say and how she would behave in Tweedy's office on Monday morning. Ted Havers' name continued to crop up in her murder investigation. She reckoned that Murray would persist with the prison officer conspiracy. But she wasn't concerned about Murray. It was Tweedy she must convince. Ultimately, he would have the final say on whether to bring an assistant chief constable from another jurisdiction to St Anne Street for questioning. When she thought about it, the decision would be made by an officer senior to Superintendent Tweedy. Most likely, the chief constable of Merseyside Police would make such a call.

Murray and Wilson joined her in Tweedy's office first thing. Immediately, Tara went on the offensive.

'Can you please confirm for us, Alan, whether Ted Havers was already present at Briarwood Manor on that Christmas Eve when you were searching for an alleged prowler?'

Murray seethed, but Tara had backed him into a corner.

'Yes, ma'am,' he answered.

'To be clear, he was inside the house when you and Constable Farnham escorted Elizabeth Winters to her home after finding her in the lane?'

'Yes, ma'am.'

'Well, thanks for that, DS Murray. You've been very helpful. Eventually.'

The room was silent for a moment, the atmosphere potent. Tara fumed, Murray was admonished, and Tweedy absorbed the enormity of the information before him. Astutely, Wilson said nothing and gazed at the floor.

'It is feasible, sir,' said Tara, 'that Ted Havers was the man in Elizabeth's bedroom during the afternoon and therefore was present when she reported her daughter missing.'

Tweedy didn't seem entirely convinced by her logic. 'And you're basing this on the information provided by Mr Sawyer?'

'Yes, sir. He told us that the Winters' housemaid had heard activity in the bedroom. Elizabeth had a dubious reputation. She was renowned for having romantic trysts with younger men.'

'Did the housemaid confirm that it was Havers?'

'No, sir. Unlikely, perhaps, that she would have recognised him.'

'So, we can't be certain about who was in the bedroom with Elizabeth. Considering what you have said about her reputation, it could have been anyone. Is it possible that Havers arrived at the house around the same time that Alan and his colleague began searching for Rebecca?'

'I suppose so,' Tara replied, grudgingly.

'Before you accuse a respected senior officer of involvement in a serious crime, have you any possible motive to support the theory that Havers is responsible for killing Lloyd?'

'If Lloyd had information that was a threat to him.'

'Such as?'

'Maybe Havers wanted to cover up his failings from the Rebecca investigation. It could be that even now he does not want his affair with Elizabeth to be revealed.'

'And what about the other victim, Angela Campbell?' Tweedy had swept all aside with this one question. Tara had nothing to link Havers with the death of Campbell. To her annoyance, Murray suddenly resurrected his confidence.

'That's why this still points to the prison angle,' he said. 'Lloyd was killed because he was embroiled in the goings-on at the jail. Aside from her relationship with Cunningham, Angela Campbell is a complete innocent in this.'

Tara didn't need Tweedy to say it. She knew, she felt that all opinions favoured Murray's analysis and she was floundering. Yet again, she felt a fool.

But Tweedy had always lent sympathy and understanding to his officers.

'We'll not discard your theory, Tara. But for now, let's just park it until we have concrete evidence that Havers is connected to both victims. If we do bring him in for interview, I would hope that we could present him with a *fait accompli* rather than our supposition.'

'Yes, sir.'

On the way back to her desk, Tara soaked up tears with a tissue and blew her nose. Never had she felt so humiliated. She ignored Murray's clumsy attempt to soothe her. At that moment, if someone had accused her of petulance, she couldn't argue.

It was the unfortunate Wilson who was summoned. He looked on as Tara thumped her bag down on the desk and rummaged inside for a pack of tissues. Then she tossed the bag on the floor and slapped her keyboard for no apparent reason. Her computer wasn't even switched on.

'Ma'am,' he said to interrupt her fraught actions.

'I need your help with a few things, John. Get Paula to help and under no circumstances tell Murray anything of what you're doing. Is that clear?'

'Yes, ma'am.'

Tara rose to her feet and gazed across the office. Murray was engrossed in something on his computer. She didn't care what it was or what he was doing. She didn't want him involved in her work at all.

'Let's talk outside, John. I need some fresh air.'

It was only when they reached the front door of the station that either one realised it was chucking down outside, the rain pelting on car roofs. At least she was free of the office and DS Murray. The pair stood in reception as Tara handed out instructions.

'As you heard in Tweedy's office, Sawyer has provided another lead in this case, but that doesn't mean I trust him entirely. If he was the father of Rebecca's unborn child, then possibly he had motive to kill her.'

'He would have motive even if he wasn't the father,' Wilson suggested. 'If Rebecca had been unfaithful to him then he may have sought revenge.'

'Yes, of course. Hadn't thought of that. Sawyer refuses to say if he was the father or even if he was still in a relationship with Rebecca at the time of her death. I need to confirm it either way. I want you to contact their college in Cambridge. Get a list of people who were students at the same time as Sawyer and Rebecca, even better if you can trace friends of the pair. Try to find someone who knew what went on between Sawyer and Rebecca, someone who knew if they were still in a relationship at the time of the murder. Who knows, you might even discover another candidate for the father of Rebecca's baby.'

As their conversation continued, the two officers had parked themselves at one end of the reception desk. Sergeant McLachlan busied himself at a computer station, greeting colleagues as they passed by.

Tara retrieved a notebook from her handbag and flicked through the pages.

'This,' she began, still searching, 'is the name of the woman who was the housemaid at Briarwood Manor. Sawyer gave it to me. See if you can trace her. She was interviewed by Sawyer for his book, but that was published three years after Rebecca's murder, so it must be fifteen years since that interview took place. She could be anywhere.'

McLachlan had tuned into Tara and Wilson's conversation.

'Find her without contacting the Winters family,' Tara continued.

'Yes, ma'am.'

'We can do without another complaint from Assistant Chief Constable Havers that we've been harassing the family... And don't forget, John. Not a word to Murray.'

'I understand, ma'am.'

'I'll let you get started,' said Tara. 'I have other things to do.'

'OK, ma'am. I'll keep you posted.'

Wilson sauntered off, while Tara mulled over the orders she'd given to her DS. She hoped she hadn't forgotten anything. She felt bad about instructing Wilson to keep Murray out of the loop. The pair were friends as well as colleagues.

'Penny for them, ma'am,' said McLachlan.

Tara was startled by his voice but managed to smile. Then she realised that he was expecting a reply.

'Nothing I can share, Sergeant.'

'I see, X-rated, are they?' He laughed at his own joke, but Tara was already walking towards the door. He watched as she hurried through the downpour to her car.

CHAPTER 63

Plastic storage boxes were strewn across her lounge floor, some filled with clothing, others with books, CDs and DVDs, although who still used these? Streaming was the thing nowadays, and she pondered a ludicrous notion of whether it'd be possible to advance her murder inquiry simply by downloading a murder mystery solving app.

Although she was looking forward to her fresh start in Hoylake, she had no enthusiasm for packing. How could she have accumulated so much in less than ten years in this flat? She thought of the memories she'd amassed in the same period. While books, CDs and clothes were reminiscent of pleasant moments, her mind was a simmering cauldron of painful visions peppered with a few good laughs. It should be the other way around. But sadly, not for her.

Such introspection brought more discomfort, and finally she had to escape her flat and head out. She'd given Wilson his orders, but there were several issues she wished to clarify for herself. Rather than battle opposition to her theories regarding Lloyd and Campbell, she should try to unhinge the belief that errant prison officers were responsible for the killings. By venturing out alone she was again ignoring Tweedy's instructions. Her disobedience was becoming habitual.

The rain had abated in mid-afternoon as she drove onto the long tarmac strip of the beach car park at Crosby. Despite the insipid weather, a dozen cars were dotted along the seafront. Only one held Tara's interest. It was a blue Jaguar SUV driven by Graham Benson. She had intended to speak with him at his home, but when she'd arrived he was driving off, and she decided to follow. She realised his activity might be entirely innocent, but she followed the car anyway. When Benson stopped at Crosby, facing out to sea, Tara drove on by, parking six spaces further on. She could see Benson, his attention focused on his mobile phone. She wanted to question him again. It was desperation really, but she hoped that he might slip up and contradict his original responses. Now the situation looked interesting. Do people drive several miles from their homes just to use their mobile, she wondered. She didn't have to wait for long to discover the reason why Benson was there. Tweedy would have a fit if he knew she was stalking a murder suspect without support.

After five minutes, Tara saw a dark grey Vauxhall Grandland speeding into the car park and pulling into a space next to the Jaguar. She watched as Lydia Jennings jumped out and climbed into the blue SUV. With the Vauxhall between her car and Benson's, Tara could no longer see inside. She considered the possibilities. It could be an innocent meeting between work colleagues, albeit that one of them was currently suspended. Or they were having an affair. Perhaps they were discussing their roles in the murders of two people. She didn't have much time to ruminate further.

A car pulled into the space next to hers. The driver looked at her and smiled. Tara stiffened in her seat. Another vehicle slid to a halt behind her car, blocking any chance of escape. Two men in dark clothes emerged from the second car. Tara attempted to lock her doors, but she was too late. Her door swung open, and hands reached inside. She gripped the steering wheel, but the man grabbed the collar of her jacket and hauled her from the seat. Momentarily, her lower body was trapped by the seatbelt. The second man opened the passenger door, leaned inside and released the catch. Screaming and thumping at the horn, Tara was dragged from the car. The kicking started before she hit the wet ground. A punch to her stomach forced the wind from her. Then a boot struck her face and blood spurted from her mouth. Passing out would be relief, but she was aware of every kick. She curled to a foetal position, but it didn't stop the pain. She prayed for an end; any kind of end would do. Her death would be sufficient, but she doubted these animals would stop at that.

It lasted seconds but felt an eternity. When the kicking finally ceased, she dared to look skyward. Her view was obscured by the face of a man she'd met before.

'I told you to stay out of it, DI Grogan. Leave it alone, or you won't survive our next meeting.'

Tara couldn't see through her tears. She threw up, and her vomit splattered over his boot. He wiped it on her body when he kicked her again. Then she heard new voices.

'What the fuck?' said one.

'Nothing to see here,' said the man who'd threatened her.

'Leave her alone, what the hell are you doing?' said a female voice.

'Mind your own business. No more, Grogan, understand?'

Tara was faintly aware of doors slamming and cars roaring off, but still there were people standing over her.

'DI Grogan? Holy shit!' said Benson. 'What the hell's going on?'

'Police and ambulance,' Jennings said into her mobile. 'Crosby beach car park.'

'Leave me alone, please,' Tara begged. She stared blankly, confused by the people who'd come to her aid. Why was Benson still here?

CHAPTER 64

'How many times, Tara love?'

Kate held her friend's hand, perhaps the only part of her body that was not in pain. Tara's face, bruised and swollen, was not such a beguiling colour. Kate's eyes overflowed with tears.

'I refuse to lose you too,' she said.

Tara appreciated the friendly face but not as much as the intravenous dose of analgesic to relieve the pain in her ribs, her back and throbbing head.

'Please, Tara, give it up. Let this be the last time. This job is killing you.'

Tara gently squeezed Kate's hand and attempted a smile. Her lower lip had several stitches and it stung with the slightest movement.

'I can't give it up, Kate. What would I do?'

'God, Tara, anything you want, love. Anything that doesn't put you in hospital.'

The door of the private room on the ward opened slightly and the head of John Wilson peered round.

'Sorry,' he said. 'I'll come back later, ma'am.'

Tara struggled to sit up, groaning with the effort.

'No, John. It's all right. Have you any news for me?'

'I'll leave you, Tara,' said Kate, placing a kiss on Tara's forehead. 'I'll come back this evening.'

'Thanks, Kate. Don't forget you're still coming to live with me.'

'I know, just take things easy for now.' Kate looked sternly at Wilson as if to warn him against bringing dangerous police business into the room.

'Everyone sends their best, ma'am.' Wilson sat on a chair beside the bed as Kate closed the door behind her.

'Did you get the short straw?' Tara asked.

'Oh no, ma'am. Volunteered. Besides, I didn't think you'd appreciate a visit from Murray just yet. I brought a couple of magazines and some grapes. I hope they're OK. I don't really know if you're into reading.'

'They're fine, thank you.' She glanced at the covers of *House & Home,* and *Hello!* 'My vision is still blurred but I'll read them later. So, tell me the biz.'

'It can wait, ma'am. You shouldn't be working, not while you're in here.'

'I need to, John. I'll go mad otherwise. What have you got for me?'

'It was easier than I'd first thought,' he began. 'I got the details of four people from the alumni office at the college, who may have known Anthony Sawyer or Rebecca Winters.' He pulled a notebook from the side pocket of his suit jacket and flicked over several pages. 'I haven't had time to meet any of these people, ma'am, but I did speak to two of them by phone.'

'OK, let's hear it.'

'The first one is Clarissa Montgomery; her married name is now Anderson. She lives in London. She had shared a room with Rebecca. They had been reasonably close, she told me.'

'Did Rebecca confide in her?'

'Seems so. Clarissa knew that Rebecca was pregnant at the time of her death, but Rebecca had refused to divulge the name of the father. She was certain though that Rebecca and Sawyer were still an item when she was killed.'

'So, it is likely that Sawyer was the father of her baby. Good to know but it doesn't remove the suspicion from him having killed his girlfriend.'

'I also called a man named Alexander Teddington, a friend of Sawyer's at Cambridge. He told me that they hadn't spoken since their student days. He lives in London too. When I mentioned Sawyer's relationship with Rebecca, he took a deep breath before saying anything. His view was that Sawyer's relationship with Rebecca was a stormy on/off affair. His opinion of Rebecca wasn't great. He reckoned she had been fast and loose with several students, and at least one of the dons. Then I asked him if he was aware that Rebecca had been pregnant.'

'What did he say?'

'He knew all right. It was the talk of his social group. He doubted that Sawyer was the father, though. He said that Sawyer was furious when rumours of the pregnancy began to circulate. He wasn't happy to have his name associated with it.'

'So, he knew that he wasn't the father?'

'It would appear so. Teddington suggested that a certain Cambridge don was "the supplier of the seed" as he put it. He didn't know for certain.'

'And who was this don?' Tara asked.

'His name was Prendergast. He would have been close to sixty at the time. He died five years ago.'

'That fits with what Sawyer told us about Rebecca having slept with older people,' said Tara. 'So, our friend Sawyer gets very upset because his girlfriend is pregnant, and he is not the father. Maybe Rebecca had already finished with him, and he couldn't handle it. That would be a motive for murdering her.' It dawned on her she'd been saying that for quite a while and failing to gather proof. 'And, if Stephen Lloyd had information to prove that Sawyer was the killer and Sawyer became aware of it, then he also had a motive for killing Lloyd? But then we get stuck over the attack on Tyrone Cunningham and

Angela Campbell. Great story, John, but it hasn't got us much further.'

'I might have something to help us with that, ma'am?' said Wilson with a gentle smile.

'How so?'

'You asked me to trace the woman who had been the housemaid at Briarwood Manor. I asked Bleasdale to deal with it while I checked things with Cambridge.'

'And?' Tara could hardly contain herself. Her DS, at times, displayed an overly tranquil manner when delivering dramatic news.

'The woman left her job at Briarwood Manor within a few weeks of Rebecca's murder. She was interviewed three years later by Sawyer for his book *Road to Nowhere*. At that time her name was Angela Price and she would have been in her mid-twenties. Since the interview with Sawyer, she has married and subsequently divorced. Her married name was Campbell.'

'Angela Campbell?' Tara yelped from the sharp pain as she straightened on her bed. 'The same Angela Campbell?'

'Yes, ma'am.'

CHAPTER 65

'Would you excuse me for a few minutes, John? But don't leave the hospital.'

'Ma'am?'

'I need to get dressed,' said Tara, struggling to get out of her bed. 'If you wouldn't mind passing me my clothes. They're in a bag inside the locker.'

Wilson obliged his DI but couldn't help protesting.

'Ma'am, I don't think this is a good idea. You can hardly move. You should be resting.'

'Just be quiet and do as you're told, DS Wilson.'

'Ma'am.'

Wilson placed the carrier bag containing Tara's clothes on the bed then stepped outside. He immediately called Superintendent Tweedy.

A short while later, the room door edged open and out limped a dishevelled Tara. The only clothes in the bag were those she'd been wearing when attacked. Her trousers and T-shirt were splattered with blood. She didn't look much better than when she'd been admitted the day before.

'Right, let's go,' she said, wincing with every step. 'You can drive me to St Anne Street. I need to speak with Tweedy before doing anything.'

'You'll have to get past the nursing staff first.'

'Don't worry, I can take care of them.'

* * *

Thirty minutes later, having limped past the nurses' station on the ward, waving goodbye and ignoring the protestations of the sister, Tara perched gingerly on a chair in Tweedy's office. Her boss was alarmed by her appearance because clearly, she should be recuperating in hospital. But Tara had no time for sympathy or comments as to where she should be. Now, she had her murder investigation by the throat. She wasn't about to let go.

Tweedy listened intently as Tara and Wilson reported the latest information regarding Anthony Sawyer and Angela Campbell.

'It's likely, sir,' Tara explained, 'that Angela Campbell had been the intended target of her attackers, and not merely the unfortunate companion of Tyrone Cunningham. And I think we can now discard any involvement from our friends at Liverpool Prison.'

'I gather that Graham Benson and Lydia Jennings came to your aid when you were attacked,' said Tweedy.

'Yes, sir.'

'What were you doing at Crosby Beach?'

Tara winced more with irritation than pain at having to go over the events surrounding her beating. Perhaps it was the trauma of her attack, but she struggled to give a plausible answer.

'I went to Benson's house, sir. I wanted to ask some questions about his movements on the night of Lloyd's murder. When I got there, he was driving off, and I decided to follow.'

'But you had already asked Benson to account for his whereabouts. He'd told you nothing. What did you think you were going to hear this time?'

Tara felt the heat rise in her swollen cheeks. She had no answer for her boss.

'I'm not sure, sir,' she said.

'I had also instructed you to stay away from the prison officers whilst the investigation by prison authorities was ongoing.'

'That wasn't helping us to solve a murder, sir.'

'Did you discover anything further regarding Benson?'

'No, sir. Only that he met with Lydia Jennings at Crosby. I didn't get to ask why.'

'But you now believe they can be dismissed from our enquiry because they came to your rescue?'

'I think so. Why would they help me if they were behind the attack in the first place? Doesn't make sense.'

Tweedy was silent for a moment, but Wilson had a question for them.

'How did your attackers know that you'd be at Crosby Beach, ma'am? If Benson noticed that you were parked nearby, maybe he called them in. He comes to your rescue, and no one suspects him of being involved.'

'Or else I was followed,' said Tara, peeved at how the discussion was turning.

'I would not discount Benson and his colleagues from our thoughts just yet,' Tweedy said.

'But what about Angela Campbell?' Tara blurted. 'She's linked to the death of Rebecca Winters. Surely, everything suggests that whoever killed Rebecca has murdered Lloyd and Campbell.'

'I agree that your recent discovery about Ms Campbell is intriguing, but you cannot yet dismiss the suspects associated with the prison.'

'Yes, sir.'

'I would prefer that you return to hospital, Tara, or at least go home and rest,' said Tweedy.

Tara grumbled to Wilson as they left Tweedy's office. She had no intention of returning to hospital or going home.

'You will have to drive, John.'

'Ma'am?'

'We need to speak with Tyrone Cunningham. Now.'

CHAPTER 66

Murray, who had done little else but loiter in the office for the past two days, jumped to his feet when Tara and Wilson came into the room.

'What's happening, ma'am? Anything I can help you with?'

Tara couldn't decide what she expected from Murray or what orders to give him. She was in too much discomfort from her aching ribs and bruised legs.

'Nothing for the time being, Alan.'

Murray retreated looking sheepish. He watched despondently as Tara and Wilson left the office.

'Do you think it's possible, John, that Alan is involved in this?'

'How so, ma'am?'

'Is he passing information on my whereabouts to whoever attacked me?'

They were in the lift and as the doors opened on the ground floor Tara stepped into the path of Sergeant McLachlan.

'Hello, ma'am,' he said, looking intrigued by her appearance. 'Welcome back. I hope you're feeling better.'

'Yes, thank you, Sergeant,' Tara replied.

He stepped around her to enter the lift.

'No way, ma'am,' said Wilson, resuming their conversation. 'Murray would never do that.'

'I can't trust him at the moment, not since he withheld information from me about his involvement on the night of Rebecca Winters' murder.'

'Even so, Murray is loyal to you. He would never do anything to hurt you, ma'am. He is not a bent copper.'

'I know. I'm just peeved with his attitude.'

Even as she spoke, Tara's mind switched to another individual. She turned to see the lift doors closing and glimpsed the expression on McLachlan's face.

* * *

'Tell me about Angela,' said Tara, standing on the doorstep of Cunningham's house. The man made no effort to invite the detectives inside.

'Not again,' Cunningham protested. His eyes scanned Tara's battered appearance, but he made no reference to it.

'You have not been truthful with us. Angela was the real target when you were attacked, isn't that correct?'

'Bollocks!'

'Someone wanted her silenced over what she knew about the murder of Rebecca Winters.'

'Don't know what you're on about, cop. Now clear off and leave me alone. I have packing to do.'

He attempted to close his door, but Wilson pressed his hand against it.

'Oh no, you don't,' said Wilson. 'We haven't finished, Mr Cunningham. Now, why don't you invite us inside and we can talk nice and friendly.'

Resignedly, Cunningham held the door open for Tara and Wilson to enter.

'Cup of tea would be nice,' said Wilson as their host continued to fume. But Cunningham did as Wilson had suggested and, in the kitchen, filled a kettle with water. Tara rested her body against a table and drew a long breath. She was struggling to keep going but knew that she must get answers quickly from this man. Wilson noticed her discomfort and pulled a chair out from the table for her to sit.

'What did Angela know about the murder of Rebecca Winters?' she asked.

Cunningham shook his head defiantly.

'I have no idea what you're on about.'

Tara lost her temper. 'Listen you, we're trying to find your girlfriend's killer and the killer of Stephen Lloyd. We can't do it without your help. Either you tell us what you know, or I'll drag you down to the station and, believe me, I will think of something to charge you with, and you'll be back inside before you know it.' Her voice weakened as her anger rose, but it had the desired effect.

'Right, OK. Calm down, missus, will ya?' Cunningham finished preparing tea, while Tara proceeded with her questions.

'Were you aware that Angela was linked to the Winters family?'

'Not until a few weeks ago. Didn't come up in conversation till then.'

'And why did it eventually come up?' Tara asked.

Cunningham filled three mugs with hot water and dunked a single tea bag into each. He removed a carton of milk from the fridge and set it on the table. 'Help yourselves,' he said.

Wilson ploughed straight in, but Tara was more concerned with hearing what Cunningham had to say. The man sipped from his mug, wincing from the pain that persisted in his jaw.

'I mentioned to Angela that one of my mates was about to be released from prison. When I said his name, Angela started asking me a load of questions.'

'Did she tell you of her connection to the Winters family?'

'Yes. She told me that she had been a cleaner at their house. She'd been there on the day the murder happened.'

'And?'

'Not much else. She didn't think that Lloyd had done the murder. She'd given a statement to the bizzies at the time, but nothing ever came of it. She was never called as a witness at Lloyd's trial, and afterwards she thought it best to keep out of it. Besides, she'd packed her job in by then.'

'Why did Angela believe that Lloyd was innocent?'

'She didn't tell me, but she asked to meet Stephen when he was released. I reckon she was going to tell him what she knew about it. That night in The Docker's Rest I told him about Angela, and we organised for her to meet him the following week. But then Stephen got killed. Then Angela. Shit!'

Cunningham twitched and wiped tears away with his sleeve. He left the kitchen and returned a few seconds later puffing on his vaporiser.

'Did Angela share what she knew about Rebecca's murder?'

The man shook his head.

* * *

'Bare-faced liar!'

'Ma'am?'

'That sneaky little shit is still not telling us everything,' Tara fumed as she eased her body into the car. 'I really don't understand some people. His partner and his friend

201

are dead, he was injured, and yet he isn't prepared to help us catch those who did it.'

'But now it's all pointing to the murder of Rebecca Winters,' said Wilson. 'Whatever happened back then has led to the murders of two more people. You were right all along, ma'am.'

CHAPTER 67

Every inch of her body was either in pain or so stiff she could scarcely move. Lying in bed staring at the ceiling as the dawn broke over the city, Tara wondered if her life would feel different once she'd moved to Hoylake. Would she feel relaxed there? Would all her stress miraculously disappear?

Easing from her bed, she opened the curtains and lingered by the window. Ignoring the dank morning view, she planned her day. Her plans did not involve staying at home to rest but she didn't feel up to driving herself so, padding to the lounge, she lifted her mobile and called Wilson.

'You'll have to drive me around, John.'

'Tweedy said that you had to rest, ma'am.'

'I am resting. That's why you're going to drive. I'll see you in twenty minutes, DS Wilson.'

'Yes, ma'am.'

She had a shower, struggled to dress and attempted to eat some cornflakes, giving up after a few mouthfuls. With stitches in her lip, it was not a sensible food to eat. She abandoned her coffee also and paced around the flat making notes of things to be done before her house move.

* * *

'Where to, ma'am?' Wilson asked as she settled into the car.

'Anthony Sawyer first, I think,' she answered with a sigh. This time she hadn't made an appointment with the author, thinking it best to catch him off-guard.

Wilson pulled into a cul-de-sac in the Tarbock area close to the M62. Tara gazed at the variety of detached bungalows and semi-detached houses, surprised by Sawyer's choice of place to live. She had pictured him in a modern city apartment with bustling social amenities on tap. Then she recalled that Sawyer had a partner. Could be the house was more hers than his.

Sawyer's consternation when he opened the door of the bungalow was spread over his face. Tara had not considered him a nervous type, but this morning he struggled to form a sentence.

'Em, DI Grogan! What's happened to you?'

'Hazards of the job, Mr Sawyer,' said Tara. 'I'd like a quick word if you don't mind.'

Sawyer, wearing a faded T-shirt and navy joggers, stepped back allowing the detectives to enter. He rubbed at his bristle then swept a hand through his hair. Tara relished his discomfort.

'What's the problem?' Sawyer managed to ask.

They stood in a lounge cluttered with books, newspapers and magazines.

'Sorry. I was working,' the author said, clearing books from the sofa.

'We won't keep you long,' said Tara, but she availed herself of the seat. 'On the day of Rebecca's death, had you visited Briarwood Manor?'

Her direct manner flummoxed Sawyer. He didn't answer straight away. 'Can I get you coffee?' he looked from Tara to Wilson.

'No, thanks. If you wouldn't mind answering my question,' Tara said.

'Well, I need some,' he said, escaping from the room. Tara frowned at Wilson but rose from her seat and followed. Sawyer was already pouring coffee from a percolator when she entered.

'I did visit the house on that day,' he replied at last. 'Or it may have been the day before.'

'Come on, Mr Sawyer. Surely you remember which day it was. You wrote a book on the subject.'

'I didn't kill Rebecca, Inspector.'

'I haven't accused you of anything, but you have not been completely honest with me. You know more about what happened on that Christmas Eve than you have so far shared, and you have a motive for killing Rebecca.'

'But I have helped you. I told you about the gaps in the police investigation. I told you about the housemaid.'

'Did the housemaid have information about you? Something that would implicate you in Rebecca's murder?'

'Of course not!'

'When did you last see the woman that you knew as Angela Price?'

'I can't remember. I'm sure I will have a note of it somewhere. It was years ago when I was writing the book.'

'And you haven't seen her since that time?'

'No. Why are you asking me this?'

'What do you know of Angela Price since you interviewed her?'

'Nothing. Like I just told you. I haven't laid eyes on her since.'

Tara reverted to the subject of her first question. 'Why did you visit Briarwood Manor on that Christmas Eve?'

The author shrugged.

Tara was not impressed. She could see he was struggling to produce an answer. 'Surely, you remember. It was the day your girlfriend died. Did you speak to Rebecca?'

'Yes.'

'And?'

'I asked her how she was doing. We had quarrelled at Cambridge before she left for the holidays. I wanted to clear the air before Christmas.'

'What did she say to you?'

'It was personal. Look, Inspector, I'm saying nothing further. If you want anything from me, you'll have to arrest me, and I will bring my solicitor to any interview. Please leave and let me get back to work.'

'One last question, Mr Sawyer,' said Tara. 'Did you know Angela Price's name after she married?'

He shook his head. 'No. Why is that important?'

'It was Campbell. Angela was the third victim in this whole affair.'

Sawyer's eyes widened. 'I didn't realise. Now please leave.'

He went to his front door and held it open for the detectives. When they'd stepped outside, the door slammed behind them.

'Touchy,' said Wilson.

'Yes. But he's holding something back,' said Tara. 'We'll invite him to the station later and get him to place his visit to Briarwood Manor in the timeline of events for the day Rebecca was murdered.'

'You don't believe that he's our killer?'

'Until this visit, I regarded him as a strong candidate. I'm not so sure now, considering his surprise on hearing the name Angela Campbell.'

CHAPTER 68

'Someone associated with Briarwood Manor on Christmas Eve nineteen years ago has found it necessary to kill Stephen Lloyd and Angela Campbell.'

Tweedy listened with a grave expression as Tara laid before him the fresh information she had regarding Anthony Sawyer, Tyrone Cunningham and Angela Campbell. The issue of the assistant chief constable in Greater Manchester hadn't been forgotten. As far as Tara was concerned it wasn't going away.

Tweedy sat behind his desk with his hands before him pressed together.

'Do you have an accurate list of who had been at Briarwood Manor on that day?' he asked.

'Rebecca and her mother were at home at several points during the day. Angela Campbell, née Price, worked until late afternoon. Stephen Lloyd called at the house around lunchtime, and I had it confirmed this morning that Anthony Sawyer visited and spoke with Rebecca.'

'And the other family members? Were they at home?'

'I don't believe so. Jack Winters, according to Sawyer, was in the city all day and into the evening. The same for the son Freddie, although that has never been verified.'

'And you believe that one of these individuals is responsible for the deaths of Lloyd and Campbell?'

Tara felt a sudden tingle of nerves before responding. 'There is one other person who cannot be ignored.'

She felt Tweedy's eyes drilling into her. She hated this. She knew that Tweedy hated it even more. What cop ever wants to consider a fellow officer as a villain?

'Ted Havers, sir,' she said. 'We know that Havers was in the house when Murray began searching for Rebecca. We don't know what time he arrived at Briarwood Manor, but the housemaid told Sawyer there was a man in the bedroom with Elizabeth Winters during the afternoon.'

'It's a huge leap, Tara. Firstly, to suggest that anyone other than Lloyd, the man convicted of the crime, was responsible for murdering Rebecca Winters and, secondly, to suggest that a serving police officer was involved. Then to accuse that same officer of killing two people because they could implicate him in Rebecca's murder. I just cannot make that jump. You have no evidence. You are no further on than when we last had this conversation.'

Tara's face reddened. She was again defeated and yet her instinct pushed her to protest.

'Sir, I realise that we cannot arrest Ted Havers without evidence, but can we at least invite him here to answer our questions? Please, sir. Without this, I can't take the case any further and would therefore request that you remove me from the investigation.'

Tweedy peered over his glasses, but Tara didn't baulk. It was make or break. The silence between them seemed to last for hours. Tara struggled to hold her nerve. She wanted to let go, to cry with frustration but she knew that Tweedy would see the weakness in her. It would not help her plea. She lowered her head as he at last responded.

'I realise you feel deeply about this, Tara. You know that I value your hard work and dedication. But I refuse to withdraw you from this case. You will continue to do as I instruct, just as you have done since you joined my team. Things have been difficult lately, and this investigation seems to have taken an unhealthy hold of you, but you will continue. Is that clear?'

'Yes, sir.' She rose to leave, to escape, but her boss had not quite finished.

'I will seek advice on your request to interview Assistant Chief Constable Havers. You do realise, of course, that if such an interview takes place you will not be allowed to question him directly. A higher-ranking officer would conduct such an interview.'

'Yes, sir. Would I be allowed to sit in on the meeting?'

'We'll see.'

'Thank you, sir.'

Tara retreated to her desk and couldn't prevent tears finally seeping from her eyes. Despite the aches from recent traumas, her body trembled. Yet again, she believed everyone in the room was staring but when she looked around, no one was taking notice. And why should they?

She was hardly an important person. Merely a paranoid police detective.

CHAPTER 69

It took several days to arrange but Tara's request that Ted Havers be invited to St Anne Street to answer questions was granted. She had no idea of the lengths that Tweedy had ventured to secure the meeting, but it had gone all the way to the chief constable of Merseyside Police. As Tweedy had envisaged, Tara was not permitted to participate in the interview. The chief constable would put questions to Havers. Tweedy was allowed to attend and to assist the interviewing officer. Tara was frustrated at being excluded from the proceedings and denied the opportunity to look Havers in the face as he responded to questions.

On the morning of the interview, feeling devious, Tara decided to loiter in the station's reception to await Havers' arrival. It was progress, she believed, that the senior officer had even agreed to be questioned, because his attendance at St Anne Street was entirely voluntary. But she wanted him to notice her, a reminder that behind the meeting was a detective striving for the truth about the deaths of three people.

'Morning, ma'am,' piped Sergeant McLachlan, his friendliness continuing to grate with Tara. She wasn't convinced by him and felt uncomfortable, and recently conscious of their interaction having only begun since her return to work.

'Morning, Sergeant,' she replied without looking up from her phone. She'd just sent a text to Wilson, inviting him to join her in reception to witness the arrival of Havers.

'Anything I can help you with, ma'am?' McLachlan inquired.

'No, thank you.'

Tara's intention to witness the arrival of her suspect was hampered when Brenda O'Connor, the chief constable of Merseyside Police, entered the station in readiness to conduct the interview with Havers. McLachlan telephoned Harold Tweedy to inform him of O'Connor's arrival and, moments later, he entered reception to greet the woman. Tara thought it best to get out of the way, so she and Wilson stepped outside. Their actions proved timely. Within a minute, Ted Havers climbed from a vehicle parked opposite the main door.

'Oh my God,' Tara mumbled to her companion.

'I see it, ma'am,' said Wilson.

'Ah, DI Grogan, isn't it?' said Havers, in bright and shiny uniform looking every bit a senior police officer. 'Why do I think this is all your doing?'

'Just trying to clear up a few things, sir.'

'Mm, we'll see.' He stared her down for a moment then proceeded into reception. Tara turned to Wilson.

'We must get Tweedy before he goes into the interview,' she said. 'He needs to know about that car.'

She re-entered the station reception and saw Havers chatting with McLachlan. Maybe it was her overactive suspicion, but it appeared to be more than a casual hello and announcing that he had arrived for his meeting. McLachlan listened as Havers spoke at length. Tara saw the desk sergeant place his hand on Havers' arm, alerting him to her presence. Suddenly, a more sinister feeling arose in her regard of the desk sergeant. The pair were then joined by Tweedy.

'May I have a word please, sir?' Tara called.

Tweedy instructed McLachlan to show Havers to the interview room where Brenda O'Connor awaited.

'Tara,' said Tweedy. 'You need to be quick. The interview is about to start.'

'I know, sir. A little piece of information for you. It may be significant.'

Tweedy listened as Tara told him about the blue Jaguar SUV in which Havers had arrived.

'There is a possibility that the vehicle we noted from CCTV on the night Lloyd was killed is Havers' car. We had previously believed it to be Graham Benson's. I'm going to have another look at the recordings.'

'You do that, Tara. I'll keep it in mind.'

'Sir.'

McLachlan returned to reception and looked towards Tara and Tweedy. This time he wasn't smiling. Tara let Tweedy leave for the interview. She didn't get the chance to tell him of her newly acquired suspicions of McLachlan. She'd been so wrong in suspecting Murray.

CHAPTER 70

In the detectives' operations room at St Anne Street several officers were gathered around a computer monitor. Wilson trawled CCTV footage from the locations where Stephen Lloyd had ventured on the night he was murdered. Tara and Bleasdale stood to one side of Wilson, Murray to the other. Suddenly, his participation no longer bothered Tara. Now it was McLachlan in the frame as the rogue officer involved in the threats against her. And she felt certain that Havers was behind it all.

'I don't think we'll get a definitive answer,' said Wilson. 'Not without the vehicle registration.'

'Take another look at the driver,' said Tara. They waited as Wilson retrieved the relevant frames showing the driver of a blue Jaguar SUV.

'This is the car passing through the contraflow at the roadworks in Lime Street,' Wilson explained.

Tara strained her eyes to make out anyone behind the wheel of the car.

'Can we get this enhanced? Get the tech guys to sharpen the images.'

'It has already been sharpened, ma'am,' Wilson explained. 'The streetlights reflecting off the windscreen obscure the driver's face.'

'Hell of a coincidence that Benson and Havers drive the same model and colour of car,' said Murray.

'A coincidence that doesn't help us,' Tara replied.

She wandered back to her desk and sat down wearily. Her aches and pains had not gone away. But as usual she didn't have long for self-pity.

'Ma'am,' Bleasdale called. She nodded towards the closing door of the operations room.

Tara looked up in time to see Tweedy striding to his office. She glanced at Bleasdale.

'That didn't last long,' she said, rising from her chair. The others looked on as she caught up with Tweedy.

'How did it go, sir?' She stood at the doorway of his office as Tweedy tossed a folder of notes on the desk. She thought he looked despondent before he'd even replied.

'Come in and close the door,' he said.

Tara did as Tweedy requested and sat down, waiting for him to explain.

'It did not go as well as we'd hoped,' he began. 'The chief constable was not pleased about having her time wasted. Havers refused to discuss any details of his presence at Briarwood Manor on the day of Rebecca's murder. He stated that he was there in answer to a call from Elizabeth Winters informing him that her daughter was missing.'

'Did he mention times?'

'He said that everything was on police file, and he wasn't about to confuse matters by offering fresh comment based on his memory nineteen years after the event.'

'What did he say about the absence of statements from Angela Price-Campbell?'

'Directed us again to the police files. He refused to discuss a case that had been successfully prosecuted with a man convicted of Rebecca's murder.'

'And his affair with Elizabeth Winters?'

'Alleged affair, Tara. He refused to comment on that also.'

'I suppose he provided alibis for the nights when Lloyd and Campbell were murdered.' It was Tara who now sounded despondent.

'No, he stated flatly that he had not visited Liverpool at all in the last six months.'

'Doesn't mean much,' said Tara. 'It's not likely that Havers would have gotten his hands dirty. He would have had others doing his bidding. Like Sergeant McLachlan.'

Tweedy's eyes widened.

'I think you should explain,' he said, finally sitting down.

She detected the warning in his tone. But Tara had just crossed another boundary. Firstly, she'd accused a senior police officer of two murders, and now she was suggesting that a desk sergeant at their own station was involved in a conspiracy.

'Sir, I believe that someone was tipping off the guys who threatened and subsequently attacked me. It had to be someone who knew my movements. At first, I thought, sadly, that it was DS Murray.'

'Murray? Really, Tara, what is going on? Do these thoughts of yours have any foundation?' Tweedy's face reddened. 'Alan Murray is your closest colleague. Why would you ever suspect him of colluding with criminals?'

Tara's world crashed around her. She felt pathetic facing her boss. She realised her distrust of Murray had been ridiculous.

'It's not important now, sir. I no longer believe that Murray had done anything untoward.'

'Good. I'm very glad to hear that. Now, you mentioned McLachlan. I take it you mean Sergeant McLachlan who manages our reception desk?'

'Yes, sir. But I have no firm evidence. It's just my suspicion. McLachlan seems to have taken an interest in me. It began when I returned to work or, as I now realise, since this murder enquiry started.'

Tweedy looked incredulous and couldn't help smiling. It upset Tara even more. She knew what he was thinking. That the sergeant had a crush on her or was merely being friendly. She couldn't take any more of this. She felt small and useless. Her murder investigation lay in tatters around her and here she was, trying to explain, poorly, how she believed a fellow officer was involved in the attack against her. She had nothing to present to Tweedy. No proof, only her gut instinct. She excused herself and hurried from his office. Where to next, Tara? She had no clue.

The remainder of her day dragged by until in late afternoon, she gathered her bag and coat in readiness to leave. She'd had enough and fancied the idea of another drive to Hoylake. It was something other than murder to think about. Besides, there was little to be achieved by remaining at the station. She was struggling to don her coat, hoping to slip out quietly, when Bleasdale called her over.

CHAPTER 71

Following his marriage to television producer Trudy Mitchell, Murray and his new bride had moved into a cottage in a quiet lane in Glazebury. It wasn't far from the M62 where Trudy had easy access to Media City in Salford and Murray could reach St Anne Street. Both had embraced the change from city apartment living to relaxing countryside.

Murray left the station in late afternoon. He was looking forward to a quiet night in with Trudy, an Indian takeaway and Netflix. Trudy had been working in London the previous week and had visited friends over the weekend. They knew well from painful experience that absence did not make the heart grow fonder. It led eventually to estrangement and bitter divorce. Their jobs would strangle any relationship if they didn't make the effort to spend time together.

Rain lashed his windscreen as Murray drove in the centre lane heading from the city. He pressed the console to make the call and immediately Radio 2 cut out and Trudy's name appeared on the screen. She answered swiftly, she too was currently on the M62 heading home and nearing her turn-off at Risley.

'Don't tell me,' she said. 'You want me to choose for both of us.'

'I was just about to say that,' Murray replied, chuckling. 'I'll pick up some beer. Would you like a bottle of wine?'

'Yes, please. I'll have that nice merlot we had last week if you can get it. What time will you be home?'

'On my way. Hold on a minute.'

There were no further words from Murray, but the line remained open, and Trudy could hear what happened next.

The spray from a lorry momentarily denied him a clear sight of the way ahead. As the wipers cleared the windscreen, he had little time to react. Instinctively, he hit the brakes. The vehicle to his right and marginally ahead had swerved suddenly. It clipped the front of Murray's Ford and he swerved to the inside lane. The lorry he'd overtaken slammed into him. Smashing into the crash barrier, he scraped to a halt facing in the opposite direction. Drivers were braking hard and a myriad of vehicles miraculously came to a halt without further collision. The car that had first collided with Murray was already out of sight.

'Alan?' Trudy called. There was no reply. 'Alan, are you OK? What happened?'

* * *

'Ma'am, this is CCTV footage recorded near the scene of the attack on Cunningham and Campbell,' Bleasdale explained. 'We've just received it from Huyton station.'

'You found something?'

'Might have.' Bleasdale navigated to the relevant place on the recording. Tara stared at the black and white images, firstly of a dark coloured vehicle slowing down to make a left turn and disappearing from view. A few seconds later, another vehicle, lighter in colour, inched through the region captured by the camera.

'What am I looking at?' Tara asked, weary from it all.

'The recording is from a traffic camera on Queen's Drive at the time of the attack on Cunningham and Campbell. It doesn't capture any of the incident. It's a quarter of a mile to the scene, off East Prescot Road, but it's these two vehicles that are interesting. The dark vehicle, a KIA Sportage, may hold the assailants. That's why it is slowing down and turning onto East Prescot Road.'

'Perhaps.'

'It's the second vehicle, moving slowly that is more significant.'

Bleasdale opened a still image on the screen.

'This was taken from the traffic recording where Queen's Drive meets Mill Bank, several junctions beyond the murder scene. The traffic lights were red at the time, and the lighter-coloured vehicle is stationary. It's a Jaguar SUV.'

'And you got the registration?'

'Yes, ma'am. The vehicle is registered to a Ms Joanna Noble.'

'I don't understand, Paula. Who is she?'

'She has the same home address as Assistant Chief Constable Havers.'

CHAPTER 72

Limping down a long corridor, Tara could scarcely believe that she was back at Aintree Hospital just a week after her overnight stay. It felt as though her life revolved around hospitals, police stations and crime scenes. Not the most heartening daily existence. Pushing open the fire door, she stepped into the ward and spotted Trudy Mitchell pacing the floor outside a bay and talking on her phone.

When she saw Tara, Trudy waved and pointed to the bed where her husband lay.

Tara sighed with relief to see Murray sitting up and tucking into the evening hospital fayre – steamed cod, mashed potatoes and garden peas.

'Hello you,' Tara said. She leaned over and kissed his forehead.

'Ma'am, thanks for dropping by.'

'You gave us all a scare, especially Trudy. You can't make her a widow just yet.'

'Had a lucky escape,' Murray said. 'A bang on the head and a stiff back.'

'The neck brace suits you. It hides the double chin.'

'Thanks a lot.'

'Tell me, what happened?'

Tara noticed him checking on Trudy's whereabouts before replying. 'A bloody idiot cut me up on the M62. Then a lorry hit me from behind and shoved me onto the hard shoulder. Would have been a hell of a mess if he'd pushed me to the outside lane. Car's a write-off; it blended nicely with the crash barrier. Hopefully, my dashcam has picked up the culprit. They didn't stop at the scene.'

'Definitely an accident then?'

Murray looked puzzled.

'What else could it be?' he said with a shrug.

'Just wondering,' said Tara. Trudy was coming towards them. 'Since I'd been attacked...'

'Attacked?' said Trudy, sounding alarmed. She gazed at her husband then Tara.

'Just work, sweetheart.'

Tara stayed for a few more minutes, enough to be polite, she felt, then bid Murray and Trudy goodbye. On her way home, she made a mental note to get access to Murray's dashcam recording. She couldn't believe it was an accident. Murray was an excellent driver.

CHAPTER 73

'Morning, ma'am, any news on DS Murray?'

Tara glared at the desk sergeant.

'I would have thought you already knew the latest, Sergeant McLachlan.'

'Sorry, ma'am. I don't know what you mean.' His smiling face clouded over.

Tara approached the desk and spoke quietly to prevent any passers-by from hearing. 'I think you know exactly what I mean. I'm quite sure you took note of when DS Murray left here yesterday.'

'And why would I do that, ma'am?'

Tara believed she was a good judge of when someone was lying to her, but she discerned only bewilderment on McLachlan's face.

'So you could pass the information to whoever it is that you feel loyal,' she said. 'In answer to your first question, DS Murray is fine. He had a lucky escape. It will not detract him from doing his duty. You can tell your master that his latest warning will not stop me either.'

'I'm sorry, ma'am. I don't understand. If you're suggesting that I am in some way bent, then you're wrong about me. I was just showing concern for a colleague and trying to be friendly.'

Tara examined his brown eyes, but she was never going to find truth in McLachlan's gaze. She had been rash in judging Murray, but surely, she couldn't be wrong about this desk sergeant. Someone in this station had to be passing information to those who had threatened her and possibly had tried to kill Murray. Feeling small for having succumbed to the temptation to challenge the man, she walked away from the desk. McLachlan held his smile, but Tara realised there was no going back. If she was right about him then it didn't matter, but if she'd got things wrong again, she'd just made a fool of herself to an innocent colleague.

As she pushed open the door to the office she was intercepted by Wilson.

'Morning, John. Did Paula tell you about the CCTV recordings of the vehicles on Queen's Drive?'

'Yes, ma'am, but it's not enough to prove that Havers was involved in the attack on Cunningham and Campbell,' Wilson replied.

A voice of reason was not what Tara wanted to hear. She wanted to drag the assistant chief constable all the way back to St Anne Street. Sweat the truth out of his smug face.

'It proves that he lied about the last time he visited Liverpool,' she said. 'That's sufficient grounds to question him again.'

'What if it was his partner driving the car on that evening? It is registered to her.'

Tara ignored the comment and proceeded to her desk. Her mind switched to other matters. She had already instructed Bleasdale to obtain the dashcam footage from Murray's car and statements from possible witnesses to the accident. She wondered if Murray had been targeted because of his connection to her investigation, or was he more acutely embroiled in the events of Christmas Eve nineteen years ago?

* * *

By the time she'd sat down, Tara was already weary of the day and again struggling to see a way ahead with her investigation. Her aching limbs didn't help her mood. She had not even removed her coat when Bleasdale approached looking pleased with herself, or at least happy with life.

'Morning, ma'am. How's Murray?'

'He's fine. Had a lucky escape.'

'That's good to hear.'

'What have you got for me?' Tara noticed her sympathetic smile.

'Nothing to report, ma'am, sorry. I was just wondering what you want me to do next.'

Tara looked despondent. 'I'm all out of ideas, Paula. If Ted Havers is involved in these murders, he has covered his tracks well. Like any experienced cop could do, I suppose.'

'We're expecting some fresh CCTV recordings from the guys in Huyton,' Bleasdale offered as consolation.

'There must be hundreds, if not thousands, of vehicles picked up by cameras. Besides, we have already identified the vehicle involved.'

'You mean the blue Jaguar registered to Havers' partner? Are you going to interview her?'

'How do I do that? Havers would cry harassment. Our chief constable wasn't happy at having to question a senior officer regarding a murder. She was not impressed by the paltry evidence we provided.'

'You never know, ma'am, we might get something more from CCTV.' Bleasdale strolled away, leaving Tara without a clue to her next move.

Tara quickly decided that if she was ever going to solve this case, she would have to disobey her boss, again.

CHAPTER 74

The house, once a family home, looked forlorn, unused, neglected. The dull and slime-coated walls were a blemish on the skyline of a crisp autumn afternoon. Tara gripped the wrought-iron gates with both hands and pondered the secrets that lay within the sealed building. What conversations had taken place inside before, during and since that fateful Christmas Eve? Would she ever discover what had really happened to Rebecca Winters?

She'd brought Bleasdale along, not just for company but to act as a sounding board for the ideas germinating in her mind.

'Why do you think the Winters family closed the place up like this?' Bleasdale asked. 'Obviously, there were painful memories, but surely they could have sold it.'

'They did. Six years after Rebecca's death. Another family lived here for seven years before selling it again. The next purchaser was a health care company. The intention was to convert the house into a residential care home, but the company went bust before any work was done. Ownership has been in dispute since the company went into administration.'

'Such a shame,' said Bleasdale.

'A waste of a good house,' Tara agreed, and couldn't help thinking of her new purchase. 'I had wondered if it was worth taking a look inside, but it has probably changed quite a bit since the Winters lived here.'

'It wouldn't do any harm to have a peek,' said Bleasdale, who was already heading for the same spot in the fence they'd used to enter the grounds on their previous visit.

'I was hoping you would say that,' said Tara, following. 'But how will we get in?'

'We might be able to manage it.'

Bleasdale strode towards a relatively modern extension at the rear of the house. It was a slate-roofed, single storey kitchen and conservatory. She pulled a wheelie bin up to a doorway and clambered onto it. Tara rushed to help, holding the bin steady as Bleasdale reached to the porch above the doorway, hoisted herself upwards and managed to slide onto the roof. She called down to Tara.

'You'll have to do the same, ma'am, but wait there until I check the window.' The young detective scaled the roof to its ridge, then crawled towards the main structure of the house. 'I noticed this window on our last visit. We might be able to get in this way.'

Unlike the windows of the ground floor, it had not been bricked up or secured with metal bars. Bleasdale tried to release the catch by pressing against the frame, but it was seized with old paint. Sitting down on the ridge, using her hands to steady her body, she raised her foot and pressed against the pane until the glass cracked then fell away, most of it landing inside the house.

'You can come up now, ma'am.'

Tara, feeling stiff, eventually struggled onto the roof with less dexterity than her colleague. While she clambered along the ridge, Bleasdale reached inside, loosened the catch and slid the window open. The pair entered the house and used the torches of their mobile phones to cast light on the gloomy interior. They were faced with a bare room that smelled of damp and felt ice-cold. Venturing onto the landing, they found a rather grand staircase and a hallway below, empty but in surprisingly good condition. Tara had expected a scene of devastation, rotting wood, peeling wallpaper, and cobwebs, but the interior of what had been a family home prior to its sale was relatively pristine. The floors were polished wood, and only a couple of the steps on the central staircase creaked beneath their feet as they descended to the hall.

'Very classy,' said Bleasdale. 'Could still be lived in. It's all in good nick.'

Each room was empty of furniture but in good decorative order. Even the kitchen still had its built-in appliances, a dishwasher and a double-door refrigerator. Tara said little as she gazed around. She felt slight disappointment that there was nothing to find, something to indicate who had once lived here. Not even a picture on the wall.

'What are you thinking, ma'am?' Bleasdale asked.

'I'm thinking, what a waste of time this is. How the hell are we ever going to crack this case?'

Once outside, and after a painful descent from the annexe roof, Tara stood dejected, while Bleasdale awaited their next move.

'I will understand if you're not comfortable about doing this, Paula, but I want to try something else before going back to St Anne Street.'

Bleasdale looked puzzled and could only wait for her boss to explain.

'I want to speak to Jack Winters.'

CHAPTER 75

He checked his phone. It was ten past nine, and he had no further messages. His feet were ice-cold, and he couldn't believe the nerves in his stomach. He should never have agreed to this. It was the stuff of thriller movies and Ludlum novels. A late-night rendezvous and for what exactly? A new version of the truth or another helping of lies and deceit. But he wanted to look the man in the face. He wanted to see his pain, all nineteen years of it, and know that it would never leave him.

Of course, in finally uncovering the truth of what happened to his darling Rebecca, he was probably hastening the end of his own pitiful existence. His peace at learning the truth would be fleeting. But he wouldn't go down without a fight. His killer would still pay.

It hadn't taken long to regret not doing more for his own safety. They'd chosen a dark and lonely place, not merely for privacy but, he now realised, to suit their own ends. Bile rose in his throat. He should drive away. Now. This was crazy. There must be another way to get to the truth.

He turned the key in the ignition but as the engine burst into life, he knew that he was too late. He watched as a vehicle, its lights on full beam, emerged from the darkness of the lane and swung into the car park. Truth or run, he must decide now.

CHAPTER 76

Paula Bleasdale smiled politely and bid Tara a good morning. Tara returned the greeting but did not engage in further chat. Her embarrassment ushered her to the precarious sanctuary of her desk. It was one thing for her to have deliberately flouted the instructions of Harold Tweedy, but it was totally unprofessional to drag a young and dedicated officer down with her.

The only relief from an awkward situation had been Jack Winters rushing past them as she and Bleasdale entered his apartment building.

'Please, Mr Winters.' Tara could hear her desperate tone. 'I only want to ask you one question.'

'Leave me alone! My wife has taken ill. I have no time for your games.'

He had stormed past the two detectives – one, no doubt relieved, the other yet again frustrated.

Scrolling through her emails, paying them scant attention, Tara realised that Jack Winters, when he had a spare moment, would probably lodge another complaint regarding her unprofessional conduct.

She was shaken from her preoccupation by Wilson who had to tap her on the shoulder to gain her attention.

'Ma'am, some more news from our study of CCTV.'

'Hit me with it,' she said with little enthusiasm. It will hardly be earth-shattering, she thought.

Wilson placed several sheets of paper before her. They contained lists of vehicle registrations.

'These registrations were collated from all available cameras in the vicinity of the Angela Campbell murder scene around the time of the incident.'

'There must be hundreds here, John,' Tara sighed.

'But just one of interest to us, ma'am.'

Her desk phone rang, and she lifted the receiver to hear the cheerful voice of the officer she had accused of corruption. His professional tone made her cringe. Was there no end to the discomfort she'd brought on herself?

'Good morning, Sergeant.'

She waited for McLachlan to state the reason for his call and hoped it had nothing to do with her outburst twenty-four hours earlier. Maybe he was calling to inform her that he'd lodged an official grievance against her.

'There is a lady wishing to speak with you, ma'am. She says it's urgent.'

'Put her through.'

'She's here in reception, ma'am.'

Tara fumed; she didn't need the interruption.

'What's her name?'

'It's a Ms Chrissie Black.'

'I'll come down.'

'Thanks, ma'am.'

Tara put Wilson off and made her way down to reception. Her initial confusion evaporated in the elevator when she recalled that Chrissie Black was the partner of Anthony Sawyer. She wondered why the woman had reason to meet with her.

Black was not what Tara had pictured. Seated by the station entrance was a prim-looking woman, probably in her forties with pinned up fair hair and dark-framed glasses. Tara, of course, had no reason to think of the woman in any way at all other than as the partner of Anthony Sawyer.

She introduced herself and Black got to her feet.

'How can I help you, Ms Black?' Tara detected an uneasiness in the woman, her eyes darting around, her handbag clutched tightly to her body.

'Anthony asked me to contact you. He told me not to worry, but…'

'What is it, what's wrong?'

'He didn't come home last night. I think something has happened. He left me a note. It said that if he hadn't returned home by this morning, I was to give you this.'

She fumbled with the catch on her bag then eventually produced a flash-drive and gave it to Tara. The action hastened the point where she broke down in floods of tears.

'I didn't know what else to do,' she sobbed. 'He usually calls me if he's going to be late.'

'Come upstairs and we can figure out what to do.'

Tara, with her arm around the woman she'd only just met, led her to the lift. McLachlan looked on with a puzzled face.

'Anything I can do, ma'am?'

'No, thanks, Sergeant.'

Tara fetched a chair and sat the woman down beside her desk, placing a box of tissues within reach. She asked Black to explain all that she knew of Sawyer's recent activities. While she listened, she inserted the flash drive into her computer and waited for the safety scan of the device to run.

'I'm sure Anthony will be fine,' Tara said. 'He knows how to take care of himself. Have you reported him missing?'

Black shook her head and blew her nose.

'I thought I could do that here. What do you think could have happened? Do you know what he was doing last night? Why would he tell me to come to a police station?'

'Let's see, shall we?'

Tara scrolled down the list of files on the flash drive. It consisted mainly of chapter numbers as individual files, but the last item was entitled, 'What really happened on the road to nowhere.'

She double-clicked on the icon and the file opened. The Word document contained only a few pages of text.

'What does it say?' Black asked.

'You didn't read it?'

'No. I only found it this morning along with the note from Anthony. I brought it straight here.'

Tara summoned Bleasdale to her desk.

'Paula, would you mind taking Ms Black to the canteen for coffee. I'll join you when I've read through this document.'

'But why can't you tell me, Inspector?' Black protested amid her sobbing.

'I won't be long, Ms Black. Please go with DC Bleasdale.'

As the two women departed, Wilson seized the opportunity to re-engage his DI.

'Not now, John,' Tara snapped, engrossed in the text on her screen. The DS retreated without another word.

Tara read Sawyer's document. It appeared to be an account of what he believed had occurred on Christmas Eve nineteen years ago and of the issue that had festered and finally erupted in the murders of Stephen Lloyd and Angela Campbell. She did not agree with all of it but, merged with her own deductions, she now knew who was responsible for the recent deaths.

CHAPTER 77

Elizabeth spluttered a mouthful of strawberry yoghurt over her clean nightdress. The nurse quickly wiped it up with a napkin.

'Come on, Elizabeth, just one more spoonful. You've had a difficult time these last few days. We need to get your strength back.'

The nurse attempted another spoonful, but Elizabeth, sitting upright in her bed, swiped it away with a growl. The room door opened and in stepped Jack Winters. Elizabeth growled again, her arms flailing to keep the nurse and her spoonful of yoghurt at bay.

'Good morning, sweetheart,' said Jack. 'Are you misbehaving for Gemma?'

'She's been fine, really,' said the young nurse. 'She's eaten some Weetabix and a slice of toast. And you've had a nice cup of tea, isn't that right, Elizabeth?'

The former chief constable aimed a wobbly finger at the nurse.

'Rebecca! My Rebecca,' she managed to say.

'No, love. That isn't Rebecca,' said Jack, aware that he was correcting his wife. Nurse Gemma did have a slight resemblance to their long-dead daughter, Jack thought and, evidently, Elizabeth had thought the same.

'I'll take over, Gemma. Let you get on,' said Jack. 'I won't be staying long this morning.'

'Thanks, Mr Winters. See you later, Elizabeth,' said Gemma on her way out.

Jack sat down close to the bed.

'I've brought you some chocolate for later,' he said, placing a small bar of Dairy Milk into the cabinet drawer.

'Rebecca.'

'I know, love. Gemma does look like our Rebecca.'

'Rebecca!'

'Please stop now. You don't have to keep saying her name.'

Elizabeth glared at her husband and for a moment, could not have looked more lucid.

'My Rebecca came to visit,' she said quite clearly.

'No, love. Rebecca didn't come.'

CHAPTER 78

Three police vehicles swept into the car park on Lifeboat Road in Formby. Tara remembered that she'd left Chrissie Black in the care of Bleasdale. The pair were probably still sitting over coffee in the station canteen waiting for her to join them. But there had been no time to check in with them. When she had finished reading Sawyer's document, she'd asked Wilson to issue an alert for a missing person. She feared, however, for news of the discovery of a body somewhere on Merseyside. Immediately, the alert matched with a live report on the discovery of a car close to the beach at Formby. The vehicle was registered to Anthony Sawyer.

'Some blood spatter across the bonnet, but we haven't found anyone,' a uniformed officer explained to Tara and Wilson. They saw the red blotches on the white bodywork of the author's Skoda.

'Anyone searching the area?' Tara asked.

'Just getting underway, ma'am. It'll take a while. A lot of sand dunes around here.'

The absence of a body lying close to the car gave Tara some hope. Maybe the author had escaped his attackers. She drew a deep lungful of fresh sea air then puffed through her lips.

'Why do these things always happen in such lonely places?' she said, more to herself than anyone else.

'Not much we can do, ma'am,' Wilson offered. 'There's nothing significant inside the motor.'

'It's all right, John. Doesn't matter now. I just hope that Sawyer is OK. That if he was attacked, he has survived, and we'll find him soon.'

'Who do you think…?'

'Oh, I know, John. This time I know. As soon as we can get away from here, you and I are going to make an arrest.'

Their conversation was interrupted by shouts coming from a path leading to the beach.

'Over here! We need an ambulance!' a uniform called.

* * *

Wilson drove them away from the beach at Formby. An unconscious Anthony Sawyer had been found among the dunes. He had suffered a serious head injury and subsequent loss of blood. A night spent in the open had led to hyperthermia. Tara could do little but pray that the author survived. These past weeks it seemed she'd done little else. Her confidence was rock bottom. She visited such negative thoughts with a regularity that merely added to her doubts. But this morning, having visited yet another crime scene, the site of a vicious attack, she was glad to have stuck with her instincts.

'You're certain about this, ma'am?' Wilson asked. He couldn't take his eyes off the road, so he didn't see her glaring at him.

'Yes, John. I believe I'm right this time.'

He smiled at her reply. 'The car registration that I was trying to tell you about when we were interrupted. It was his car, ma'am. It confirms that he was in the area when Angela Campbell was murdered.'

'Thank you, John. I'm sure that will be of help.'

They stopped opposite the apartment building in Birkdale. Tara climbed from the car, her aches ignored, and hurried towards the entrance as Wilson followed. She was soon to be thwarted, however. There was no reply from Winters' apartment. Of course, Tara sighed, it could never be this simple. She bounded out, again Wilson trailing behind her. It was only a few minutes' drive to the Summer Breeze Nursing Home.

'He was here earlier this morning,' a young nurse in the foyer of the home explained.

'Would it be possible to see Mrs Winters?' Tara inquired.

The woman looked doubtful, her eyes darting from Tara to Wilson.

'Just for a couple of minutes,' said Tara.

'I suppose it would be all right.' The nurse led them along a corridor, and at a secure doorway she entered a code on a panel and showed them into a ward. The name Elizabeth Winters was on the door of a room beside the nurses' station.

'Why are we doing this, ma'am?' Wilson whispered out of earshot of the nurse.

'While I'm talking, have a look around, just in case Winters has left any indication of what he's up to.'

The nurse opened the door and spoke to Elizabeth who lay staring at the television showing *Escape to the Country*. 'You have visitors, Elizabeth.'

The woman took no notice of the activity.

Tara resisted the idea of addressing Winters as ma'am. The woman hadn't been a serving officer for years and never during Tara's time. 'Hello, Elizabeth, how are you today?' she said.

Wilson browsed the room with the nurse watching him.

'Did you have a visit from Jack this morning?'

Elizabeth did not respond to Tara's questions but as Wilson attempted to open a drawer of the bedside cabinet, her hand reached towards him. 'Chocolate,' she mumbled.

Wilson removed a chocolate bar from the drawer and handed it to the nurse.

'You won't be able to eat your tea,' said the nurse. Nevertheless, she broke off a square of chocolate and gave it to Elizabeth.

Tara saw Wilson shake his head to indicate that he'd found nothing of interest.

'And where has Jack gone this afternoon?' Tara asked, expecting no answer. She smiled, thinking of this still beautiful woman who had once been vibrant, powerful and in charge of Merseyside's police force. Turning to the nurse, she thanked her and made to leave.

'Rebecca!' Elizabeth blurted.

'And who is Rebecca?' Tara asked.

The nurse quickly supplied the answer that Tara already knew well. 'That's her daughter. She died a long time ago.'

'Rebecca!'

'And where is Rebecca?' Tara asked.

The nurse looked irritated by the apparently futile question, but Tara got her reply.

'Home!'

* * *

Wilson tried Jack Winters' apartment again without success. Tara viewed the building from the sanctuary of the car. The rain was coming down hard and the daylight was fading.

'Do you think he's got wind of us?' Wilson asked.

'Maybe, but I'm wondering if Sawyer was a step too far for him. He's looking for an exit.'

'He's bolted?'

Tara shrugged.

'Please, don't think me mad. This is just a hunch.'

'Ma'am?'

'Why don't I drive.'

CHAPTER 79

Heavy clouds hastened the darkness as Tara slowed in the lane. Silhouetted against the light of the western sky, the house maintained its foreboding stance. They climbed from the car, and Tara led Wilson to the place in the fence she and Bleasdale had used to gain access to the grounds.

'Creepy looking place,' said Wilson as they hurried to the front of the house.

'It was once a beautiful family home. Seems doubtful that anyone will ever live here again.'

'What are we looking for, ma'am?'

'I wondered if our murder suspect would venture here. But perhaps not.'

They circled the house but found nothing to indicate that Jack Winters had visited his former home.

'I reckon he's aware that we're after him,' said Wilson.

'If I'm right about what's happened, then he knows he's a wanted man.'

They returned to the car and drove away. Instead of making an immediate turn by the gates of the house, Tara proceeded further along the lane.

'May as well show you where Murray found the body of Rebecca Winters,' she said. As they approached the derelict building by the side of the lane, there was a car in the centre of the road blocking their way.

'That's his car, ma'am.'

Tara stopped, and as they climbed out Wilson glanced at the disused building.

'Up there, ma'am.'

Tara looked upwards to see the daunting figure of a man standing in the space of what had been a first-floor window. Wilson caught him in the beam of his torch. A rope around his neck hung from a wooden joist in what remained of the roof.

'Please, Mr Winters. I just want to talk with you.'

'Miss Grogan, it's you, isn't it? Although, I do know that you're really a police officer. A clever one, by all accounts.'

'There's no need for any of this. Things are never that bad.'

'Aren't they?'

Wilson handed his torch to Tara then slipped back to the car to call for support.

'Where's he off to?' Winters asked.

'He's checking in with the station, that's all,' said Tara. 'May I come up there and we can talk?'

'Stay where you are. I won't be here for long. Tell me, how did you know it was me?'

'I didn't know for sure and certainly couldn't prove it. I received a message from Anthony Sawyer. It confirmed my thinking.'

'Sawyer was a big mistake. I don't know why Elizabeth ever allowed him to write his damn book. She should have left well alone. Is he dead?'

'He is seriously injured but still alive. Tell me about Stephen Lloyd.'

'There's little point in discussing him, not now.'

'Why is that?'

'Because of what Sawyer told me. None of it matters. I suggest you clear off and leave me in peace.'

'No! Please tell me what happened that Christmas Eve.'

'Too late for that.'

Winters stepped from the window ledge. A hand caught his collar.

'No, you don't!' Wilson grunted. He grasped Winters by his coat and tried not to fall along with the burly man. The rope tightened around Winters' neck, and his legs thrashed as Wilson struggled to hold him. There was a crack of splintering wood. The joist above gave way. The rope slackened and both men fell to the ground. Wilson's fall was broken when he landed on top of Winters, who cried out in pain. His arm, trapped beneath him, had broken at the elbow.

'Why couldn't you let me die?'

'It's not your time, Mr Winters,' said Tara, helping the uninjured Wilson clamber to his feet.

'I'm arresting you on suspicion of the murders of Stephen Lloyd, Angela Campbell and the attempted murder of Anthony Sawyer...'

CHAPTER 80

Late getting home, Tara didn't feel like eating. She managed one glass of wine from the last bottle in the fridge and slumped into her sofa. Falling asleep from exhaustion would be the only way she could switch off this evening. There were several messages from Kate on her phone, questions about their new home, proposed arrangements to shop for furniture, and a date for a show at Adele's school. She couldn't deal with any of it, not tonight. Nothing could help her relax. She craved company; she wanted to shut herself away for months. She wanted to get drunk; there was no wine left in the fridge. She was hungry; she felt like throwing up. She hated the silence and switched on her TV. She muted the sound. She cried. She dozed off.

Cold and stiff, the only difference between her and a body in the morgue was that she was breathing. Inside, she felt dead. Another case had dragged her down. Her first investigation since Aisling's death and all she wanted was to run away. She glanced at her phone. Shortly after three. She should crawl into bed but the urge to get to work grew with each thought. Her colleagues, Wilson, Bleasdale and even Tweedy believed they'd got their man. Jack Winters, after a spell at A&E, was safe in a holding cell and later would be brought to St Anne Street for interview. Why then did she have a nagging doubt that this was not an end to it?

From the sofa she traipsed to the bathroom, casting off clothes on the way. The water from the shower gradually warmed her and she lingered, caressing her body, applying shower gel, washing it away and reapplying. A thought of

Anthony Sawyer, wondering if he had made it through the night, shook off her dawdling. She stepped from the shower and wrapped her tingling body in a towel.

She endured a bowl of muesli and a glass of orange juice, keeping an eye for alerts on her phone, although it was only four o'clock in the morning. Who, other than the likes of her, would be wide awake thinking of work at this hour? She was intent on looking her best when she sat opposite Jack Winters. What on earth for? Perhaps, in a small way, to illustrate that she was professional. That there were people in this city striving for justice. That no human being had the right to extinguish the life of another. She impatiently desired answers from Winters before she had even posed her questions.

From her wardrobe she chose a tailored jacket, slim trousers and a white blouse. She placed a silver chain with a tiny cross around her neck, her last birthday present from Aisling. She applied light make-up and brushed her cropped hair. Gathering her bag and keys, she stepped from her apartment. It was just 4.15 a.m., and she was on her way to work.

The office was in darkness when she pushed the door open and walked in. She flicked a couple of switches and several fluorescent strips flickered into life. At her desk, she logged in to her computer and inserted the flash drive she'd received from Chrissie Black. She opened the file and read the letter addressed to her and written by Sawyer.

> *Hi Tara, or perhaps in this instance I should say Inspector.*
> *I thought I should lay some thoughts before you. Maybe it will help you get to the bottom of what happened to my darling Rebecca and has led to the deaths of Stephen Lloyd and Angela Campbell. Since you are reading this, it must mean that something nasty has befallen me. Otherwise, I would be telling you face to face over a coffee.*

I should first like to state, for the record as it were, that everything I have told you so far has been the absolute truth as I know it. The one omission has been my refusal to answer your question of whether I was the father of Rebecca's unborn baby.

What follows is my updated belief of what happened on Christmas Eve nineteen years ago. It may not be entirely accurate. You may choose not to believe it. That is your decision. I realise that you are an excellent detective and will evaluate all the evidence before making judgement.

Two pages of text then described what Sawyer believed had occurred at Briarwood Manor nineteen years ago and why those events led to the deaths of Stephen Lloyd and Angela Campbell.

One thing I am reasonably certain of, and the fact that you have this file in your possession proves it, is that Ted Havers murdered Stephen Lloyd and probably Angela Campbell. A harrowing thought is that by now I may be another of his victims.

I'm sure you'll want to know how I reached the conclusion that Havers is a killer with a secret to protect. I'm truly sorry that I didn't realise this sooner.

Anyway, one thing suddenly occurred to me about the events of nineteen years ago. When you told me that Winters had contacted Havers after we'd met with him and that Havers had complained to your boss, it puzzled me. Why would Winters have anything to do with Havers, a man who'd shared Elizabeth's bed? Then it hit me. Jack Winters never knew of his wife's infidelities. It never came out at the time. And why should it? Elizabeth and Havers were at the head of the investigation of Rebecca's murder. Easy for them to suppress it. Stephen Lloyd would never have known, so it couldn't be used by the defence counsel at his trial. I think, however, that sometime around his release from prison Lloyd learned something new of what had taken place that Christmas Eve and he was going to use it to clear his name. I'll leave that for you to figure out.

Yesterday I called Jack Winters. I told him I had information about Havers and Elizabeth. He agreed to meet me to discuss. Since you are reading this letter then I guess things did not go well, but if I were you, I would check on the whereabouts of Havers. Jack Winters has a violent temper. When they were children, Rebecca and Freddie were on the receiving end of it many times.

CHAPTER 81

Jack Winters looked in pain as he was brought into the station reception. His right arm was encased in a plastic cast up to his armpit and supported by a sling. There was a gash on his forehead which had received a couple of stitches. Ironically, he had been treated in the same A&E department that his victim Anthony Sawyer had passed through several hours earlier.

Tara watched as he hobbled by without a word. Desk Sergeant McLachlan checked off the details and instructed the uniformed escorts to place Winters in interview room two. Wilson emerged from the lift and stood beside his DI. He had saved the life of Jack Winters, but the man did not look grateful for seeing another day.

'Ready, ma'am?' said Wilson.

'As I'll ever be,' Tara replied with a sigh. 'Any news of Havers?'

'Nothing yet. He's not at home or his office. Could be anywhere, I suppose.'

Tara winced. If only she'd paid more heed to the ending in Sawyer's letter. She would have realised that Havers was a likely victim of Jack Winters' rage.

'Right, let's get started,' she said, heading for the interview room as Wilson returned to their office.

A solicitor was already seated next to Winters and discussion between the pair halted when Tara entered. The lawyer, around fifty, tall with thinning hair and wearing a dull suit and yacht-club tie, stood to greet her.

'James Brough. I'll be representing Mr Winters this morning.'

'Good,' Tara replied, not wishing to ingratiate herself to another brief. She endured them, tolerated them. It was the right of the suspect, and she was happy with it so long as they didn't get under her feet.

After the formalities in commencing a police interview, Tara wasted no further time. She wanted the full story from Winters, of course, but crucially she needed to learn what he might have done with Ted Havers. It seemed that Havers had not returned home the night before and his partner had heard nothing from him.

'Tell me the whereabouts of Assistant Chief Constable Havers.'

Brough looked at Winters. Tara feared she was about to face the traditional no comment. But Winters looked bemused.

'I don't understand,' he said.

'When did you last see him?'

'Years ago.'

'Can you confirm that no harm has come to Ted Havers?'

'Not as far as I know, Inspector.'

Tara studied the man's eyes. Despite his current predicament there remained a confidence in his gaze. It was the arrogance Tara had encountered when she'd first met him. She glanced at Brough. He looked unmoved by this first exchange. Tara readjusted her thinking. Ted Havers, alive or dead, would have to wait.

'Tell me why you killed Stephen Lloyd?'

Winters' broad shoulders seemed to chuckle involuntarily when he scoffed.

'I thought that much was obvious. He killed my daughter.'

'You believe that?'

'He was convicted, wasn't he?'

'And wasn't it enough for you that he'd served his time?' Tara asked.

'Not sufficient for murder, Inspector. We lost our daughter. Elizabeth and I are serving a life sentence for what he did. Where's the justice in Lloyd walking free after just eighteen years?'

'Had you always intended to kill Lloyd when he was released from prison?'

'Yes.'

Tara hesitated, staring doubtfully at the resolute man before her. But it seemed to unnerve him; he shifted in his seat and winced from the pain in his arm.

'Tell me why you killed Angela Campbell?'

'She and her boyfriend were intending to help Lloyd clear his name.'

'And how were you aware of this?'

'Lloyd contacted me through a solicitor and told me of his intention.'

'So, you killed him? Didn't you consider that Lloyd may have been innocent?'

'Not at all. I wasn't in the least impressed by his claim.'

'Did he tell you exactly how he was going to prove his innocence? What evidence did he have that was going to help him?'

'I have no idea.'

'You simply killed him in revenge for Rebecca, and you killed Angela Campbell, your former employee, for wanting to help Lloyd?'

'Not revenge, Inspector – justice.'

Tara sat back.

'You don't like that word, Inspector? Very strange for someone who works in law enforcement.'

Tara seethed. She wanted to leap across the table and tear his face off. Before pausing the interview for a refreshment break, she had one further question.

'Did you act alone?'

Winters stared directly in her face.

'Yes, of course.'

CHAPTER 82

The news on Anthony Sawyer was promising. When Tara rang the hospital for an update, she was informed that he was stable.

She sat at her desk, while Winters and his brief sampled the station coffee in the interview room. She was startled by a voice, unaware of Tweedy's approach.

'How is it going with our guest?'

Tara shrugged.

'It's hard to say, sir. He's been willing to admit that he killed Lloyd and Campbell. On the face of it he's been co-operative.'

'Do I detect a but?'

'He's feeding me with a pack of lies. I don't understand why he's prepared to confess to the murders but withhold the true reason for his actions. Sawyer believed that Havers is the killer, but I think he and Winters acted together. I just can't figure out why. I'm not convinced by

Winters' motive for killing either of the victims. His reason for Campbell is flimsy. I don't think it's a strong enough reason that she was intending to help Lloyd to clear his name. There must be more to it than that. Winters must have perceived it as a threat, but why? How could he feel threatened by Lloyd unless he had something to hide? And what threat could Angela Campbell have posed?'

'Perhaps her boyfriend would know the answer to that question. I'll let you get on.'

Tweedy strolled off leaving Tara with a developing headache. The day is long when it begins at four in the morning.

* * *

Wilson entered the interview room behind Tara. She introduced her DS for the benefit of solicitor James Brough. Winters did not acknowledge the man who, a few hours earlier, had saved his life. Without sitting down, Tara addressed the murder suspect.

'DS Wilson will take your statement. If you are content to accept responsibility for killing Stephen Lloyd and Angela Campbell, then please include as much detail as possible of your actions. We will reference your statement with the evidence we have already gathered. I would advise that you reconsider your response to my question that you acted alone.'

Winters' face turned pale, and his mouth dropped open.

Tara could not have hoped for a more telling reaction. 'When you're finished, we can address your assault of Anthony Sawyer.'

Tara left the room. By the time she returned she hoped to have a much clearer version of events, a version to dispute the one given so far by multiple murderer Jack Winters.

* * *

Bleasdale, acting on Tara's request, had obtained the new address for Tyrone Cunningham, a homeless shelter on Queen's Drive, not far from the house he'd shared with Angela Campbell.

Two scruffy men were smoking roll-ups by the entrance to the modern building and stepped aside to let Tara and Bleasdale enter.

'All right, love?' One of them called as the other whistled. 'Fancy a bit of rough?'

Tara turned to the battered-looking man who'd spoken. 'DI Grogan, Merseyside Police. I'm looking for Tyrone Cunningham.'

The man's face paled. Mention of police induced a stutter. He shook his head. 'I... I... I d-d-don't know.'

Tara smiled mischievously, knowing she'd struck fear in the old sod. His younger companion laughed at his friend's discomfort.

Voices echoed on the stairwell, and the aroma of fish and chips with vinegar hit them as they entered a dining room on the first floor. Several people were dotted around the tables, while three others queued at a serving hatch awaiting their lunch. One of them was Tyrone Cunningham. The empty tray he was holding dropped to his side when he noticed Tara. She approached him smiling, although she was deadly serious in what she wanted from this meeting.

Cunningham looked about to run, but his good sense prevailed, and he raised his hand in defence. 'Why can't you leave me alone?'

His protests raised a few heads.

'Hello, Tyrone, it's nice to see you too,' said Tara.

'What do you want, cop? I'm about to have my lunch.'

'Don't let us stop you. We'll wait over here, shall we?' She indicated a nearby table and Bleasdale joined her.

Cunningham, looking agitated, collected his meal of fish and chips, mushy peas, and a mug of tea, then sat with the detectives at the table. He didn't speak and began to eat as if no one else was present.

Tara reckoned that he looked like a man with little hope remaining in his life. Evidently, he'd had little option when he'd vacated the house in Knotty Ash but to move into a hostel for the homeless. Tara had sympathy for the man. In recent weeks he'd lost a friend in Stephen Lloyd, had survived an attempt on his life, one in which his girlfriend had perished, and now he'd been left without a home. One didn't always appreciate the repercussions of a crime and how far reaching they could be.

'We came to tell you that we've arrested someone for Angela's murder,' said Tara.

Cunningham didn't take his eyes off his food. He seemed unmoved by the news.

'Aren't you curious who it is?'

The man shrugged and supped from his mug.

'His name is Jack Winters,' Tara continued. 'He has admitted to killing Angela.'

'So, what do you want with me?'

'The reason he has given for the murder doesn't stack up.'

'Your problem, love.'

Tara glared angrily, struggling to remain calm. Here was another candidate for having his face torn off. She pulled his plate away. It slid off the table and smashed on the floor.

'What the hell?'

'Touch that mug of tea and I'll pour it over you.'

'Take it easy, love. Who's rattled your cage?'

'Call me love once more and I'll have you in cuffs and on your way back inside within the hour.' Tara could feel the warmth in her face. Even Bleasdale seemed to baulk at her outburst.

'Jeez! Calm down, will you?' Cunningham said, his hands raised in surrender.

Tara returned to the objective of their meeting. 'Winters claims he killed Angela because she was helping Lloyd to clear his name. He remains adamant that Lloyd killed his daughter. I don't believe that was a strong enough motive for Winters to have killed Angela. But I think you know the true reason for her murder, and you haven't shared it with us. Angela is dead, Tyrone. Winters has confessed. You have nothing more to fear, so tell me the truth.'

'I'm not going back inside again.'

'Tell me, or so help me I'll drive you to the prison right now.'

'OK, OK, I hear you.' Cunningham clasped his hands as if in prayer, but it was to stop them shaking. 'Like I told you before, Angela said she had information that would help Stephen to clear his name. It was stuff about the murder of the Winters girl. I thought it was a way to make some money.'

'You need to explain.'

'She told me that none of her statement was ever used at Stephen's trial. If it had been, then she reckoned that Stephen would never have been convicted.'

'Why did her version of what happened not come out?' Bleasdale asked.

'Your lot covered it up. That was down to the guy in charge of the investigation and the girl's mother being chief constable.'

'What did Angela know about that day?' Tara asked.

'She was certain that Stephen was nowhere near the Winters' place when Rebecca died. She was adamant that the mother was in the house with a bloke. They were in bed together. None of that came out at Stephen's trial.'

Tara was hardly surprised by what she was hearing. It was the same opinion that Sawyer had expressed. It still, however, did not explain what had occurred on that Christmas Eve. But Cunningham hadn't finished.

'About a week after the girl was killed, Angela was back at work doing her cleaning. She found what looked like a blood stain on a rug in the hall. The brother, Freddie, saw her trying to clean it. He told her that red wine had been spilled during Christmas and ordered her to throw the rug in the bin.'

'You mentioned a way for you to make some money?' Tara asked.

'When Angela told me about having worked at the Winters' house and how she could help Stephen, I had an idea for getting back at the bizzies who were involved. I contacted this Havers bloke, told him what I knew and that unless he gave me twenty grand, I would tell Stephen and his lawyers.'

'You tried to blackmail a senior police officer?' said Tara.

'Didn't matter to me what he was. He had a secret and a career to protect. I reckoned he would pay up.'

'How did he react to your threat?'

'Laughed in my face. Told me I should be careful making accusations. So, I passed the information to Stephen. But he thought it was a good idea to keep at Havers.'

'You mean he was in favour of the blackmail?' said Tara.

Cunningham nodded.

Tara allowed him to drink some tea. 'What happened next?'

'That's when it all got nasty. Stephen had been released by then. Havers tracked him down and threatened to put him back inside if he tried to act on the information I'd given him. The night he was killed, we'd met to talk about our next move.'

'Was Angela aware of what you were doing?' Bleasdale asked.

'Not the blackmail. She would have freaked out. But she was happy for me to have told Stephen her story. I didn't tell her about Havers. Why is any of this important now? You said that Jack Winters has confessed to the murders?'

Tara was already on her feet.

'We need to get back to the station. Thanks, Tyrone.'

He watched the women hurry from the dining room, then, indifferent, returned to the serving hatch to fetch another portion of fish and chips.

CHAPTER 83

Bleasdale used the siren to negotiate Friday afternoon traffic in the rush back to St Anne Street. Tara was on her phone. Wilson, she learned, was still taking the statement from Jack Winters. She managed to get hold of Tweedy.

'We need a warrant for the arrest of Ted Havers, sir.' She supplied her boss with an update from her meeting with Tyrone Cunningham. To her relief, Tweedy didn't hold back in agreeing with her analysis. That was at least one battle less to fight. Her concern remained, however, that Winters, after he'd learned from Sawyer for the first time of his wife's affair, might have dispensed with the assistant chief constable.

Winters, Brough and even Wilson were startled as the door of the interview room flew open. Tara stormed in. All formalities were ignored.

'Ted Havers! Where is he?'

Jack Winters, caressing his broken arm, looked at her with a conceited smile. Slowly, he shook his head.

'I have no idea.'

'Don't, just don't. I want the truth from you, Mr Winters, or so help me...'

'Or you'll do what, Inspector? You forget that I have nothing left worth fighting for. If your sergeant hadn't intervened yesterday, I would be gone by now. I owe you nothing, least of all the truth.'

'Inspector Grogan,' Brough interjected. 'You will not get answers with this attitude to my client.'

'Shut up! A man's life is at stake and your client knows exactly what has happened. He places so little value on his own life but how dare he continue to do so with other people?'

'Inspector…'

She ignored the solicitor's protest and made for the door.

'Wilson! Get him back to a cell. Now! You can leave too, Mr Brough.'

She fumed all the way to her desk. The news she feared awaited her in the person of Tweedy. He had been wandering around the office and looked relieved to see her.

'We have a report of a burnt-out vehicle found in Knowsley,' he said gravely. 'It is registered to Joanna Noble, the partner of Ted Havers.'

'A blue Jaguar SUV?'

'Hardly recognisable now but yes. A body was discovered inside. We don't have a confirmed identification yet.'

'I understand. Thank you, sir.'

Tara hurried from the office. She met Wilson on the stairs.

'Get that man back here, right now,' she snapped.

'And his brief?'

'Him too.'

Tara spotted the solicitor in reception. He was signing out as Sergeant McLachlan looked on.

'You'll be required again, Mr Brough,' she said.

'Now?'

'That's correct. Same room if you don't mind.'

Five minutes later, Wilson entered with Jack Winters. Tara ignored him until he'd sat down, and she had begun the voice and video recorder.

'Mr Winters, you may believe that you have cleaned up your mess. It seems that Ted Havers is dead. I see no reason now why you cannot provide me with the truth.'

Winters smiled. Tara winced. In such brief encounters with the man, she had come to detest his supercilious grin.

'I'm inclined to quote Pontius Pilate, from his meeting with Jesus Christ, in that regard,' he said.

'I'm sorry?'

'What is truth?'

CHAPTER 84

It was fortunate that Tara and Wilson had no firm plans for their weekend. Friday evening moved into the night and had slipped into Saturday morning with the detectives barely noticing. Coffee and biscuits came several times. There were numerous comfort breaks and occasions when James Brough requested time alone to advise his client. Tara was relieved to have her suspect talking. How much of it was true was for a philosophical mind or, eventually, a jury to decide, if Winters were ever to plead not guilty.

'Can I assume that the body found in the burnt-out car is Assistant Chief Constable Ted Havers?'

Winters replied with a single nod.

'For the recording, please answer yes or no.'

'Yes.'

'Are you admitting to causing his death?'

'Yes. With great pleasure, yes absolutely.'

'Please explain your reason for killing this man.'

'It took nineteen years to hear of it, Inspector. I can't believe I'd been kept in the dark all that time. You'll appreciate now why I hesitate when you ask for the truth.

'When Rebecca died, I never doubted for a second that Lloyd was her killer. I believed everything I was told. He killed her because she was a beautiful young woman who had rejected his advances. When he was convicted, I was content that was an end to it. Rebecca was gone and a day hasn't passed since then that I don't think of her. Contrary to what I told you previously, I did not harbour any intentions to kill Lloyd when he was released from prison. Not until Ted Havers came to see me. I hadn't laid eyes on him since Lloyd's trial. He was a cocky man, don't you think?'

Tara wanted to agree but cocky wasn't a big enough word to describe the ego of the late assistant chief constable. It would be unprofessional for her to state an appropriate one.

'How did Havers convince you that Stephen Lloyd had to die?'

'He told me that Lloyd was about to be released from prison. Then he explained that Lloyd and an associate were blackmailing him about the investigation of Rebecca's murder. He claimed that Havers and Elizabeth had framed him for Rebecca's murder and had suppressed evidence that could prove he was an innocent man. Elizabeth's good reputation as a former chief constable would be destroyed if it emerged that she and Havers had suppressed evidence to convict Lloyd. I couldn't let that happen. Elizabeth was not able to defend herself. It was down to me to protect her. I suggested to Havers that we pay them, but it was Havers' idea to kill Lloyd. He said that no one was likely to bat an eye over the death of an ex-offender, a convicted murderer. He assured me that he could arrange things, make it look like a random attack.'

'What was your involvement in the killing?' Tara asked.

'Havers set everything up. I went along to hit the guy on the head with a hammer. Havers had people, police officers I suppose, who kept Lloyd under surveillance. Then he arranged for some queer boy to pick Lloyd up in a bar and lure him to St John's Garden. Havers and I gave Lloyd a beating, and then Havers finished him off when he ran across the road towards the tunnel.'

Tara's spine tingled uncomfortably. Accounts of a murder, especially a confession, never got any easier to hear. Images of the scene in the city centre tumbled through her mind: the CCTV recording that showed the victim escaping from St John's Garden, staggering and falling on the road, and vehicles swerving to avoid the apparent drunk.

'Why kill Angela Campbell?' Tara asked. She realised that another harrowing tale was about to unfold. How would she ever get through this night?

'Same reason,' said Winters with a sigh as if he was talking of a beloved pet that had to be put to sleep. 'Again, Havers convinced me that Angela, and that lowlife she lived with, posed a threat to Elizabeth's good name. He said that Campbell was an unreliable witness from the day Rebecca was killed, and she was the one providing the information they were using for the blackmail. Another seemingly random attack and our problem would disappear. He arranged everything. I messed up, of course.'

Tara looked inquiringly at the man.

'Cunningham survived, while Havers killed Angela. He told me not to worry. We'd done enough. Cunningham wouldn't bother us again.' Winters sat back on the plastic chair. 'So that's it, Inspector. I killed to protect my Elizabeth.'

'But you weren't finished, Mr Winters.'

'I would have been, until you showed up at my door with Anthony Sawyer.'

CHAPTER 85

'After you left my flat, I called Havers to tell him about you and Sawyer. He immediately suspected you were a police officer. You really should have used a false name, Inspector. He told me not to worry, but that I wasn't to speak with you or Sawyer again.'

'What changed?' Tara asked.

'A few days ago, Sawyer called me. He'd heard that I'd told Havers about meeting you. Something niggled him about my having any contact with Havers. So, he asked to meet with me. I wasn't keen on doing so. Didn't want him sticking his nose in again. He'd already gone way too far with that blessed book of his and then bringing you to my door.'

'What changed your mind?'

'He told me that he'd just realised there was something I was not aware of. He wouldn't explain on the phone. Insisted on our meeting. I assumed it had something to do with his relationship with Rebecca, or he was intending to write another damn book.'

'So, you agreed to meet?'

'Yes, at Formby beach. I chose the place, but he insisted that I come alone. If he got even a hint of Havers being there, then the meeting was off.'

'And did you go alone?'

Winters nodded.

'Yes. I saw no point in alerting Havers. I didn't believe that Sawyer was a threat. Merely an unwelcome irritation. I had no intention of doing him harm. I gather that he survived our meeting. I'm glad about that.'

Tara glared at the man before her. He was up to his neck in bodies and still had the gall to express sympathy. She quickly reminded him why he was seated in a police interview room.

'What did Sawyer tell you that drove you to assault him?'

'He claimed that Havers and Elizabeth had been in bed together at our home on the day Rebecca was killed.'

Tara slid a box of tissues in front of him. He wiped tears away then blew his nose. His voice faltered.

'Can't believe that in all those years I never suspected a thing. Sawyer stood with a smirk on his face. He seemed to enjoy telling me something I didn't know. It seems that Havers was not the only one. Elizabeth, he told me, had made a habit of sleeping around. I was told by Elizabeth that Havers had rushed to help us when Rebecca went missing. I knew they had been colleagues. I wish now that I'd come home early that day instead of hanging around my office party.'

'Why did you decide to kill Sawyer, the man who had provided you with the truth?' Tara asked.

'Don't you see? I couldn't let that story come out, Inspector. I still had to protect Elizabeth. I was angry too, of course. Mostly, I was seething about Havers. Suddenly, I realised that he'd goaded me into killing Lloyd and Angela, but the motive hadn't been to stop them from challenging Lloyd's murder conviction. It was to prevent them from revealing Havers' affair with Elizabeth, that he'd been in our home on the day Rebecca died and that he and my wife had covered it up. Havers and Elizabeth had kept that secret from me and then Havers had relied upon my ignorance of the fact when he got me to help him kill two people. I was well and truly duped.

'So, you took your anger out on Sawyer?'

Tara couldn't suppress her disdain of this naïve, gullible and despicable man. She had too many words surfacing to describe her contempt.

'I lost my temper. I punched him in the face, and he went down. He hit his head on a rock when he fell. Then I kicked him. But he got back on his feet and ran off. I went after him; I had calmed down quickly; I wanted to help him, but it was pitch dark. After a few minutes in the cold, I gave up and returned to my car. I waited for about twenty minutes. He didn't appear, and I drove home. So, you see, Inspector, I didn't intend to kill Sawyer.'

'Moving on to Assistant Chief Constable Havers,' said Tara, reaching for the latest information on the burnt-out SUV and the body found inside.

'I'll keep it short, Inspector. I killed the lowlife. I was waiting for him as he left his office. Made him drive to some place I can't even recall. I stabbed him then slit his throat. It seemed a fitting end to burn his car with him inside it. I killed him for what he had enticed me to do and for nineteen years of my not knowing the truth. There's that word again. Afterwards, I felt it appropriate, with nothing remaining to live for, that I should end things at the very spot where our nightmare had begun, the place where Rebecca had died. Elizabeth, thank goodness, will never know any of this. It would have been a reasonable end to things, until Sergeant Wilson decided that I was worth saving.'

Tara had one last truth to seek.

'Thank you for your co-operation, Mr Winters. There is one issue remaining.'

The man waited expectantly, while Tara gathered her notes and closed a folder.

'What happened on the day Rebecca died?' she asked. This was a truth that still mattered. Innocent blood had been spilled on a freezing Christmas Eve nineteen years ago and, as a consequence, three more lives had been cut short. It was time to learn the truth.

Winters shrugged and managed a thin smile. But it was a look of bewilderment. His good hand massaged his broken arm and he grimaced.

'I don't know what you mean, Inspector.'

'Is it still your belief that Stephen Lloyd killed Rebecca at the derelict house on Firs Lane?'

'Yes, of course. He was convicted, wasn't he?'

'You don't believe that anything different occurred from what was recorded in the police file?'

Winters turned pale. For the first time during the hours of his interview there was terror emblazoned on his battered face.

'I don't understand. What haven't you told me, Inspector? I have a right to know. She was my daughter.'

'If you don't already know what really happened to Rebecca, Mr Winters, then I'm afraid I can't help you. My opinion, although I can never prove it, is that Stephen Lloyd was used as a scapegoat for whatever occurred at your home on that Christmas Eve. Rather than merely concealing his affair with Elizabeth, I would suggest that Ted Havers had been hiding a more sinister fact. Sadly, the people who knew the truth are no longer able to speak it. That includes your wife.'

Winters lowered his head and wept.

CHAPTER 86

Kate held Tara's arm outside the front door of their new home. Adele tugged her mother's hand and stamped her feet, eager to get her first look inside.

'One, two, three, let's go!' Tara called. The three of them stepped forward in unison and giggled when they were jammed in the doorway. The child trotted on, cheering as she ran to the lounge then upstairs and soon had located her new bedroom. Beaming, Tara and Kate looked in to see her sprawled on a princess' bed, admiring her palatial surroundings.

'What do you think?' Kate asked.

'It's great, Mummy. I love it. It's beautiful.'

'Wow! That's a great big word,' said Tara, delighted by her goddaughter's reaction.

'It's a hit then,' said Kate. 'Let's make some lunch in our new kitchen.'

Afterwards, as weak sunshine streaked over the back garden, the three of them decided on a short walk. Beyond the stretch of lawn and vegetable patch, they opened the gate that led onto the lane. Tara had explored it before completing the purchase of the house, but Kate and Adele hadn't stood in the lane before now.

'Where are we going, Mummy?' Adele asked.

'This leads all the way down to the beach,' said Tara, turning left.

'What if we go the other way?' Adele ran to her right, skipping along the gravel path.

'Come back, Adele. That doesn't go anywhere,' said Kate.

While Kate took charge of Adele's movements, Tara's mind reverted to thoughts of her work. This was her weekend off, for goodness' sake. She was supposed to be enjoying time in her new home, and all she could think of was a nineteen-year-old murder. The comparison was easy. Firs Lane had led nowhere, and now she stood in another lane that dwindled and was lost among the bushes.

Later in the afternoon, while Kate settled into their home, unpacking some of the many boxes scattered about the place, Tara made coffee. Waiting for Kate to join her, she scanned the morning paper. The tragic story of the Winters family had disappeared from the front pages. Jack Winters had been formally charged, and at his hearing had pleaded guilty to all but the attempted murder of Anthony Sawyer. It meant that there would be a trial. Tara's attention was drawn to a story on an inside page.

She sat on a stool at the island in the kitchen to read. The passage referred to a disciplinary hearing for prison officer Graham Benson. He had been cleared of direct responsibility for the death of prison inmate Imran Fadel. The tribunal had, however, considered several allegations of prisoner abuse relating to him and to officers under his command. The complaints were upheld, and it was likely that Benson, still on suspension, would be dismissed from the prison service and face criminal proceedings. All officers cited in the allegations were suspended from duty pending separate disciplinary hearings. Tara hoped there would be justice for Andy Greengates, Tyrone Cunningham and Stephen Lloyd for what had occurred in the prison.

Her thoughts returned to her investigation. If she had acted on her instincts sooner maybe Anthony Sawyer would not have suffered horrendous injuries from which, thankfully, he was slowly recovering. Ted Havers, also, might still be alive. His murder seemed to have pulled the shutters down on the mystery of that Christmas Eve.

She'd spent recent days tracking down the officers, working for Havers, who had stalked and attacked her. Their defence was they had believed they were performing a covert operation on a rogue detective inspector. Tara had refuted that they were on a police operation at all but were merely acting under Havers' direction as they had probably done countless times for purely criminal reasons. Their association with Havers was now under investigation and the officers would likely face charges of corruption in addition to the those relating to the attacks on Tara.

Murray confirmed from CCTV recordings at a car park in Liverpool One that a blue Jaguar SUV, registered to Havers' partner, Joanna Noble, was the vehicle used at the time Josh Yarnly had been hired to lure Stephen Lloyd to his death. It was likely that Yarnly would avoid the charge of accessory to murder since he was unaware that his actions would lead to the death of Stephen Lloyd. He would, however, face prosecution for his failure to report a crime. She had learned also that Sergeant McLachlan had served previously under Ted Havers. He was included in the corruption investigation of Havers and his rogue officers and would likely face similar charges.

CHAPTER 87

'She doesn't go to the day room now,' the nurse explained. 'Sleeps most of the time.'

Tara sat by Elizabeth's bed looking on as the once important woman slept, puffing tiny breaths through her dry lips. Even in the short time since Tara had first seen her, the woman's condition had declined. Her cheeks had collapsed inwards, as if she had no teeth, her cheekbones seemed on the verge of breaking through waxy, thin skin. Her fingers were closed around her thumbs like those of a newborn baby. There was a crust of dried bleary sleep across both of her eyes.

Tara, even if pressed, couldn't provide a compassionate reason for visiting the former chief constable. The charges against her husband were damning. He'd been implicated in the murders of three people and in the attempted murder of Anthony Sawyer. His actions seemed to have closed any avenues to the truth of what really happened to Rebecca Winters on a freezing Christmas Eve nineteen years ago. Despite it never having been her case, it still cast an uncomfortable shadow over the investigation that for her had begun with the murder of Stephen Lloyd.

'Does she mention her husband?' Tara asked.

The nurse, who was replenishing the fluid drip on a stand attached to Elizabeth's arm, shook her head.

'Nothing. No mention of anyone. She has no idea of what has occurred recently. Probably for the best, really.'

The nurse then left the room leaving Tara alone with the ailing woman. Tara checked her phone in case she was needed at the station. But she was content to stay for a while, the phone resting in her lap, and to cogitate on all that she'd learned about the Winters family.

Silly for her to think that Elizabeth would suddenly awaken completely lucid and prepared to speak the truth. It must have taken a lot of devious work for the woman to keep it hidden for so long. Tara, from the outset, had doubted and continued to doubt that Lloyd was guilty of killing Rebecca, unlike Jack Winters who had believed everything told to him by his wife and by Ted Havers. He'd believed it to such an extent that he was prepared to smudge out the truth as it had begun to emerge. He'd helped to kill Lloyd and Campbell to protect the reputation of an unfaithful wife who'd fed him lies over the death of their daughter. And when he'd learned from Sawyer that he'd been duped for years, he continued to eliminate those who knew the truth, a truth more painful than he could have ever imagined. So much so that when he believed his task was complete, he had attempted to end his own life.

Then Tara had added to the man's anguish by suggesting that Lloyd had not killed Rebecca, but that the real story may never be known since all the players had left the stage.

All except for one.

CHAPTER 88

Tara guessed that Freddie Winters would return to England to visit his failing mother. She'd requested from UK immigration to be notified when he entered the country. Freddie flew into Heathrow, and his progress through passport control was flagged. But he was not arrested, and he left the airport unchallenged. Fortuitous this morning, perhaps, that as Tara sat mulling over her investigation and the outstanding facts surrounding it, Freddie showed up at the nursing home. He'd been kept under surveillance since his arrival in Liverpool. He was pinged when he checked into a city-centre hotel and used his credit card. She couldn't be sure of the exact time of his arrival at the nursing home, but she knew he would come.

The door to Elizabeth's room opened and a man peered round.

'Oh, sorry,' he said. 'Didn't realise Mum would have visitors. I'll come back later.'

'Freddie Winters?'

'Yes. Do I know you?'

The man who bore little resemblance to his father Jack, with fine unblemished features and slight build, stepped further into the room. He wore a dark sport's jacket, blue jeans and open-neck shirt.

'We spoke on the phone once. I'm DI Tara Grogan.'

She saw the nerves rising in the man. Her presence was a cleverly engineered stroke of luck for her but an unexpected sideswipe for him.

'Yes, I remember,' he said, sounding nervous. He was certainly uncomfortable with this impromptu situation. 'But why are you here? Has something else happened?'

'No. I can't say anything has. I suppose I was just paying my respects in a way.'

Freddie didn't look convinced by her answer. She didn't care.

'But I'm glad you're here,' she said. 'I was hoping you could help with some unfinished business.'

'And what might that be, Inspector?'

'Have you been to see your father?'

'No, nor do I intend to, not after what he's done.'

Tara invited Freddie to sit, and he moved to the far side of his mother's bed and sat on the only other chair in the room.

'Your father, despite confessing to his involvement in the murders of Stephen Lloyd and Angela Campbell and to killing Ted Havers, continues to believe that Lloyd was responsible for the death of your sister. I don't believe that to be the case and I think you can help me with the truth.'

'Sorry, I don't know what you're on about. I wasn't even at home when Rebecca was killed.'

His eyes were trained on his mother.

'Are you saying that your sister was killed in your home?'

'No, of course not.'

Freddie shifted uncomfortably in his seat but his gaze remained fixed upon Elizabeth.

'Your housemaid, Angela, recalled finding what she thought was blood on a rug in the hall of your home. But you claimed it was red wine and told her to dump it.'

'This is ridiculous. Of course, it was wine. It was an accident.'

'Was it really just an accident, Freddie?'

'I meant the wine.'

'Stephen Lloyd didn't kill Rebecca. Angela Campbell was certain that he was innocent. They both died because your father wanted to protect your mother's reputation when she had been chief constable. Even when he learned what kind of woman your mother really was, he still insisted that Lloyd killed Rebecca. But you know what really happened, don't you, Freddie? Don't you think the families of your father's victims deserve some justice?'

Freddie Winters appeared to consider Tara's words. She thought him a man in crisis. He'd harboured a secret for nineteen years, maybe it would be some relief to finally unload his burden. Several moments passed before he responded.

'Can we speak, off the record, Inspector? If you try to charge me with anything I'll simply deny this conversation ever took place.'

He may not look like his father, Tara thought, but he possessed Jack Winter's cold and sardonic traits. She didn't agree to anything. She waited for Freddie Winters to tell his story.

'I worked all that morning,' he began. 'We were trying to get finished up in time for Christmas. The international markets were shutting down for the holidays. Anyway, once we got finished, I was heading to our Christmas party. About lunchtime, I got a call from my mother. She told me that a young man had turned up at the house claiming that I had invited him there for lunch. I honestly had no idea what she was on about. I asked his name, and she said it was Stephen Lloyd. My blood ran cold. I couldn't remember ever inviting him to our house. I must have been pissed or something. I would never have suggested such a thing.'

'Why not?'

'Because Stephen was gay. At the time I thought I was too. But there's no way I wanted my family to find out. Besides Stephen was not the kind of guy my parents would have warmed to, even if they'd recovered from the shock of me being gay.'

262

Tara looked at him quizzically. She didn't repeat her question.

'His background just wouldn't have gone down well with Dad.'

Tara could imagine that to be the case. Jack Winters never struck her as a tolerant man.

'I asked Mum if Stephen was still there, and I wanted to know exactly what had been said. Mum sounded amused. She accused us of getting our wires crossed and told me that Stephen had left straight away. She said that she was just calling me in case I wanted to catch up with Stephen in town or something like that. I was kind of relieved that she didn't seem to suspect anything. But all afternoon I had this uneasy feeling in my gut. Then in the middle of the office party I got a call from Rebecca. She could hardly speak for laughing. I had to go outside just to hear what she was saying. "I've just met your new friend," she said. "Can't wait to tell Mum." Tell her what? I asked. "That her precious Freddie is wired the other way around." She was giggling like crazy. If she'd been standing next to me, I would have thumped her. Typical bloody Rebecca, always taunting. "I know all about you and Stephen meeting at Rainbow Glory. I know it's a gay club. Then he shows up at our house for lunch. What on earth were you thinking, Freddie boy? But it's all right. I gave him a lift back to town and he told me everything, every spicy detail. The poor soul had had to walk all the way from the bus stop to Firs Lane on such a cold day only to be told by our dear mother that his lover wasn't at home. He is very good looking, though. I admire your taste." I screamed down the phone for her to stop. Then she threatened to tell Mum and Dad over Christmas dinner, just for a laugh. I knew that I had to get home. I had to shut her up.'

Freddie paused and watched as Elizabeth stirred on the bed, but her eyes did not open.

'Did you go home?'

Tara's information had been that Freddie and Jack arrived home around the same time in the evening after Rebecca had been reported missing.

'I couldn't settle at the party thinking of what my sister could be up to. I realised she would use it against me to get something she wanted. That was always the way with us. Our playing together would turn to teasing, trying to outdo each other until things went too far and one or both of us got a roasting from Dad. Knowing his temper, I'm not surprised he had the nerve to kill those people. So yes, Inspector, I hurried to get home. It was just getting dark when I drove through the gates. There was a man standing in the drive. At first, I thought it was Stephen. I was confused because Rebecca had said that she had driven him into town. I stopped and lowered my window and when I saw that it wasn't Stephen, I asked the guy if I could help. He seemed upset, tears were running down his face. But he said he was OK. He told me that he was a friend of Rebecca's, and he was just leaving. He went to a car, climbed in and I watched him drive away. I didn't think much about him. He was just someone else that Rebecca had annoyed.'

Tara realised that the man Freddie had encountered was probably Anthony Sawyer who had admitted to visiting Briarwood Manor on that Christmas Eve.

'Once I got inside it was all kicking off.'

'What do you mean?'

'Rebecca and Mum were having a fierce argument at the top of the stairs. Neither one even saw me.'

Freddie wiped at his eyes with the back of his hand. Tara spotted a box of tissues on the bedside table and passed them over.

'Thanks,' he said taking a handful to blow his nose. Tara waited until he'd composed himself.

'What was the argument about?' she asked.

'The two of them were in full flow when I walked in. Rebecca was her usual taunting self. "What are you going to do now, Mother? Send me to my room? Order me to forget what I've seen? Don't tell Dad? Is that the deal?" I had no idea what was going on. I called up to them. Mum was fuming, and she looked really shocked to see me, but neither one spoke to me. Just kept laying into each other. Mum was yelling, "It's not your business to tell your father." Then Rebecca swore and said she was going back to Cambridge. Mum grabbed her by the arms, and Rebecca tried to wriggle free. Mum was telling her that she had to keep her mouth shut. I immediately thought that Rebecca had spilled the beans about Stephen and me. "One word about this to your father and I'll tell him your piece of news," she said. I was certain then that Rebecca had told on me, but I was wrong. Suddenly they were arguing over Mum knowing that Rebecca was pregnant. She seemed shocked that Mum already knew. I didn't even know at that point. I couldn't help smiling at that. My sister had a secret as well as me. But they were arguing about something else. I was so confused. I was a mere spectator. Then Rebecca let my secret out. Even now her words still ring in my ears. They were the last words she ever spoke. "What about your precious son, Mother? Your darling Freddie is gay! That boy who was here earlier is Freddie's gay lover." Mum was screaming at her to stop but Rebecca wouldn't let it go. "Which secret would you like me to keep from Dad, yours or Freddie's? You obviously care little about mine." Mum took a swipe and caught Rebecca on the face. She reeled back screaming. Next thing I know she's tumbling down the stairs. She landed at my feet. I heard the crack when she hit the floor. Mum rushed down after her and when I looked up there was a man I didn't know standing on the landing, stark naked. I realised then that my sister had found Mum with her lover. That's what they'd been fighting about.'

Tara sat without speaking. She could fill in most of the remaining details, but she waited for Freddie to compose himself. He reached for another handful of tissues. Elizabeth gave a sigh but remained asleep.

'I knew Rebecca was dead before Mum even reached her. There was blood on the floor, but her head sat at a funny angle and her eyes were open. I guessed her neck was broken. Mum was hysterical and I tried to pull her away. She wrestled with me and then I realised that she was telling me to go, to get out. I didn't understand but she screamed in my face and told me to get out and go back to work.'

'Why do you think she did that?'

'Well, I had gone outside; didn't know what to do or what to say or who to call. Mum came after me. She'd calmed down a bit although she was crying. She told me not to say anything to anybody, to go back to work and she would call me when it was time to come home again. Under no circumstances was I to contact Dad or the police. Do you know, Inspector, I found that instruction the strangest of all. My mother, the chief constable, had just killed her own daughter and from the way she spoke to me I knew things were not going to play out as they should. I did as she ordered. I went back to my office Christmas party and had several stiff drinks. A while later I got a call from her to say that Rebecca had been reported as missing, and I had to come home. She reminded me that I was to say nothing to Dad about anything. She said she was protecting me.

'Over that Christmas she explained what she'd done after I'd left the house. I don't think I took it all in at the time. Not only had I witnessed the death of my sister, but it was obvious that Mum had been having an affair. I asked her why she didn't just report that Rebecca's fall had been an accident. It seemed the right thing to do. Apparently, her lover, Ted Havers had offered to back her as a witness. But Mum said that would mean revealing her affair and she didn't want that to come out. It was her idea to move Rebecca out of the house and make it look like an opportunistic murder. She and Havers knew what to do, how to make things look suspicious. She even pretended to be a distraught mother out searching for her daughter when a police patrol, that she had organised, showed up.

'I suppose the worst part was her remembering that Stephen had called at the house earlier that day. Not only was she fitting him for the murder of her daughter, but she was putting a stop to my relationship with him. I suppose if she'd realised about the other guy, Anthony Sawyer, having been at our house, she might have tried to pin Rebecca's death on him. I learned months later that he and Rebecca had been a couple for a while in Cambridge. I realised just how callous a woman my mother was but like Dad I just wanted all of it to be over.'

'Your family life must have been terribly strained after that.'

'Mum and I had always been close. Even my sister's death didn't change that. Besides we now had a shared secret to protect. I had no feelings for Dad, nor apparently, had my mother. Funny thing was that Rebecca's death seemed to bring them closer again. But it was such a strain keeping those secrets from him. I could never look him in the face. In the end, I moved out of the house and as soon as I had the chance, I got out of the country too.'

'Did you ever consider the injustice of Stephen Lloyd being convicted for killing Rebecca?' Tara, although she now had learned yet another version of events, couldn't empathise with the man.

'My family came first. Mum and I had to keep our secret. It was an accident; she didn't deserve to go to jail or to lose her career and her marriage.'

'What about Stephen's career?'

'It was bad luck for him.'

'Don't you realise that if you'd told the truth three people would not have died at your father's hands?'

Tara got to her feet. Freddie had clasped his mother's withered hand. She had no sympathy for any member of the Winters family save Rebecca.

'Freddie Winters, I'm arresting you for attempting to pervert the course of justice.'

Winters listened to all of Tara's official caution then raised a conceited smile.

'I told you this off the record, Inspector. I'll deny everything I've said.'

'Well, Freddie, I'm sure you wondered why I was here with your mother this morning. I knew exactly when you returned to England. I'd been expecting you to call. You are the only person left to provide the truth to this sorry mess.'

She held her mobile phone aloft.

'I thought it wise to record our conversation. We'll see how we go in court, shall we?'

Freddie turned pale and released his mother's hand. Elizabeth opened her eyes and stared vacantly at the ceiling.

CHARACTER LIST

DI Tara Grogan – Liverpool detective of serious crimes.

DS Alan Murray – Tara's closest assistant.

DS John Wilson – Newly promoted officer in the team at St Anne Street station.

DC Paula Bleasdale – Youngest member in Tweedy's squad.

Detective Superintendent Harold Tweedy – Senior officer in charge of squad.

Stephen Lloyd –Recently freed after serving 18 years for the murder of Rebecca Winters.

Tyrone Cunningham – Former prison mate of Lloyd.

Andy Greengates – Prison inmate and friend of Lloyd and Cunningham.

Graham Benson – Prison officer.

Lydia Jennings – Junior prison officer.

Ted Havers – Assistant Chief Constable, Greater Manchester. SIO of the Rebecca Winters murder investigation.

Jack Winters – Husband of Elizabeth and father of Rebecca and Freddie.

Rebecca Winters – Cambridge student, murdered 19 years ago.

Elizabeth Winters – Mother of Rebecca and Freddie. Former Chief Constable of Merseyside police.

Freddie Winters – Brother of Rebecca.

Anthony Sawyer – Author of book about the murder of Rebecca Winters.

Josh Yarnly – Student.

Stella Ramsey – Manager of The Docker's Rest pub.

Kate – Tara's closest friend.

Sergeant Dave McLachlan – Desk sergeant at St Anne Street station.

If you enjoyed this book, please let others know by leaving a quick review on Amazon. Also, if you spot anything untoward in the paperback, get in touch. We strive for the best quality and appreciate reader feedback.

editor@thebookfolks.com

ALSO IN THIS SERIES

AN EARLY GRAVE (Book 1)

A tough young Detective Inspector encounters a reclusive man who claims he holds the secret to a murder case. But he also has a dangerous agenda. Will DI Tara Grogan take the bait?

THE DARING NIGHT (Book 2)

Liverpool is on high alert after a spate of poisonings, but DI Tara Grogan is side-lined from the investigation. Yet when she probes into the suicide of a company executive, she becomes sure she has a vital lead in the case. Going it alone, however, has very real risks.

THE SILENT VOICES (Book 3)

When bodies turn up on a Liverpool council estate, DI Tara Grogan goes undercover to get inside information. But she risks everything when the cover story she adopts backfires. Can she work out the identity of the killer before she is exposed and becomes a target?

LETHAL DOSE (Book 4)

Investigating the death of a journalist, DI Tara Grogan stumbles upon his connection to a number of missing women. Is it possible the victim was actually a serial killer? Tara closes in on the truth but can she evade a fatal jab?

LETHAL JUSTICE (Book 5)

When a body is found, cruelly crucified on a makeshift wooden structure, DI Tara Grogan suspects it is the work of a secretive religious cult. Focusing on this case and with her guard down, she becomes once again the target of a man with murder on his mind, among other things. Will the wheels of justice turn quick enough to save her from an awful fate?

LETHAL MINDS (Book 6)

Following a murder, a drugs feud in a notorious Liverpool estate is kicking off when a missing woman's body is found in the Irish sea. DI Tara Grogan has her attention divided, and someone with a grudge to bear has her in his sights.

All FREE with Kindle Unlimited and available in paperback.

MORE FICTION BY THE AUTHOR

THE MOURNE MOUNTAIN MURDERS

Father and daughter Sidney and Ursula make an unusual private detective team. But hitherto they've survived the tough streets of Belfast. Yet when curiosity gets the better of them and they probe into a murder, they'll attract the unwanted attention of a nasty criminal gang. Can they outwit the mob, or are their days numbered?

BOUND TO RUN

A romantic getaway in a remote Lake District cottage turns into a desperate fight for survival for Alex Chase. If she can get away from her pursuer, and that's a big if, she'll be able to concentrate on the burning question in her mind: how to get revenge.

THE WIFE'S BOYFRIEND

Charlie Geddis is thrown out by his wife but, determined to win her back, decides to prove that her new boyfriend, a property developer with a lot of assets, is in fact a lying crook. In the process, he becomes embroiled in a web of bribes, infidelities and possibly a murder.

All FREE with Kindle Unlimited and available in paperback.

OTHER TITLES OF INTEREST

THE DCI GAWN GIRVIN SERIES
by Linda Hagan

Meet DCI Gawn Girvin, a detective who gives little away about herself, but one determined to solve the toughest of serious crimes with her sharp mind and steely resolve. Working in one of the roughest cities in the British Isles, she is no stranger to danger. Her cases also take her onto mainland Britain and further afield, tackling incidents that answer to the name of murder. How people react to this fearless Belfast detective is one thing, whether she'll let it affect her is another.

All FREE with Kindle Unlimited and available in paperback.

THE YORKSHIRE DETECTIVE MYSTERY SERIES by Ric Brady

Ex-DCI Henry Ward seemed finally ready to enjoy retirement and quiet walks on the beautiful Yorkshire Moors with his loyal terrier Tessa. But soon enough he stumbles across a case after another of suspicious crimes, from murder, to kidnapping and abduction. Not getting involved doesn't seem to be an option. With the help of his nosey neighbour Jean, he can't but lend a helping hand to the local force, whether they like it or not.

All FREE with Kindle Unlimited and available in paperback.

www.thebookfolks.com

Printed in Great Britain
by Amazon